When reason flees—love takes the field!

"HANG IT, LUCY," Perry said furiously, turning her to face him and grasping her shoulders. "Is it so impossible for you to say you're sorry?"

Lucienne stared at Perry with mouth agape. Her lips began to tremble, and two tears rolled down her cheeks. Perry winced, overwhelmed with shame at his unkind outburst. "Blast!" he muttered, "I'm so sorry, Lucy. I—"

Not quite knowing what he was doing, he cupped her face in his hands. The dark, tear-filled eyes had not moved from his face. Whatever had possessed him to speak to her that way?

Before he realized it, he was kissing her . . . as he'd wanted to do since he first laid eyes on her . . .

—————

THE ACCIDENTAL ROMANCE
A Regency Love Story by
ELIZABETH MANSFIELD

Elizabeth Mansfield

The Accidental Romance

CHARTER BOOKS, NEW YORK

THE ACCIDENTAL ROMANCE

A Charter Book/published by arrangement with
the author

PRINTING HISTORY
Charter edition/August 1988

ISBN: 1-55773-060-1

Charter Books are published by The Berkley Publishing Group,
200 Madison Avenue, New York, NY 10016.
The name "Charter" and the "C" logo
are trademarks belonging to Charter Communications, Inc.

PRINTED IN THE UNITED STATES OF AMERICA

10 9 8 7 6 5 4 3 2 1

Chapter One

The black-hooded curricle seemed to loom up out of nowhere. As soon as her phaeton wheeled round the corner Lucienne glimpsed it. She gasped, pulled the reins to the right and managed, with consummate skill, to keep the horses from colliding. But she could not avoid a collision of the carriages themselves. The front corner of her phaeton crunched against the side of the curricle with enough force to jar her almost completely from her seat. The sounds of cracking wood and neighing horses were horrifying.

Both carriages shuddered to a halt, causing the traffic on the busy London street to come to a standstill. Despite an icy and persistent drizzle, the pavement was immediately thronged with curious onlookers. The driver of the curricle, a gangling young man with a shock of red hair curling out from beneath his high-crowned beaver hat, leapt out and ran at once to steady the horses. Lucienne, recovering her balance, did not hurry to climb down from the driver's seat. She merely readjusted her rakish riding hat to its proper angle while eyeing the scene with an expression of extreme disgust on her lovely face. It was bad enough, she said to herself as she stared at the ugly gouge in the front of her equipage, to have an accident at a time when she was already late for her appointment, but to have it when she was driving her brand-new phaeton with the high wheels and the beautiful blue-lacquered finish was the outside of enough! The only consolation in this disastrous occurrence was to be found in the fact that the horses had not been hurt.

She threw the reins to her tiger (a stocky, muscular, sharp-

1

eyed lad who'd already jumped down from his perch at the rear and was surveying the damage with calm inscrutability) and slid down from the driver's seat. *If I were a man,* she muttered to herself, *I would throttle the driver of that blasted curricle to within an inch of his life!*

The watchers on the pavement were probably glad that the furious creature who'd just alighted from the phaeton was not a man, for she was a delight to look upon. The lady was tall and built on lines that could only be called statuesque. From the top of her rakishly tilted, plumed hat to the tips of her modish leather half-boots, she was impressive. The hat (a creation of devilish charm that must have cost the wearer a plump bundle) sat upon a bed of glossy brown curls that had been carelessly pinned up away from the lady's neck only to bounce entrancingly with every movement of her head. Her eyes were large and black and were now positively glowing with fire. Her skin had a golden smoothness that would have gleamed even without the droplets of rain that sparkled on her cheeks. She had a strong but softly rounded chin, and her lips were full and expressive, although at this moment they were turned down at the corners in a manner that clearly revealed her disgust and impatience at finding herself in this predicament.

The women in the crowd were quick to notice the elegance of the close-fitting town coat of blue worsted that draped her shapely curves to perfection, the tantalizing effect (at the neck and bottom of the coat) of the show of cream-colored ruffles of the gown beneath, and the obvious costliness of her yellow leather riding gloves and matching half-boots. The men, however, were conscious only of the overall effect: that of a woman who, though imperiously angry, was so lovely she riveted their eyes.

The lady's tiger, himself impressive in his gold-trimmed livery, ran up behind her and held an umbrella over her, but she paid not the slightest heed to him. She stood glaring at the driver of the curricle until he'd finished examining the horses and turned round. He was a pleasant-faced fellow of not more than twenty-five years. Only average in height, he appeared taller because of his lean, long-limbed form and his tall hat. He had a pair of mild blue, bespectacled eyes, a broad nose and a mouth that curved up slightly on one side (giving him a permanent air of amusement, as if the world around him provided him with an endless supply of things to laugh at). But the characteristic that immediately caught one's eye was the color of the hair that protruded from beneath his beaver. It was so bright a red that it seemed to brighten up his face, as if, even on this rainy afternoon, he carried about his own supply of sunshine. In short, he was that rare sort of fellow whom everyone finds instantly likeable. But Lucienne, at that moment, did not find him so. The fact that he seemed to be smiling in the face of this irritating occurrence only served to increase her displeasure.

The young man was obviously relieved by the result of his examination of the horses, both hers and his, and was about to reassure the lady that all was well when the fury of her expression startled him into momentary silence. He peered at her a bit myopically from behind his rain-spattered spectacles. "I'm very sorry about all this, ma'am," he said affably, removing his soggy hat.

"Sorry? Is *that* all you have to say?" she demanded, putting elbows akimbo.

He gave her a shy smile that creased his cheeks with an appealing innocence. "Yes, ma'am. Except that I can relieve you of any worry you may have about your horses. They, and mine, too, seem to have escaped completely unscathed."

"No thanks to you," she snapped.

He blinked at her again. "I beg pardon, ma'am?"

"You heard me. Why didn't you watch where you were going?"

"I? Why didn't *I* watch?" His eyebrows lifted in bewilderment at her accusation. "I don't like to contradict a lady, ma'am, but you came round that corner so quickly that I couldn't have avoided you even if . . ." He paused and bit his lip, shyly keeping himself from saying anything more.

"Even if what?" Lucienne prodded impatiently.

"Even if my horses had wings," he said, softening the words with another of his sweet-tempered smiles.

The fascinated people on the pavement, who might at first have been inclined to take the side of the lovely lady, suddenly offered their allegiance to the soft-spoken, sweet-tempered fellow by laughing at and applauding his sally. But Lucienne was unmoved by his good nature. She glared up at the speaker with renewed anger. "Are you trying to place the blame on *me*, you buffleheaded gudgeon?"

This was greeted by the crowd with a loud boo. The "gudgeon" lifted his eyebrows. "Well, you *did* take that turn with rather too much speed, you know, ma'am," he pointed out quietly. "One should slow one's vehicle to a walk when making turns, especially in this part of town, London traffic being what it is."

"Aye, that's tellin' er, lad!" shouted a man on the street. "Give 'er what-for!"

Lucienne drew in an infuriated breath. "Are you presuming to lecture me on how to *drive?*" she demanded of the fellow icily. "I'll have you know that I've been taking corners since I was ten. If you weren't such a ham-fisted clunch you could have maneuvered your blasted curricle out of my way."

The tall fellow's mild expression did not change. He merely made a gesture that invited her to take note of the narrowness of the street. "There's no room here for such a maneuver, you see," he pointed out calmly. "Since you didn't pause at the corner before taking your turn—"

"It's *you* who should have paused, you makebait!"

"A real sharp tongue ye 'ave on ye, dearie," hooted a woman on the pavement as a number of voices jeered along with her.

"No, ma'am, that's not so," the red-haired man insisted quietly, speaking to Lucienne with the patience of a tutor toward a recalcitrant and somewhat slow-witted pupil. "I was proceeding straight ahead. You were making a turn. The driver making the turn has the responsibility of—"

"Don't you *dare* speak to me as if I were a child! And don't speak to me of *responsibilities* either! All of this is *your* responsibility, and you know it! My beautiful new phaeton is utterly *ruined* because of your ham-handed driving!"

The red-headed fellow lost nothing of his good nature. "In the first place, ma'am," he explained with a gentle firmness, "your phaeton is far from ruined. It can easily be repaired and will look good as new. In the second place, although my curricle has sustained some damage, too, I am quite willing to overlook it. And in the third place, I've just pointed out that my driving was not at fault here."

The crowd cheered, making Lucienne clench her teeth wrathfully. "May I point out to *you*, you weasel," she hissed, "that it was you who ran into me, not the other way round? If you were a man instead of a worm, you'd admit it!"

Her insulting words and tone failed to shake his relentless good humor. But they also failed to shake his belief in the rightness of his position. "Sorry, ma'am, I can't admit any such thing. You, I'm afraid, ran into me."

"That is an out-and-out *lie*. I was well into my turn before you and your blasted curricle appeared out of nowhere." She turned to her tiger. "Isn't that so, Jason?"

Jason, the tiger, knew where his bread was buttered. "Yes, ma'am," he agreed promptly.

"There, you see?" Lucienne said triumphantly to the stranger.

This last was greeted by the crowd with loud and prolonged hoots.

"No, ma'am, I don't see," the fellow said, ignoring the support from the mob. "I don't see how your tiger can be used to substantiate your case at all. He was riding on the back of your phaeton, was he not? From there, he couldn't possibly have been able to observe what was occurring in front."

Lucienne drew herself up to her full height. "Do you have the temerity to stand there and accuse me of *fraudulence?*" she queried loudly, the noise from the crowd and her inability to think of a good answer increasing her fury. "You, Sir Rudesby, should be given lessons in manners. No gentleman speaks to a lady so!"

"I believe, ma'am," he suggested humbly, "that that is an argument *ad hominem*."

"And what, may I ask, is an argument *ad hominem?*"

"It is a fallacy in logic, ma'am, where the arguer attacks the opponent's character rather than the issue at hand." He grinned, tossing back a dripping lock of hair from his forehead. "It is usually used when the arguer is at a loss."

His grin only enraged her more. "Oh, you fancy I am at a loss, do you? Well, I'll show you whether I'm at a loss or not!" With that, she snatched the umbrella from the tiger's hand and, shutting it quickly, proceeded to beat the poor fellow about the shoulders and arms. "There!" she cried, swinging the umbrella like a club. "Take *that,* you clumsy oaf! And that! How's *that* for an argument *ad hominem?*"

The lanky fellow, habitually easy-going and not prone to explosions of temper, laughed and tried to fend off the attack by putting up his arms and taking a few steps in retreat. The crowd was enjoying the scene hugely, laughing and applauding noisily whenever she swung and missed. But after a few moments of this ludicrous, one-sided battle, the curricle-driver decided he'd had enough. Without seeming to exert any effort, and without the slightest show of temper, he pulled the "weapon" from her grasp and tossed the umbrella to the hooting, jeering crowd on the pavement.

While Lucienne watched frozen-faced, the sturdy Jason ran over to the mob and attempted to recapture the umbrella, but a shabbily dressed old crone had already snatched it up. Waving it like a banner and chortling happily, she scooted off down the street with her loot. While the crowd cheered her on, she disappeared from view more quickly than anyone might have thought possible for a creature so old and bent.

Lucienne, furious at having been forcibly disarmed, turned back to her adversary and glared at him with venom. "You clod-crusher, you not only lost me my umbrella, but you hurt my wrist!"

"Did I, ma'am?" he asked without a touch of irony, despite the fact that *she*'d been trying to hurt *him* only a moment before. "I *am* sorry. That only goes to prove how harmful this sort of quarrel can be. Don't you think it's time to stop this foolishness? I'm quite willing to admit defeat. You win."

Lucienne could only gape at him. "I *win?* Whatever do you mean?"

"I mean, ma'am, that the . . . er . . . force of your argument has convinced me to accept full responsibility for this unfortunate contretemps. I am at fault, if you say so. Send the bill for all the repairs to me, Perry Wittenden, at Wittenden House in Charles Street."

"Good heavens!" she gasped, the wind having been taken from her sails. "Are you really serious? This is a very sudden surrender."

"Yes, but there's no use prolonging this, is there?" he asked, his guileless smile reappearing. "I'm already drenched, and you soon will be, since I've disposed of your umbrella. By the way, you may as well add the cost of the umbrella to the bill. I'm guilty of throwing it away, after all." He bowed, placed his beaver on his wet head and started toward his curricle. "Good day, ma'am," he added pleasantly over his shoulder.

"Humph!" was all the surprised Lucienne could manage in response.

"Oh, one thing more," the fellow called to her as he climbed up onto the box of his carriage. "If you please, ma'am, I would appreciate it if you'd also send me a bill for your very charming hat. The rain has quite ruined the plumes."

As the curricle moved off down the road and the crowd began to disperse, Lucienne remained in startled immobility. "Now, *that*," little Jason murmured as he watched the curricle disappear down the street, "is as sweet a gen'leman as ever I met up wiv."

"Sweet? Ha!" Lucienne snorted scornfully, shaking herself from her reverie, turning on her heel and striding to her damaged carriage. "He's as sweet as a cobra. That so innocent, so good-natured smile of his was nothing more than a ploy. He behaved in that disgustingly conciliatory manner only to show me up!"

"Show you up, m'lady?" the tiger asked with feigned innocence as he helped Lucienne up to the driver's seat. He was well aware that his mistress had behaved like a fishwife, and he knew that she was as aware of it as he. "I dunno whut ye mean," he insisted with wide-eyed naiveté.

She threw him a look of disdain as she took the reins. "You know perfectly well what I mean, you imp. He played the affable gentleman just to make me feel like a petulant cross-patch. Offering to pay my bills when he knew perfectly well that the crash was all my fault! What *brass!* The cheeky makebate! If I were a man, I'd call him out!" And with that, she rapped the horses smartly with her whip and drove off, leaving the little tiger to catch up with the carriage as best he might.

Chapter Two

Lucienne Gerard lifted her eyes from her teacup and stared at her aunt in surprise. "Aunt Chloe! You *know* him?" she gasped.

"Of course I know him," Lady Gerard declared. "His mother and I were the best of friends until she passed on." The wiry little lady studied her niece with renewed interest. She'd listened to Lucienne's spirited and detailed account of her accident with amused attention, but it wasn't until she learned that the driver of the curricle was Perry Wittenden that her interest was really piqued, for Perry's family was very well known to her. "We came out the same year, Perry's mother and I. But she died when Perry was born, and her husband took the boy up north to be raised by his grandmother. That was why I couldn't keep in close touch with the family. But I've met the boy from time to time over the years. I remember being invited to the Wittenden estate when the old Earl remarried. That was in 1806, I believe. Perry was a shy fifteen-year-old then, all legs and elbows. But when he smiled at me or peered at me with that intent stare of his, he quite melted my heart. I've always been interested in his development. He called on me a few months ago when he first moved down to London. He seemed to me to be just the sort of man I like—the kind who's soft-spoken and modest but has an inner, unobtrusive self-confidence. Some say he is too reserved and reticent, but I don't believe those qualities are flaws, do you? One might do worse than be reticent. I have the greatest affection for him. There's not a sweeter boy in the world than Perry Wittenden."

Lucienne listened to her aunt's praise of the fellow with an expression that was both dubious and glum. It was extremely irritating to Lucienne to discover that her darling aunt, with whom she'd never had a word of disagreement, could describe the odious curricle-driver as the sweetest boy in the world. Lucienne had been a guest at her aunt's London house for almost a month, and this was the first time she wished she were back home in Yorkshire. Her aunt had been invariably understanding and sympathetic to her moods during this visit, but today, just when she badly needed some sympathy, her aunt was failing her. This had turned out to be the worst day she'd spent since she came to town, and that run-in with the curricle was quite the last straw. Why didn't her aunt understand?

She put down her teacup and strode across the room to the fireplace. The warmth of the flames soothed her, and she remembered feeling a similar glow of warmth when she'd wakened that morning. The day had started out so well. Her abigail, Trudy, had wakened her with the news that her new carriage was at that moment being delivered. She'd jumped out of bed, drawn back the drapes from her bedroom window that overlooked her aunt's curved driveway and stared down at her new phaeton. There it stood, gleaming in the sunshine in all its bright blue elegance. Her blood had danced with excitement. All her life she'd dreamed of driving a high-perch phaeton through the streets of London, and now this shiny creation, with its huge, yellow-spoked wheels, was going to make that dream a reality. She'd dressed herself in her favorite riding clothes and her most dashing hat, had kissed her aunt good-bye (promising to return in time for tea), had stopped in Albemarle Street to pick up Owen (her about-to-be betrothed, Sir Owen Tatlow) and had tooled off to drive him through the park. But somehow, from that moment on, everything had gone wrong. First the day had turned rainy. Then Owen had found fault not only with the color of the phaeton (which he'd termed vulgar) but with her driving style (which he'd called rash). They'd had a brief but violent quarrel, she'd turned the horses back to Albemarle Street, and then, only minutes after she'd set him down, she'd had the accident.

She returned to her aunt's house an hour late for tea. Her

clothes and spirit (the former having already been considerably damped by the inclement weather and the latter by the quarrel with Sir Owen) were positively sodden because of the encounter with the curricle, but she expected to be warmed and soothed by the sympathy her usually doting aunt would offer in response to her tale of woe. Instead, her aunt was taking the young man's side against her!

Lucienne turned round from the fire and faced her aunt accusingly. "I don't see how you can call that Wittenden fellow *sweet* after all I've told you," she objected.

Lady Gerard merely stirred her tea placidly. "But, Lucy, my dear, there's nothing you've told me that reflects discredit on Perry. He behaved in the calmest, most gentlemanly way. While you, as you've as much as admitted to me, behaved like a hoyden."

"Yes, I did, but only because the fellow was so nauseatingly *pleasant,*" her niece retorted in disgust. "Such unremitting good nature at a time when any normal person would be snarling in fury is enough to make me suspicious of his motives. Good God, Aunt Chloe, why wasn't the man *livid?* Not only had I run into him, but I was abusing him verbally, striking him with my umbrella, and all the while keeping him standing about *in the rain!* And all he did in response was to smile that innocent smile of his and offer to pay for the damage, not only to my phaeton but to my *hat!*"

Chloe Gerard laughed. "Did he, really? What a delightful thing to do! I fail to see, Lucy, my love, what sinister motive he could have for doing *that.*"

"His motive, my dearest aunt, was to make me look like a screaming hysteric to the crowd while he, meanwhile, won their admiration and affection by showing off his repulsive rationality and good nature. You may think he's the sweetest boy in the world, but I think he's a gawky, stuffy, sanctimonious humbug."

Aunt Chloe hid a smile. "Then it's just as well you met Owen Tatlow before I roused myself to invite Perry Wittenden to dinner, for if you hadn't succumbed to Tatlow's advances, I fully intended to introduce you to Perry."

"Introduce me to that . . . that spectacled spindleshanks?" Lucienne asked, appalled. "You must be joking."

"Not at all. That spectacled spindleshanks, as you call him, has more wit and charm than you can imagine. You might have suited each other very well."

"Not in a thousand years," her ladyship's niece declared with finality.

Lady Gerard lifted her cup to her lips and calmly sipped her tea, eyeing her niece with affectionate disapproval over the teacup. Lucienne was both a joy and a problem to her. She loved the girl like a daughter, but she did not approve of the way her brother-in-law had raised her. He had utterly spoiled the girl. Lucienne Gerard was the only child of her brother-in-law, Sir Matthew Gerard, and his wife Millicent. Poor Millicent had been childless for a dozen years after her marriage to Matthew, exactly as Chloe herself had been. But while Chloe and her now-deceased husband had adjusted to being deprived of offspring and had made full, busy lives for themselves in London, Millicent and Matthew had hidden themselves away in Yorkshire and mourned. Years later, when they'd completely given up hope, to their utter astonishment a child was conceived. When she was born and found to be healthy and normal, their joy was unbounded. But Millicent's health was never the same after childbirth, and in only a few months she died.

The child, however, was sturdy, bright and beautiful from the first, and Matthew's delight in her never faltered. Little Lucienne could say or do nothing that her father did not find pleasing. He admired her every word, praised her every act and indulged her every whim. When she exhibited a talent for the pianoforte, he hired the best teacher available and sent to Italy for the finest grand piano made. When she showed an agility on horseback, he bought her several fine horses and built an addition to his stables. He gave her a suite of rooms of her own and furnished them with the finest of Sheraton and Chippendale pieces. Her numerous wardrobes and chests were crammed with all sorts of apparel, and her jewelry box contained some of the most exquisite pins and necklaces to be found in all of England. When Chloe pointed out to him that his daughter's figure was as lithe and shapely as youth, nature and a talented dancing master could contrive, the father decided that all her gowns should be worthy of her, and from then on they were made by a fashionable *modiste* who was handsomely paid to travel to Yorkshire from Paris twice a year to fit her. There was nothing the girl wanted that her father would not give her.

Cosseted and pampered, Lucienne grew to believe that she was a superior young woman, more beautiful, more clever and more gifted than the ordinary. Her Aunt Chloe (who from the first had taken to the child and did her share of pampering her by visiting Yorkshire frequently, buying her niece expensive clothes and playthings, and showering her with affection) could not deny that Lucienne *was,* in fact, very beautiful, clever and gifted. What troubled the aunt was that she feared the girl was too aware of her gifts. Even Chloe's closest chum, Jenny Rutherford, had commented that what Lucienne lacked was modesty.

It was not becoming, Chloe thought with a sigh, for a young woman to be so sure of herself and so certain that all the good things of life were her due. What would happen when life dealt her—as life was inevitably wont to do—a severe disappointment? How would Lucienne handle disappointment and frustration when she'd never been inured to it? Perhaps it would have been better for her to have had more disappointments when she was younger.

Of course, as Chloe had said to Lady Rutherford in the girl's defense, Lucienne had behaved with admirable strength when, at age eighteen, her father had fallen ill. It was the year they'd all looked forward to, for Chloe was to give Lucienne a magnificent London come-out that season. They'd planned it for years, and Lucienne, who'd never spent more than a few days in town, could hardly wait. But when her father had had the stroke, the girl cancelled all their plans for her London season and stayed at his side. For five years she remained fixed in Yorkshire, supervising his care with uncomplaining, cheerful devotion. It was only now, with her father so much improved, that he and Chloe were able to convince Lucienne to spend a few months in town.

The girl did have character, as even Jenny Rutherford had agreed; her devotion to her father was proof of that. Perhaps Chloe was foolish to be concerned about the girl. Nevertheless, she couldn't keep a nagging inner voice from whispering warnings that all was not quite as it should be with Lucienne. Look at how badly she'd behaved during the accident, for one thing. And for another, why had she decided to accept the hand of Sir Owen Tatlow after knowing him only a fortnight?

Chloe's dearest wish was to see Lucienne married. Indeed, the primary purpose of this visit to London was to arrange a suitable match for Lucienne. Having missed her come-out five years ago, the girl had had no opportunity to meet eligible young men. Not in Yorkshire. Buried in the country with no family but an ailing father, she'd lived in a society made up almost exclusively of elderly neighbors. Over the years she'd managed to find a few young female friends and to meet one or two young men who'd become suitors, but such a limited society did not offer opportunities for the girl to make a match as splendid as she deserved. Thus, beautiful and desirable though she was, she'd reached the advanced age of twenty-three without having made a suitable connection. It was essential, therefore, for the aunt to rectify the situation by helping the niece to make the most of this London visit.

Chloe had made careful plans. She had many friends besides Lady Rutherford among the *ton,* and she'd told them all of her niece's arrival. The friends, having heard from Jenny Rutherford as well as from Chloe herself of the girl's beauty, cleverness and wealth, had sent so many invitations to parties, routs and balls that Chloe and Lucienne could have kept themselves occupied every evening of her stay if they'd wished. Chloe carefully weeded out all but the most promising affairs, and she cheerfully escorted Lucienne to the selected festivities several times a week.

There was no doubt in Chloe's mind that Lucienne would attract a number of suitors in a very short time. The schedule she'd worked out in her mind was a simple one: Lucienne would make the rounds of the social events her aunt had laid out for her, and after a month or two she would have gathered about her enough suitors to make a choice among them. By the end of the season—three months hence—Lucienne would choose from among them someone suitable to wed. That someone would, of course, have wealth, character, background and intelligence to match hers. Chloe hoped it would be someone like Perry Wittenden, who, besides having all of the qualities the aunt considered basic, had the additional advantages of charm, wit, and an unusual modesty. Nothing less would do for Lucienne.

But to Chloe's astonishment, Lucienne had not taken a month or two to acquire a circle of suitors; she'd done it in a week. And she'd not waited out the season to make her selection from among them; she'd done it in a fortnight. And she'd chosen, of all people, Sir Owen Tatlow, who'd been introduced to her by Jenny Rutherford in spite of Chloe's objections. (Jenny rarely listened to Chloe's advice in these matters, considering herself a far better matchmaker than her friend.)

When Jenny challenged her friend "to give me even one reason why Sir Owen is not right for your Lucienne," Chloe could find nothing specific to say against the fellow. Many of London's matchmaking mamas would have been delighted to snare him for their daughters. It was Jenny Rutherford's opinion that he qualified on every one of the basics, and had, in addition, the most remarkable good looks. He was so tall, broad-shouldered and slim-hipped that he seemed molded by the gods to wear the fitted breeches and narrow-waisted coats that were the rage. His dark curls, cut in the fashionable Brutus style, were thick and charmingly tousled, falling in profusion over a noble forehead. His nose, mouth and chin were almost Greek in their perfection, and if his expression sometimes revealed a touch of haughtiness or self-satisfaction, his good breeding quickly masked it over.

But it was that touch of smug self-satisfaction that troubled Chloe. Lucienne, too, had a trace of self-pride in her character. Wouldn't the pairing of two such top-lofty personalities be dangerous? Wouldn't the pridefulness of one tend to encourage the pridefulness of the other? Chloe couldn't help fearing that they would bring out the worst in each other.

Of course, these were not the sort of thoughts she could express aloud. She never even confided her misgivings to Jenny Rutherford. She kept her thoughts carefully hidden. If Lucienne fancied herself in love with Owen Tatlow, it would not sit well with her to hear her aunt say that *two smug creatures might make one bad pair*.

She glanced over at her niece speculatively. The girl had turned back to the fire and was staring down morosely at the flames. The aunt felt a twinge of sympathy for her beloved niece. Lucienne had had the worst of the encounter with Perry, and the lowering experience had depressed her. But in truth Chloe was glad it had happened; Perry and Lucienne were now known to each other. If Chloe could only find a way to bring them together, Lucienne might learn to appreciate the boy's excellent qualities. She might make a comparison in her mind between Perry's quiet but strong virtues as compared to Owen's smug and shallow ones. She might even grow to see how much more suitable Perry might be for her to wed. Perry, modest and soft-spoken, was just the sort of influence Lucienne needed. If Chloe could convince Lucienne to choose Perry over Owen Tatlow, she would feel much more confident of Lucienne's future happiness. But how could such an event come to pass? Lucienne, who was not the sort to change her mind easily, had already decided on Owen. What was even worse, she'd already come to the conclusion that Perry was a—how had the girl put it?—a sanctimonious spindleshanks.

Chloe sighed and refilled her teacup. "By the way," she asked her niece innocently, "why didn't you bring Owen to tea? I thought you were to spend the afternoon together."

"I didn't ask him," Lucienne muttered, kicking at the fender despondently. "I'd had quite enough of him today."

If that, her aunt said to herself, *is the sound of a young woman in love, then I've forgotten what love is.* She twirled her teaspoon round and round in her cup, keeping her eyes on her niece's bent head. Something had better be done about this betrothal, she thought, before it was too late. But what was there to do? Lucienne was unlikely to listen to any advice she might offer or to any criticism she might make of Owen. The only thing she could do was to concoct a plot designed to keep Lucienne from taking the final step. She did not know at the moment what plot she might concoct, but she would think of *something.* It was not too late, after all. Lucienne was not yet wed.

Chapter Three

Chloe, lulled into complacency by the rift between Lucienne and Owen Tatlow, let five days pass without managing to concoct a suitable plot to bring her niece and Perry Wittenden together, but on the evening of the fifth day she witnessed something that shook her into action. She and Lucienne had returned from the opera, and she'd gone upstairs to bed. Lucienne had remained behind, saying she wished to have a cup of tea before she retired. After undressing, Chloe decided to keep Lucienne company and, donning a robe, came downstairs. On reaching the foot of the stairway, she was startled to hear voices emanating from the morning room. She walked toward the sounds, wondering who could have come calling at such a late hour. As she neared the door she heard Lucienne's voice. "No, I don't think I've been sulking too long," the girl was saying. "Your behavior was quite unforgivable."

"My dear girl," a man's voice responded, "murder may be unforgivable. Dishonesty may be unforgivable. Unfaithfulness may be unforgivable. But a bit of loving criticism should not be considered so."

Chloe peeped round the doorframe into the morning room. The room was lit by only a brace of candles on the table and the moonlight flooding into the room from the bow window. In the dim light, Chloe could see Owen Tatlow standing behind Lucienne in the window embrasure, attempting to coax her to turn round and face him. Chloe had to admit to herself that they made a magnificent-looking couple. Moonlight was shedding its silver glow on both their dark heads (particularly Lucienne's, bent and turned away from her betrothed in an

attitude of charming rebuff) and outlining Owen's broad
shoulders and admirable profile as well as Lucienne's statuesque shapeliness. They were both so strikingly tall and handsome in the magical light that the scene would have taken
Chloe's breath away had she not been stiff with surprise and
disapproval.

"Is that what it was?" Lucienne was asking Owen softly.
"Loving criticism?"

"What else?" Pressing his advantage, he grasped her
shoulders and pulled her round. "Do you think I want to see
you hurt by careless driving?"

"My driving is not careless," she insisted, nevertheless permitting him to put a finger under her chin and lift her face to his. "I
am more expert than you realize at handling the ribbons."

"If that's so, then I need more time to grow accustomed to
that bravura style of yours. If I judged you too harshly, I do
beg your forgiveness." He smiled down at her in full confi-
dence that he'd won her over.

"Do you beg my forgiveness for criticizing my taste in
phaetons, too?" she asked, a small, coy smile turning up the
corners of her lips.

"I'll beg forgiveness for anything you wish, if it means
you'll smile like this at me again," he murmured, bending his
head to her and adding wickedly, "but don't ask me to *ride* in
that garish contraption."

Chloe fully expected Lucienne to flare up at that, but Lucienne, although she stiffened, was swept into a close embrace
before she had time to object. Chloe, her eyes widening,
watched as Lucienne visibly wilted in Owen's arms. The troubled aunt blinked, observed the reconciliation for a moment
longer and then backed away from the door. She tiptoed up
the stairs and hurried back to her bedroom where she sat
brooding until she heard Lucienne bid her visitor good night
and come upstairs.

Chloe climbed into her bed and pulled the covers up to her
neck, feeling unwontedly glum. She was becoming more and
more certain that Owen, handsome and charming though he
might be, was not the man for her niece. If something was to
be done, she told herself, it had to be done soon.

The next morning she went into action. She rose early and

went to her writing table as soon as she'd dressed. She wrote a note to Perry, inviting him to dinner the following week. Perhaps it was an impulsive act, she realized (for, if he accepted, she would have to round up at least nine other guests, select a menu, hire extra kitchen help and make all sorts of other hasty preparations), but the embrace she'd witnessed the night before had made the situation seem urgent, and she could think of nothing better to do.

She rang for Kelby, her butler, and handed him the letter, instructing him to have one of the footmen carry it round to Wittenden House at once and to wait for a reply.

She barely had time to clean the nib of her pen and close the lid of her writing desk when Kelby returned to her door with the announcement that the Ladies Haversleigh had called and were awaiting her in the downstairs sitting room. Chloe blinked up at him with upraised brows. Both Lady Frances Haversleigh and her spinster daughter, Evaline, were frequent callers, but since the object of their visits was always to engage in trivial conversation, Chloe often instructed the butler to make her excuses. This time, however, it was obviously too late to avoid them. "Oh, dear," she sighed, "not the Haversleighs now!"

"I'm sorry, your ladyship," the butler said with a touch of chagrin, "but one of the footmen admitted them while I was up here with you, and I'm afraid he's already informed them that you are at home."

"Oh, well, never mind, Kelby," she said, rising reluctantly. "Just be sure to come in with a reminder that I have a noon appointment, if they stay beyond half an hour."

Chloe found her guests sitting side by side on the sofa, their attention utterly absorbed by a magazine that the tall, angular, overdressed Lady Haversleigh held on her lap. "Good morning," Chloe said from the sitting-room doorway, noting with amusement that the closeness of her guests' heads as they bent over their reading was causing the plumes of their bonnets to entangle.

Lady Haversleigh looked up eagerly, thus knocking her hat askew. "Ah, there you are, Chloe, my dear," she said in her high, piercingly clear voice. "I hope we haven't called too early."

"No, not at all, Fanny," Chloe assured her, bending down and kissing her cheek. "And Evaline, how charming you are looking in that bonnet."

Evaline (who, having reached the advanced age of thirty-five without ever having received an offer, had long since accepted the fact that her prospects for marriage were nil and had consoled herself by making herself a reputation as a woman of high style) patted her black-and-white striped bonnet with a smile of satisfaction. "Thank you, Lady Gerard," she murmured modestly. "My milliner assures me that stripes will be all the crack this season. I think stripes on hats are vastly amusing, don't you?"

Chloe perched on a chair opposite the sofa and looked over at her guests with curiosity. The angular Lady Haversleigh and her equally bony daughter were infamous gossips, and they made a habit of calling on Chloe every time they heard a new on-dit that they suspected Chloe had not yet caught wind of. They loved nothing better than finding audiences whom they could shock with tidbits of scandal. "Have you *heard*—?" was the way they began every conversation. Chloe couldn't help wondering what bit of juicy information they were about to disclose today.

Lady Haversleigh's first words this morning were completely in character. "Chloe, my dear, have you *heard* of the commotion the new issue of *West Ender's Monthly* has caused?" she asked at once. "Everyone is snickering over it."

"Oh, yes, everyone," Evaline said in support. "It's vastly amusing."

"No, I haven't," Chloe admitted, smiling at Evaline's repeated use of the expression 'vastly amusing'. It was probably as much in vogue this season as stripes.

The two guests exchanged delighted glances. "She hasn't heard," Lady Haversleigh told her daughter with real pleasure.

Chloe sat back in her chair, quite ready to listen. She was not averse to gossip that was not malicious. Gossip was often entertaining, and since she was forced to spend half an hour in the Haversleigh ladies' company anyway, she might just as well be entertained as bored. "Well, Fanny, what is it everyone's snickering about?" she asked with sincere interest.

"They are snickering, my love, about the disclosures in the

Whistledown Diary in the current *West-Ender's Monthly*,"
Lady Haversleigh said, holding up the magazine she'd had on
her lap. "Haven't you read it?"

"No, I don't subscribe to it. It's a periodical for men, is it
not?"

"No, not necessarily. I admit it has too many pages of
political commentary, but there is always something in it
worth a lady's attention."

"This month, for instance," her daughter put in, "there's a
report of Lady Holland's dinner for the Prince. And every
issue contains the names of those in our set who are traveling
abroad. And—"

"Yes, indeed," her mother interrupted impatiently, "there
are many such fascinating items. No need to enumerate them
all, Eva, my love. But, Chloe, everyone's favorite is the
Whistledown Diary."

"Oh, yes, *everyone*'s favorite," Evaline echoed. "It's vastly
amusing."

"The Whistledown Diary?" Chloe knit her brows. "I think
I've heard it spoken of somewhere. Did Jenny Rutherford
mention it to me, I wonder?"

"Yes, I'm certain she did," Lady Haversleigh said. "One
hears it spoken of everywhere one goes."

"Does one really? Why can't I recall—? What *is* it, exactly?"

"It's a . . . a kind of essay that appears monthly in the magazine. This fellow Whistledown writes it. He claims it is
culled from pages in his diary."

"From his own diary? That *is* strange."

"Well, it's not *really* a diary, Mama," Evaline objected.
"There's nothing of an *intimate* nature in it."

"That may be so, Eva, but one feels that he's really *experienced* everything he writes about."

"That's true," the daughter agreed. "One does."

Lady Haversleigh turned back to Chloe. "In any case, intimate or not, the diary is most entertaining. One never knows
just what Whistledown will decide to write about. Last week
he wrote about the types who sit about in his club."

"His *club?*" Chloe sneered. "That sounds terribly dull."

"But you see, my dear, it wasn't dull at all. The particularity of his observations makes everything he writes so fascinating." She giggled. "He wrote, in that piece, that it struck him as strange that these fellows, who are the greatest loafers in the world, will always have the correct time. Remember that one, Eva, dearest?"

"Oh, yes. He also wrote that clubs are places for men who prefer armchairs to women! We found it so droll, especially when he went on to describe, quite wickedly, the various types one finds there, like the fellow who sat snoring in his chair all day and then, when he got up to go, was asked where he was off to. 'I've so much to do,' the fellow replied, 'that I'm going home to bed.' It was vastly amusing. Mama and I laughed and laughed."

"Yes, and another time he wrote a verse about how different a cup of tea can taste at different times."

"Tea? He wrote about tea?" Chloe asked in disbelief.

"Yes. I know it sounds peculiar, but I assure you that you'd have enjoyed the poem as much as I did. Whatever he writes about, he makes it all so charming and amusing! Everyone seems to quote him lately. They all say that the Whistledown Diary is very much like the Roger de Coverly Papers in the old *Tatler*."

"Truly, Fanny?" Chloe asked dubiously. "The Roger de Coverly Papers? It can't be as witty as all that."

"But it is, I assure you," Lady Haversleigh insisted. She turned to her daughter. "Speaking of wit, can you repeat that little verse he wrote about wit in the last edition, Eva, my love? You remember it, don't you?"

"About wit?" Evaline wrinkled her brow in concentration. "Oh, yes, I think it went something like this:

> *To those who say I'm witty,*
> *Here's a truth I've kept concealed:*
> *Though true wit's something like a lance,*
> *I use it as a shield."*

Chloe smiled in appreciation. "That *is* good, isn't it? It says something of the writer's character that he uses his wit in self-defense rather than to attack others. I rather like that."

"You see?" Lady Haversleigh chortled. "I knew you would."

"And there's the vastly amusing couplet everyone's quoting," Evaline said, "that goes: 'The girls who can't dance are often heard saying/ How very badly the musicians are playing.'"

"And surely Jenny Rutherford must have told you what he wrote about Henry Brougham and the Prince," Lady Haversleigh added.

"No," Chloe said interestedly. "What was that?"

"It was after Brougham made that speech about Prinny's wild expenditures. Well, Prinny was reported to say that Brougham 'handled the truth carelessly,' so Whistledown wrote that handling truth carelessly was better than *not touching it at all*."

Chloe laughed. "Prinny must have raged when he read that! Quite a fellow, this Whistledown. Who *is* he?"

"I don't think his identity is generally known," Lady Haversleigh said. "A name like *Whistledown* is surely a pseudonym."

"But we've strayed from the point, Mama," Evaline pointed out. "You haven't told Lady Gerard about the latest to-do he's wrought."

"No, I haven't." Fanny smiled a wicked smile. "It's a most delightful to-do, Chloe. Everyone's trying to guess the identity of the woman."

"Woman?" Chloe asked with a touch of disapproval. "He wrote about a woman?"

"Yes. A Lady. Someone in our set, I have no doubt. It's all quite tantalizing."

"Perhaps you should wait for Lady Gerard's niece to join us before you tell the story, Mama," Evaline suggested.

"Oh, but I have no idea when Lucienne will come down," Chloe admitted. "She didn't go to bed until the wee hours, I'm afraid, and she was still abed when I looked in on her a little while ago. She may not come down at all this morning."

"Well, then," Lady Haversleigh said, leaning forward eagerly, "I may as well proceed. The story in Whistledown's Diary this month has to do with a mysterious lady with whom he had an encounter."

Chloe's interest was caught despite herself. "An encounter? A *romantic* encounter?"

"Oh, no, not romantic at all. Quite the contrary."

"Yes, quite the contrary," Evaline echoed. "The encounter was with the Lady's *phaeton*. Vastly amusing."

Chloe blinked. "Her . . . phaeton?"

"Her phaeton," Lady Haversleigh repeated, nodding firmly. "It seems that our diarist was driving his curricle when this unnamed lady ran into it with her rather dashing phaeton—"

"A high-perch, I have no doubt," Evaline put in.

"Are you talking about a . . . a collision?" Chloe asked, feeling a sudden twinge of uneasiness.

"Yes, just so."

"Good God! Let me understand this." Chloe's uneasiness was becoming a decided clench of alarm. "Are you saying that this Whistledown wrote that his curricle collided with a high-perch phaeton?"

"The phaeton collided with *his curricle*," Lady Haversleigh corrected, "although the lady would not admit it. Instead, she berated him in loud and unseemly terms and even beat him with her umbrella!"

Chloe felt the blood drain from her face. "Her umb-b-b-rella?" she stammered, gaping at her guests.

"Yes, did you ever hear of anything so vulgar?" Evaline asked gleefully.

"Well, I . . . I . . ."

"That's why Whistledown calls her his Lady-Shrew," Fanny chuckled.

"Lady *Shrew?*" Chloe's stomach knotted tightly. "He called her a . . . a Lady Shrew? And he described the whole encounter in the *magazine?*"

"Yes, isn't it delicious? Everyone's been reading it. And now everyone is trying to guess who the Lady-Shrew is."

Chloe stared at her, appalled. "Everyone is trying to guess her . . . her *identity?*"

"Yes, exactly."

Chloe put a shaking hand to her forehead, her thoughts whirling about in confusion. There seemed little doubt that the collision described in this 'diary' was the one experienced by

Lucienne, for how could there have been *another* such accident involving a high-perch phaeton, a loud argument and a
battle with an umbrella? Yet the occurrence had befallen
Perry, not this diarist fellow! Was it possible that *two* such
accidents had happened? No, it was not possible. There were
too many similarities to be coincidental. There was only one
person in London who could be Whistledown's Lady Shrew,
and that person was *her niece!* Somehow this Whistledown
chap had heard the story (perhaps he'd witnessed the accident
himself or heard tell of it at his club) and had decided to write
about it as if it had happened to him. However it had come
about, the conclusion was inescapable: Her darling *Lucienne*
was the shrew that all of London wanted to identify!

Chloe clenched her fists tightly in her lap and glanced up at
her guests. They were eyeing her curiously, as if to ascertain
her reaction to their news. If she gave the slightest hint of
what she was thinking, the Haversleigh ladies would guess. In
record time, they would spread the true identity of the "shrew"
all over town. To prevent this, she had to pretend to be enjoying what she'd heard. Although the effort might kill her, she
had to put a good face on this. She lifted her eyes and forced a
smile. "How vastly amusing," she said brightly.

"Yes, isn't it?" Lady Haversleigh giggled.

"Vastly amusing," Evaline agreed. She leaned forward, her
eyes gleaming cattishly. "Mama thinks the Lady in Question
might be Sybil Sturtevant," she offered.

"Sybil Sturtevant? How can you possible say *that?*" Chloe
found it hard to disguise her disgust. It would have been con-
venient to encourage Fanny to do her conjecturing down the
wrong path, but Chloe could not permit herself to allow the
Haversleighs to malign someone who was completely innocent. "That's just silly," she declared firmly. "Sybil Sturtevant
has been a model of good behavior since her betrothal, and
everyone says so."

Lady Haversleigh snorted. "Perhaps she has, but you may
take my word that it won't last. She's always been a wild,
mischievous creature, and the leopard doesn't change its spot,
you know."

"That scarcely seems an adequate reason for you to suspect
her of—" But Chloe was spared further argument by the

sound of a knock at the door. It was the butler. "I beg pardon, my lady," Kelby said with smooth impassivity, "but I believe you've forgotten that you've an appointment at noon."

The Ladies Haversleigh, having accomplished their mission very satisfactorily, were quite willing to take the hint. They rose to their feet and bustled to the door. "We had no idea it was so late," Lady Haversleigh murmured, bestowing a peck on Chloe's cheek.

"So good to see you, Lady Gerard," Evaline chirped, kissing her other cheek.

Chloe watched them walk down the hall. Then, with a gasp, she ran after them. "Oh, I say, Fanny," she called, trying to sound casual, "I'd love to read the diary for myself. May I borrow your copy?"

"Of course, my dear." Lady Haversleigh handed the magazine over. "Keep it as long as you like."

"And be sure to show it to Lucienne," Evaline added as they went out. "She's bound to find it vastly amusing."

Chapter Four

With the *West-Ender's Monthly* clutched in her hand, Chloe scurried back to the sitting room, dropped down on the window seat and nervously flipped through the pages, looking for the Whistledown Diary. She found it prominently displayed on Page Three. To her surprise the text was in verse rather than in the Roger de Coverly–style prose that Fanny had led her to expect. Her eyes raced over the lines. She found the word *shrew* repeated several times, but, to her intense relief, this first, quick overview revealed no hint of Lucienne's identity. She sighed, took a deep breath, curled her legs up under her and began to read in earnest:

THE WHISTLEDOWN DIARY

By Peregrine Whistledown

noted in my diary this second day of April, eighteen hundred and sixteen:

A Strategem for Shrews

A man whose murder I would fain contrive
Is he who first told Ladies they could drive.
He put good horses' reins in female hand
And undermind the safety of our land!

These female drivers are a group two-fold:
One half too shy, the other much too bold.

It takes the shy ones (always smiling sweet)
A month of Sundays just to cross the street.
But, oh, the Bold! They're something to beware!
With eyes alight and breezes in their hair
They bowl along, their carriages a-sway,
And woe betide whoever's in their way.

I met a "Bold" today, to my regret—
A brush with death that leaves me shaking yet!—
Who turned her phaeton (not once looking round)
At such great speed that two wheels left the ground.
'Twas thus the Lady, driving with panache,
Encountered my equipage with a crash.
We heard wood crack, we felt our senses jarred;
Though horses were unhurt, each coach was marred.

Quite shaken, but unbloodied, I climbed down
To find I faced a Raging Fury's frown.
The driver *looked* a Lady, top to toes,
But never judge a Lady by her clothes!
Invective, accusations and abuse
Poured out of her, but never an excuse.
No word of penitence! She heaped, instead,
Umbrella-blows and insults on my head.
Before too long the watching crowd all knew
Her ladylike facade disguised a Shrew!

Petruchio, when taming Kate the Wild,
Was rough and rude, and soon he made her mild;
But times have changed, and now it will not do
For me to play Petruchio to *my* shrew.
When faced with a Virago, loud and cross,
A Gentleman, today, is at a loss,
For Social Laws decree that, come what might,
With females he must always be polite.
Though *she* may shriek or give his cheek a whack,
He must not even *think* of striking back.
So . . . since I am a Gent. in birth and name,
I meekly smiled and bowed . . . *and took the blame*.

But then and there she changed! To my surprise
My Lady-Shrew just gaped and blinked her eyes
In disbelief that I, despite her slurs,
Would take the blame that patently was hers!
Her lips compressed, her cheeks grew rosy red;
She dropped her eyes and turned away her head.
Not one more curse or insult could she vent:
Her words dried up in Sheer Embarrassment,
And she became, for all the world to see,
The Image of Chagrined Humility!

So, Fellows: when *your* shrews are vile and trying,
This strategem is yours for the applying:
When Ladies grow unladylike and shrill,
We men must turn more gentlemanly still.
If, when they strike, we turn the other cheek,
They soon will learn the world's won by the meek.
'Twas well for *Shakespeare's* Shrew to have a Taming,
But as for us, we'll give *our* shrews a SHAMING!

Chloe stared at the page. "Good *God,*" she muttered under her breath, "I don't know whether to laugh or scream." Who was this Whistledown, anyway, and how had he learned about Lucienne's accident? There was a great deal about this that was confusing, but one thing was certain: Lucienne's reaction would be violent. Whoever this Whistledown fellow was, Lucienne would have his head on a plate!

Chapter Five

Chloe read the verses yet again. This time a laugh reluctantly bubbled up inside her. Evaline Haversleigh was right; the deuced thing *was* vastly amusing. If she could be sure that Lucienne's name would never be linked to this account of the accident, she would feel no animosity toward its author, for she did not find his report in the least vituperative or vengeful. He hadn't intended any harm, she was sure. And no harm would come of it *unless* Lucienne had been unwise enough to relate the story of her accident to someone else—to anyone *at all* (except her trustworthy aunt, of course). If she *had* told someone, the connection between her and the shrew of this "diary" would surely become known, and *then* the harm would be very great indeed, for the poor girl would have to spend the rest of her days in London living down the epithet "Whistledown's Shrew."

It was a little past noon, and Chloe was reading the poem for the third time, when Lucienne wandered in. The girl was yawning and stretching in languorous indifference to her surroundings, to the problem the Haversleighs had brought to her aunt's attention, and even to the time of day. "Good morning, Aunt Chloe," she said cheerily.

Chloe, who'd been so engrossed in her reading that she hadn't heard her niece come in, stated in surprise. "Oh, Lucy, my love! You're awake."

"And about time, too, isn't that what you're trying so hard not to say?" Lucienne teased.

Chloe's startled look was immediately superceded by a fond smile. Although the girl was sleepy-eyed, disheveled and

29

carelessly robed in an extravagantly ruffled dressing gown and bedroom slippers, Chloe found her delightful to gaze upon. Lucienne, with her magnificent hair tumbling over her shoulders and the rosiness of sleep still lingering on her cheeks, looked to her doting aunt like a beautiful goddess, superior to and unaware of the petty squabbles of ordinary, earthly beings. How could anyone, the aunt wondered, call this lovely creature a shrew?

But this thought immediately caused Chloe's smile to fade. The word *shrew* brought to mind the poem she'd been reading, and, feeling instinctively guilty, she dropped her eyes and hastily closed the magazine.

The movement caught Lucienne's attention. "Goodness, Aunt Chloe, what were you studying with such fascination?" she asked as she crossed the room to plant a kiss on her aunt's forehead.

Chloe, without knowing why, tried awkwardly to shove the periodical out of sight behind her on the window seat. "It's nothing important, my love. How are you feeling this morning? Did you sleep well? Are you hungry? Do you wish to take some breakfast now, or will you wait for luncheon?"

Lucienne laughed. "So many questions!" But the words had no sooner left her tongue than it occurred to her that her aunt's manner was unusual—that she was trying to hide the magazine she'd been perusing and that her questions had been more like nervous reflexes than sincere inquiries. Lucienne peered down at her aunt curiously. "You seem unusually abstracted, dearest. Has something in that magazine upset you? Let me see it."

"No, it's nothing. We'll talk about it later." She got up, put an arm about her niece's waist and tried to urge her out of the room. "Come to the breakfast room, love, and we'll see if Kelby can find some coffee and muffins for you."

"Just a moment, Aunt Chloe. Stop trying to distract me. Something is wrong here."

"Wrong? What makes you think there's something wrong?"

Lucienne frowned down at her diminutive aunt from her superior height. "You said, first, that nothing was wrong, and then you said we'd talk about it later. If nothing's wrong, then what is there to talk about later?"

Chloe gave a rueful laugh. "Your logic is deucedly disarming, my love. Very well, then, we'll talk about it now, if you're certain you wish to face it before you've breakfasted."

"Face what, for heaven's sake? One would think there was something terrible about *me* in your blasted magazine."

"That's just it, Lucy. There is."

Lucienne stared at her. "About me? You're joking."

"I wish I were." With a sigh, she dropped down on the sofa and gestured toward the window seat where the magazine still lay. "Look at page three."

Lucienne gaped at her for a moment in disbelief and then strode to the window. She picked up the periodical, her expression more puzzled than frightened, found the page and read the verses.

Her face retained its puzzled expression for several moments, but by the time she'd reached the poem's halfway point she began to wince, and by the time she'd read it all, she was quite pale. "Good God!" she exclaimed in an awed whisper as she slowly sank down on the window-seat.

"Yes, exactly," Chloe said drily. "I couldn't have expressed it better myself."

But Lucienne barely heard her. She continued to stare at the verses in stupefaction. "I can't *believe* it! This . . . this *tripe* . . . it *is* about me!"

"So it seems. There can hardly have been *another* collision in which the lady involved struck the man with an umbrella. But I wouldn't call the piece *tripe*."

This brought Lucienne's head up sharply. "No? What would you call it, then? You can scarcely call this *verse mongering* literature."

"Perhaps not. But the Haversleighs called it vastly amusing, and half of London agrees with them, it seems."

"*Half of London?*" Lucienne echoed with dismay. "You can't mean it."

"I'm afraid I do."

"If you're trying to make me believe that half of London subscribes to this idiotic periodical, you may save your breath, because I *won't* believe it! I've never even *heard* of the . . ."

She looked down at the cover impatiently. ". . . the *West Ender's Monthly.*"

"I don't have any idea of the number of their subscribers, my love," her aunt explained patiently, "but it's not an idiotic periodical, I assure you. It's a political journal of good repute. But what is more relevant to our problem is that the Whistledown Diary itself is widely circulated and often quoted."

"Widely circulated? The Whistledown Diary? But . . . *why?*"

"It's evidently a consistently entertaining piece of writing. Fanny Haversleigh says it's being compared to the Roger de Coverly Papers."

Lucienne snorted in disgust. "Fanny Haversleigh must be a fool!"

Chloe shook her head. "Fanny may be a gossip, but she's not in the least a fool. And speaking of gossip, you haven't even considered the worst part of all this, my dear, and that is the gossip that will result."

"Gossip? I don't know what you mean. What gossip?"

"As the Haversleighs were delighted to inform me, guessing the identity of Whistledown's 'shrew' has become a favorite game in the drawing rooms of the *ton.*"

Lucienne's lovely, dark eyes widened in horror. "Oh, Aunt Chloe, *no!*"

"Yes, Lucy, my love, I'm afraid it's so. I can only hope that you've told no one but me about the details of your accident. If no one knows, no one can connect you with the lady in the verse."

Lucienne's brows drew together. "Let me try to remember. "No . . . no, I don't *think* I told anyone."

"Are you sure, Lucienne? Not even Owen?"

"No, I don't think I did. Owen and I quarreled that day, you know, and I haven't permitted him to speak to me since . . . until last night, that is. And last night, I didn't mention the incident, for I had no wish to give him additional cause to criticize my driving."

"Then we've nothing at all to worry about," Chloe declared with relief, jumping up from the sofa. "Let's forget the entire matter and have a bit of luncheon."

"Forget the matter?" Lucienne glared at her aunt in angry astonishment. "How can you expect me to forget the matter, Aunt Chloe? This Whistledown creature called me a *shrew!* I ought to sue him for *slander!*"

"But, Lucy, dearest, that's *silly.* You can't do that."

Lucienne put her chin up pugnaciously. "Why can't I? The man insulted me in public print!"

"I wouldn't say that. He didn't *name* you, after all."

"But he *meant* me. What if I *had* told someone about the collision? It would be all over town by now that Lucienne Gerard is the Whistledown Shrew! A fine muddle I'd be in *then,* wouldn't I? It's no thanks to him that I'm not!"

"Then there's certainly no need to *thank* him," Chloe said with tongue-in-cheek logic. "But there's no need to sue him, either. You can't claim he *slandered* you if he didn't *name* you. Besides, if you institute a suit for slander, everyone *will* learn the shrew's identity."

"There, do you hear what you just said?" Lucienne accused, jumping to her feet. "Now *you* are calling me a shrew!"

"Now, Lucienne, *really!*" her aunt said reprovingly. "I know you're upset, but you can at least be fair."

"Very well, perhaps I accused *you* unfairly but I'm not unfair about *him.* And as for my point about slander, you needn't behave as if I'm making a royal to-do over this, Aunt. The man called me a 'Raging Fury and a 'virago', he said that I was shrill, that I shrieked and cursed, that only my clothes were ladylike, and several other such imputations. I've never been so insulted in all my life! You cannot expect me to *ignore* it!"

"Of course I expect you to ignore it," Chloe declared firmly. "There's nothing else you *can* do. You don't even know who *wrote* the blasted thing."

Lucienne gave a bitter laugh. "You can't be serious, Aunt Chloe. Do you take me for a fool? Of *course* I know who wrote it."

Chloe blinked. "How can you? Whistledown is obviously a *nom de plume.* Fanny says that no one knows who he is."

"Nonsense. There is no question at all that the writer is your despicable Perry Wittenden!"

Chloe gaped at her in sincere bewilderment. "Perry? You think it's Perry?"

"Of course it is. He's the one with whom I collided, isn't he? Who else could have related the tale in that knowing way?"

Chloe shook her head, refusing to believe it. "Just because it's written in the first person doesn't mean that Perry wrote it, my love. He may have related the story to someone. Or perhaps the author himself witnessed the collision. More likely, the tale was bruited about by some other witness. Then the writer heard about it and decided to write it as if it had happened to him. I understand that writers do such things all the time."

"Perhaps they do, but not this time. Look here, Aunt Chloe, at the author's name. He calls himself Peregrine Whistledown. Wittenden, Whistledown. Do you think the similarity in the sound of the names is merely coincidental?"

Chloe took the magazine and peered at the name intently. "I wonder . . ." she mused, sinking down upon the sofa again. "Whistledown . . . Wittenden. I suppose it *is* possible . . ."

"It's more than possible," her niece insisted, perching on the sofa beside her. "What about the given name? Perry is short for something, is it not? What is your Perry's real given name? Isn't it Peregrine?"

"I don't know," Chloe answered, looking at her niece in confusion. "I've always called him Perry. It might be Percival, might it not?"

"Then he'd be called Percy."

"Yes, I . . . I suppose he would," the deflated Chloe admitted, sagging back against the cushions and putting a hand to her suddenly throbbing temple. "I'm beginning to believe you're right about this."

"Good," her niece said with satisfaction, "but you needn't look so heartbroken about it. If Perry Wittenden wishes to publish his diary for all the world to see, it certainly is no fault of yours."

"No, love, that's not what troubles me. I'm told that there's nothing intimate in his diary-style writings. In fact, I'd be quite proud of him if . . ." She shut her eyes and sighed. "It's just unfortunate that he chose *you* to make sport of."

Lucienne rose majestically from the sofa and strode to the door. "You needn't trouble yourself about *that,* Aunt. In the first place, he doesn't know who I am, for I never gave him my name."

Something in her niece's voice made Chloe open a wary eye. "And in the second place?"

"In the second place," the girl declared between clenched teeth, "*I shall make that dastard sorry he ever took pen in hand!*" And with those ominous words, she stormed out of the room in a swirl of ruffles.

Chloe groaned. What mischief, she wondered uncomfortably, would her hot-tempered niece concoct to accomplish that threat? For the first time since her niece had arrived, she felt sorry she'd invited the girl. Trouble was looming like a thundercloud, and Chloe feared that she would be as incapable of preventing it as she would of holding back a storm.

A sound at the door forced her to open her eyes and sit erect. It was Kelby again. "The footman has returned from Charles Street, your ladyship," he informed her, "and he's brought Lord Wittenden's response."

Chloe gaped at her butler in horror. She'd completely forgotten that less than an hour ago she'd invited Perry to dinner. But in that one brief hour since she'd sent the footman with the invitation, the whole situation had changed. Good heavens, what had she done? She couldn't have him come *now.* At *best,* Lucienne would be certain to refuse to sit down with the fellow, and God only knew what the *worst* might be!

Wordlessly, she put out her hand for Perry's note and, staring at the envelope as if it contained a blood-stained instrument of torture, she waved the butler from the room. *Perhaps he will say he is not free,* she told herself, breaking the seal. *He is certain to have more interesting things to do in the evenings than come to dine with an old lady like me. I needn't be so uneasy about this.*

But those words gave her only momentary comfort, for after one quick glance at the neatly inscribed words she knew there was no hope. The note was brief, pleasant and to the point. He thanked her for her invitation and declared that he'd be delighted to dine with her. "Good God!" she muttered aloud. "What do I do now?"

Chapter Six

At first Lucienne could do nothing but seethe. She locked herself in her room for the rest of the afternoon, refusing to take either luncheon or tea. The more she thought about that insulting doggerel, the angrier she became. Wittenden's words—"her ladylike facade disguised a shrew"—reverberated in her head, each syllable clanging like the stroke of a too-loud gong. She paced round and round her bedroom, occasionally pressing her fingers to her temples, but if the gesture was an attempt to press the memory of those humiliating verses out of her mind, it was in vain. More and more of those painful phrases came back to her. "A virago loud and cross," he'd written... and "if *your* shrews are vile and trying..." (wherein the words, *like mine,* were very distinctly implied). *His* shrew, indeed! His implications were as degrading as they were dishonest. She had certainly not been as vile and trying as he was suggesting in those blasted verses! At worst one might say that she'd been a *bit* cross and *perhaps* a bit trying, but to be called shrill, vile, a virago and a shrew was going much too far!

The *insolence* of the fellow! How *dare* he malign her so dreadfully! Her feelings toward him were positively murderous. If she were a man she would call him out! But of course, if she were a man, this never would have happened. If it had been a *man* who'd collided with Wittenden's curricle, Wittenden couldn't have called him a shrew. There wasn't a word in English—at least, none that she could think of—that was a masculine counterpart of *shrew.* The worst he could have called a man in a like situation was *hothead* or *churl,* neither of which were particularly humiliating epithets. But a hot-headed *woman* was a *shrew*, and there were few words in the language more insulting than that.

She could, she supposed, ask Owen to challenge the fellow in her name and fight a duel for her sake. She was certain that Owen, who looked to be a head taller and two stone heavier than Wittenden, would have no difficulty in besting the fellow with a sword. And oh, how very satisfying it would be to see Wittenden writhing on the ground, bleeding from a sword wound and groaning in agony! That sight would surely be sweet revenge.

She would not wish the wound to be mortal, of course. It would not do for Owen to be brought before the magistrates for murder. But illegal dueling, if it did not result in serious injury, was often overlooked by the authorities. In fact, it was unlikely that any charges would be brought against Owen; Wittenden would surely not wish his humiliation to be made public. He would probably do nothing but crawl home, defeated and degraded, and nurse his wound in silence. Yes, a duel would give her much satisfaction, especially if it resulted in Wittenden's being left with an ugly scar to remind him forever that there was a price to pay for calling Lucienne Gerard a shrew.

But, truth be told, she didn't really want to ask Owen to fight a duel for her. Such a request would require that she reveal to him the full facts about the accident, and for some reason the prospect of relating the details to him was distasteful to her. Owen could sometimes be rather stuffy, she had to admit, and he'd indicated earlier that he disapproved of her tendency toward hoydenish behavior. In addition, they'd already quarreled about his remark concerning the reckless way she drove. She had no wish to give him another opportunity to lecture her on the subject. It was even possible that he might tell her that she *deserved* the set-down that "Whistledown" had given her. If he *did* take it on himself to say something like that, she would be furious, and the resulting rift between them might be irremedial. No, all things considered, she would be wiser to keep Owen out of this . . . to keep him completely ignorant of the fact that "Whistledown's shrew" was the very girl to whom he'd offered his hand.

Thus Lucienne reluctantly gave up the idea of a duel. But there were other ways of getting revenge. She was not without ideas. She perched upon her bed and gave serious consideration to a scheme to send Wittenden a hugely overinflated bill for the repairs to her carriage. However, she soon rejected that idea. Not only had she too much pride to ask for money for the repairs when she knew in her heart that she'd caused the damage, but she also realized, from what Chloe had told her, that Wittenden was wealthy enough to feel no suffering from paying such a bill, no matter how greatly she inflated it. *Where is the joy of revenge,* she asked herself as she fell back against the pillows in disgust, *if the victim doesn't suffer?*

Then she considered writing her own version of the incident and offering it to the *West-Ender's Monthly* for publication. That was a *splendid* idea! She would compose a satiric counter-attack in verse, so devastating that Wittenden would not be able to show his face in public again. She leaped from the bed, sat down at her writing table and picked up a pen. Ten minutes later, however, she rejected that idea, too. It took her merely those ten minutes of trial and error to realize that writing verse was not as easy as it seemed and that she did not have the talent for satire that her adversary had.

Somewhat chastened, she threw herself upon the bed again. Her mind, searching about in desperation to find the satisfaction she sought, returned to her original intent: to institute a suit for slander against Wittenden. It would be lovely, she thought, her lips turning up in a wicked smile, to see Wittenden manacled hand and foot, hauled away to prison and put on trial. How she wished such an occurrence would come to pass! She could see it all in her imagination . . . how, on the day of his trial, she'd dress herself in a splendid costume, seat herself right in his line of vision and let him watch her as she smiled in cool disdain while he wriggled miserably in the dock. How she'd laugh while the judges would attack him with nasty questions, accuse him of making scurrilous accusations against a lovely and innocent female, deride him for defaming a lady's reputation while hiding behind a *nom de plume*, and at last sentence him to long years in a *dingy* gaol with no company but rats! It was a most delicious scenario.

But after thinking about it carefully she realized that her

aunt's two objections to the plan (one, that she'd have to identify herself as the shrew in order to instigate such a suit; and two, that it would be difficult to prove he'd slandered her when she was not named or even physically described) were too strong to be overthrown.

She was just beginning to despair of ever concocting a satisfactory scheme when an idea dawned upon her that was so naughty, so devilish, so irresistibly *wicked* that she jumped up again and danced around the room in glee. It was a wonderful scheme, and the more she thought about it, the better it seemed. It had no drawbacks, no danger, and it could be instituted almost at once. And all she needed to set it in motion was the assistance of her abigail.

Trudy, the abigail her aunt had engaged especially for her, was the perfect choice for the role Lucienne wanted her to play. She was the right age for the part, had a delightful streets-of-London way of speaking, and had just the air of pathetic innocence that Lucienne required. Lucienne rang for her at once.

When Trudy came in, Lucienne ordered her to sit down. The sweet-faced, sad-eyed abigail blinked in surprise. "Sit down, Miss Lucy? Me?"

"Yes, of course, you. Sit down, Trudy, please. Here, you can perch beside me on the bed."

The maid demurred. "I cain't be sittin' down now, Miss. It's almost dinnertime, and you ain't dressed."

"Is it as late as that? Oh, dear. Very well, you can do up my hair while we talk. Listen carefully, Trudy, for I want you to do a very great favor for me. I want you to enact a role for me . . . just as if you were in a play."

"A *play,* Miss? Me?" the abigail inquired, her brows rising in astonishment but beginning to brush the tangles from her mistress's tousled hair anyway.

"It's not really a play, Trudy. But you're to act a role as *if* it were a play."

"Act a role? Me?"

Lucienne expelled an exasperated breath. "I wish you'd stop asking 'Me?' in that way. Since there's no one else in the room with us, who else can I be talking to? Of *course* I mean you."

"But I ain't no actress, Miss Lucy. I ain't never even *seen* a play."

"That doesn't matter. It's not a play, really. It's just a bit of . . . of pretense."

Trudy's brush halted. "I don' understan', Miss. What sort of pretense?"

"It's difficult to explain, I'm afraid, but it will be very easy to execute, Trudy, I promise you. There's no need to look so frightened, really there isn't. You won't even have to say a word. All you'll have to do is nod your head when I ask you a question. You can nod your head, can't you?"

"Yes, I s'pose I cin nod me 'ead."

"Good. Now, the situation is this. Tomorrow we're going to pay a call on a gentleman of my acquaintance—"

"*We*, Miss Lucy?"

"Yes, we. You and I. But we'll pretend that we've just met . . . that I've not known you before. I'm going to say I found you in a river tavern, hungry, tearful and . . . well . . . in the family way, if you know what I mean."

The abigail dropped the brush. "Did ye say . . . wut I tho't ye said? In the f-family way, Miss?"

"Yes, that's what I said. You know what I mean, don't you? Breeding. Expecting. With child."

"Ye wish me t' pretend I'm . . . *breedin'?*" the abigail asked, horrified.

"Yes, exactly."

The maid stared at Lucienne's reflection in the mirror, her mouth agape. "Oh, *Miss*," she breathed, "I *couldn't—!*"

"Nonsense," Lucienne said flatly, bending down, retrieving the hairbrush and thrusting it into Trudy's hand. "Of course you can."

"B-but, Miss Lucy, I don' understan' the game 'ere. You know I ain't wed. I'm a good girl, see, a real good girl. I couldn't—!"

"Will you stop babbling, Trudy, and listen to me? I know you're not the sort to get yourself in that kind of trouble. This is only a . . . a *trick* I'm playing on someone."

"Trick? What do ye mean, trick?"

"You'll see. It'll all become clear when we . . . er . . . perform it. Please say you'll do it for me. It will all be over in a few minutes, and then you can forget all about it."

The maid studied her mistress with bemused suspicion. "I don' wish t' be disobligin', Miss Lucy, but I don' know what yer askin' of me. You want me t' go wi' ye to some gen'leman's house an' pretend I'm in the family way?"

"Yes. Exactly."

"But how'm I t' pretend it if I don' do nothin' but nod me 'ead?"

"I'll do all the speaking, you needn't worry about that." Lucienne jumped up and grasped the girl by the shoulders. "Please, Trudy, say you'll do it! There won't be any trouble over this, I promise. Have I ever broken my word to you?"

The girl lowered her eyes. "No, cain't say ye 'ave. But you've never asked me to pretend to be breedin' afore, either."

"Trudy, please. It would mean such a great deal to me."

Trudy sighed. "Well, if it's so important t' ye . . ."

Lucienne threw her arms about the dubious girl. "Thank you, Trudy! It's very good of you to agree. You have my undying gratitude."

Trudy shrugged. "That's as may be," she muttered as she urged her mistress to return to the chair so that she might resume her work on the tangles, "but I 'ope no one'll ever get wind o' this scheme o' yours, Miss."

"No one will, I swear it. No one will ever hear of this. It will all be over before you know it. We'll never even mention your real name to the gentleman, so your reputation will not be at all affected. And when it's over, we need not ever tell a soul. You have my solemn word you won't be sorry."

"I 'ope not, Miss Lucy. I truly 'ope not," the maid said with feeling, rolling her eyes heavenward, "'cause if me ma ever 'eard tell that I wuz breedin' . . . even *pretend* breedin' . . . ye cin lay odds I'd be *very* sorry indeed."

Chapter Seven

Perry Wittenden stared at the letter in his hand, wondering what to do. It was a brief missive from his father, the sort of letter the old Earl always wrote, in which he made brusque comments on the state of the government, reported that everything was satisfactory at home, and extended terse good wishes for his son's continued health and happiness. This time, however, he had let slip a little phrase that hinted that Perry's grandmother was ailing. Perry, with a slight constriction of worry in his chest, studied the letter carefully for other clues concerning his grandmother's condition, but there were none.

Perry wondered if he should make a journey home. He was reluctant to do so, for his grandmother would be certain to take offense at his assumption that she was really ill. She was the sort who hated to admit an infirmity. If he came running up to be at her bedside, she would berate him soundly. "One would think I was at death's door!" she'd be sure to exclaim.

Besides, it would be awkward to have to leave London right now. The social season was just beginning, and he had accepted at least a dozen invitations. Why was it that problems of this kind always came up at the worst times?

Perry, who'd been forced to spend his first twenty-four years dividing his time between the seclusion of the Wittenden estate in Norfolk and the cloistered, scholarly world of Harrow and Oxford, was delighted to be living at last the dashing life of a bachelor in the heart of the most vibrant metropolis in the world. His Charles Street townhouse in London's West End was only steps away from the clubs of St. James and the theaters and opera houses of King Street, the Haymarket, Covent Garden and Drury Lane; a mere stroll took him to Westminster, Buckingham Palace and the homes of most of his friends; and it was only a short ride to the City where his business agent was housed and to Fleet Street where the office of the *West-Ender's Monthly* was located. He was now where he always wanted to be, doing what he'd always wanted to do. He'd never been so happy and busy before.

In less than a year, he'd made himself at home. He had many friends with whom he dined or gamed at White's; he had a steady stream of invitations from the leaders of society (all of whom would have admitted, if asked, that his wealth, titles and what Lady Jersey had termed his "intrinsic amiability" made him high on the list of Desirable Catches on the Marriage Mart and thus a favorite of all the hostesses of the *ton*); he had the interest of several lovely young ladies, a couple of whom were putting out lures for him, and, best of all, he had a magazine publisher who thought so well of his casual writings that he was printing them pseudonymously in his magazine every month. Perry couldn't have wished for a more satisfying life.

There was only one fly in the sweet ointment of his London existence—the absence of his family. He had hoped that his father and his grandmother would pay frequent visits to London, but they hadn't come. His father's second wife was something of a recluse who detested the social whirl of London, and the old Earl was reluctant to leave her. And his grandmother, who would have been delighted to spend some time in town being escorted about by her beloved grandson, had suddenly begun to feel the effects of age and reluctantly admitted that she was becoming too frail to make the long trip. Despite the excitement of his new life, Perry missed them.

He certainly missed them at this moment. He missed his grandmother so much, in fact, that the thought of remaining in town while she might be lying at home ill became suddenly repugnant to him. Shrugging, he made his decision: He would go home at once. It would be better to face his grandmother's ire than to spend the next few weeks worrying about her condition. He rang for Magnus, his butler-valet, and ordered him

to pack a bag and to arrange for the carriage to be brought to
the door within the hour. Then he removed his coat, sat down
at his desk in his shirtsleeves and began to write apologetic
notes to those hostesses whose invitations he'd accepted for
the next few days.

He'd already composed a sizable pile of letters when he
came across a note in his appointment book reminding him of
the dinner invitation from Lady Chloe Gerard. He'd written an
acceptance only yesterday. He hated to reverse himself now.
He was very fond of Chloe; she was lively, spirited, intelligent
and maternally affectionate. In addition, she was the one person in the world, other than his father, who had known his
mother intimately. His father never spoke of his deceased first
wife, but Chloe loved to reminisce about her. Perry always
found conversation with Chloe fascinating and had been antic-
ipating dinner in her company with real pleasure.

He chewed the tip of his pen, studying the date of the
invitation. May fifteenth. That was six days hence. He might
very well make it back to London by that time, if the situation
at home was not serious. He would not break the appointment,
he decided. If it came to pass that his grandmother's condition
was serious, he would write to Chloe from Norfolk.

That final decision made, he tossed his pen aside, took off
his spectacles and wearily rubbed the bridge of his nose.
Then, with a purposeful sigh, he replaced the glasses and rose
from his desk. He was reaching for his coat when he heard
Magnus clear his throat. He looked round to find the butler
eyeing him from the doorway. Magnus, whose protruding
stomach and triple chin gave him a look of lordly dignity,
usually kept his facial expressions impassive and unreadable,
but at this moment Perry was surprised to note that the butler's
brows were raised in a manner that clearly expressed curiosity. "Yes, Magnus?" he asked, puzzled.

"There's a pair of . . . er . . . ladies asking to see you, my
lord," Magnus replied, the corners of his mouth turned down
in his effort to keep from grinning.

"Ladies?" Perry froze in the act of slipping his arm into his
coat. "Did you say *ladies?* Here? But it's almost nine at
night!"

"Yes, my lord, I know," the butler said, crossing the room

in imperious dignity and helping Perry on with his coat.

"Didn't you ask their names?"

"I asked, my lord, but they would not supply them. One of them explained that her name would mean nothing to you but that you would recognize her face."

"Would I indeed?" Perry muttered drily. His brow creased in an endeavor to recall a nameless face. "How strange! I can't imagine . . ."

"Shall I send them in, my lord, or do you wish me to send them away."

"No, I'll go out to them. But don't go too far away, Magnus. I haven't much time. I may need your help to get rid of them if they are inclined to linger."

Perry walked quickly down the hall, buttoning his coat. The two ladies stood waiting in the foyer, one hiding timidly behind the other. The foremost one, a startlingly pretty young woman, was wearing a fur-trimmed spencer and a feathered *bergere* hat that looked quite fashionable. The other was drabbly draped in a gray cloak and black bonnet that had seen better days. He gave them each a tentative smile but addressed the braver of the two. "You wished to see me, ma'am?"

The woman studied him brazenly. "Lord Wittenden, is it not? *Peregrine* Wittenden?"

"Yes, that is my name. But I'm afraid you have the advantage of me, ma'am, for I don't believe I've had the pleasure of *your* acquaintance."

The woman raised a pair of shapely eyebrows. "Oh, but you have," she insisted. "Look at me closely, my lord. Don't you recognize me? Unless I'm very much mistaken, you even *wrote* about our encounter in the *West-Ender*."

Perry adjusted his spectacles and stared at her for a moment. Then his brow cleared. "Of *course!* The lady in the blue carriage! How do you do, ma'am?" Relieved that the mystery had been so quickly and easily solved, he grinned at her with friendly warmth. "Have you come for your checque?"

"Checque?" Lucienne was confused. She'd expected neither the question nor the warm greeting. "I don't know what you mean."

"I did promise to pay for the damages, didn't I? If I remember rightly, that included not only the damages to the carriage but to your charming hat as well. What does it come to, ma'am?"

Lucienne glared at him. "I have *not* come for a checque, my lord. Do you take me for a sponger as well as a shrew?"

"Sponger, ma'am?" Perry asked, the brightness of his charming half-smile dimming. "I don't understand you. It is not sponging to collect that which was promised to you."

Lucienne flicked her arm in a gesture of disgust. "You only made that promise to get out of the rain. The accident, as you insisted at the time, was my fault."

"But I'm perfectly willing to pay for the damages."

"Of course you are," she sneered. "That would be a cheap and easy way to extricate yourself from this situation, wouldn't it?"

"Extricate myself?" He peered at her in bewilderment. "I'm afraid you've lost me, ma'am. If I'm willing to pay for the damages, I fail to see what sort of 'situation' I must extricate myself from."

"The situation, my lord," she replied, enunciating each syllable with venom, "is the witch's brew you concocted when you libeled me in the public print by calling me a shrew."

"Ah, I begin to see. We are speaking of the verses in the *West-Ender*." He grinned. "If we are to speak of those verses, ma'am—and it is a subject I never tire of discussing—perhaps it would be better to sit down. Would you and your companion like to accompany me to the drawing room?"

Lucienne shook her head coldly. "No, thank you. We can say what we have to say standing right here."

"Very well, if that is what you wish," Perry said pleasantly.

"That is what I wish. Now, to return to the subject of your libelous characterization of me as a shrew—"

"But, my dear young lady, there was no libel involved. I didn't call *you* a shrew. The lady in my verse was a fiction—a character of my imagination. You are, of course, justified in assuming that you were the inspiration for the verse, but we poor writers must take our inspiration where we find it."

"Are you denying that the details of the accident in your verse were the same as what really happened?"

"The details may have been similar but they—as well as the lady—were transformed, you see. They became a fiction

. . . merely a *tale,* used to make a humorous point about men and women in society. By the time the verse was written, any connection with reality was far from my mind. The truth is, ma'am, that I didn't think of my shrew as a *real* person at all."

"It makes no difference what *you* think, my lord. All of London thinks of her as real. I'm told that the newest parlor game is guessing the identity of your shrew."

"Is it indeed?" Perry asked, his eyes lighting up. "I had no idea my verses were so widely read."

"This one seems to be. So what do you intend to do about it, eh?"

"Do about it? Why, nothing."

Lucienne stiffened in indignation. *"Nothing?"*

"Of course, nothing. What did you expect me to do?"

"I expected, my lord, that you would print an apology. A humble, heartfelt apology."

"But ma'am," he remonstrated calmly, "what have I to apologize for? And to whom?"

"To me, you nincompoop! To *me!"*

"To you? Do you mean by name?"

"No, of course not. Do you take me for a fool? Just write a retraction of the entire verse. Say that the story was exaggerated and that the lady was not as despicable as you painted her."

"Pardon me, ma'am, for being blunt, but that's ridiculous. I've just explained that the lady in the verse isn't you. She's nothing but a figment of my imagination. How can I write a retraction to a . . . a ghost?"

"Are you refusing me, then? You won't print a retraction?"

"How can I? An apology to an unnamed, nonexistent creature? I'd be making an utter ass of myself."

Lucienne's magnificent eyes flashed fire. "You'd rather make an ass of me, is that it?"

Perry sighed patiently. "You have nothing to do with it. I don't even know your name. The readers don't know it. They don't even know *mine.* You and I don't exist in this matter. There's only the pseudonymous Whistledown, his imaginary diary, and the imaginary characters who inhabit it."

"That is not how I see the matter. I have been maligned, and I want you to write a retraction."

Perry peered at her intently through his spectacles. "You appear to me a young woman much accustomed to getting what you want," he remarked in his mild, gentle-humored fashion, "but much as I regret it, ma'am, you cannot get what you want in this matter. If my verses have caused you pain or embarrassment, I'm truly sorry, but there's nothing I can do to change matters. So if you'll excuse me, ma'am, since I am a bit pressed for time, I'll call my man to see you to your carriage."

"Not yet, my good fellow, not quite yet," Lucienne said, lifting her chin aggressively. "I'm afraid you can not squirm out of this so easily. I haven't yet played my trump card."

"Oh? You have a trump card, have you?" His quirky grin reappeared. "And what's that?"

"This young woman here. Her name is . . . er . . . Violet. Say how-de-do to his lordship, Violet."

The drab young woman gulped. "How d-d-do, yer lordship," she mumbled, dropping a curtsey.

"How do you do?" Perry responded interestedly. "And what have you to do with all this, Violet?"

The woman called Violet glanced nervously at Lucienne. *"M-Me,* m'lord?"

"Violet has a *great deal* to do with this," Lucienne said firmly. "I found her at a riverside tavern, cold and hungry. She has been . . . er . . . seduced. Seduced and . . . and abandoned. The poor girl is *breeding*. Isn't that so, Violet?"

Violet, throwing the other woman a look of pure terror, nodded her head.

"Is she indeed?" Perry asked, not looking at all perturbed. "Breeding, eh? And abandoned? I'm sorry to hear it. Am I right in suspecting that you are about to make some connection with that interesting information and the subject we were just discussing?"

"Yes, my lord, I am," Lucienne declared. "The connection is simply this. If an apology for the verse does not appear in the next issue of the *West-Ender*, I shall reveal to all the world that it is you, Peregrine Whistledown Whittenden, who's responsible for this poor girl's miserable condition."

Perry blinked at her through his spectacles for one brief moment. Then, to Lucienne's astonishment, he threw back his head and laughed. He laughed so hard that tears came to his eyes, and he had to remove his spectacles to brush them away.

"I fail to see what amuses you about this, my lord," Lucienne said tightly. "Violet's situation is nothing to laugh at."

"I earnestly apologize, Miss Violet," his lordship gasped, trying to swallow his persistent guffaws. "If you are truly breeding... and abandoned, too... I'm sincerely sorry for you. I wasn't laughing at your situation, but at the suggestion that I might be held responsible." He turned to Lucienne, smiling broadly. "Do you really intend to tell the world that I'm the father of Violet's child?"

"Of course. Don't doubt it for a moment!"

The frightened abigail wrung her hands. "But *Miss,*" she hissed, "you never tol' me you was goin t'—"

"Hush, you prattle-box!" Lucienne snapped. "I told you *I* would do the talking."

"You realize, don't you," Perry pointed out, "that you'll have to explain to the world not only how you discovered this hideous secret of my past but why it concerns you? Your own identity will certainly have to be revealed as well. Are you willing to go through all that just because I refuse to apologize for my insignificant verses?"

"Yes, I am."

He shook his head in amused disbelief. "Then by all means, go ahead and do it."

Poor "Violet" moaned.

Lucienne clenched her fists. "Have you no care for your reputation, my lord? Do you wish the world to believe you to be a vile seducer?"

"I doubt if the world will believe it, ma'am. Not without proof. And, of course, you have no proof."

Lucienne smiled a gloating smile, for she'd already thought of this. "But what does proof matter in a case of this sort? Unfortunately for you, I've noticed that the world quite readily accepts the worst accusations to be the truth, even without proof."

"Ah, but not if the accuser is proved false," Perry countered cheerfully.

"The accuser? Me, you mean?" Her self-satisfied smile wavered. "And how, may I ask, can you do that?"

"Quite simply. I need only to ask Violet to describe the birthmark which is prominently placed on my body. Anyone with whom I was intimate would have to have seen it. Well, Violet?"

The abigail froze in fear, a gurgle of misery escaping from her throat.

"Good heavens," Lucienne muttered, "I suppose you *could* make inquiries of that sort in public."

"Of course I could . . . and *would*, if I had to," Perry said. Then he turned to the abigail and smiled at her kindly. "Don't be frightened. I shan't do you any harm, Miss Violet. I'll even give you a hint. Is the birthmark oval or heart-shaped?"

Lucienne put a protective arm about her maid. She, as much as Trudy, was startled by this unexpected turn the conversation had taken. She realized with a sinking heart that she hadn't thought her plan through carefully enough. She'd been hasty and probably foolish as well. But she was caught in it now, and there was nothing for it but to play out this little scene she'd initiated. Wittenden was waiting for an answer to his birthmark question. She had to say something. Thinking quickly, she reasoned that a birthmark was more likely to be oval than heart-shaped. "Violet's already confided to me that your mark is . . . er . . . oval," she declared, lifting her chin proudly. She was determined to conclude with courage the battle that she was beginning to suspect she'd already lost.

"Oval, eh?" Perry smiled at her in admiration. "That's a sensible guess. I would have chosen that answer, too, if I'd been in your shoes."

"Then my answer is correct, my lord? I've proven my point?"

"I said your answer was sensible. I didn't say it was correct. I'm not such a fool that I'd reveal the correct answer at this time. But even if your answer was correct, it would have been more convincing coming from Violet. Let's try another question, shall we? And this time, perhaps Violet will answer for herself. Violet, tell me . . . is the oval birthmark—if it *is* an oval—on my shoulder or my hip?"

Trudy shuddered. Lucienne met Perry's eye brazenly for a

moment and then looked down at Trudy, who was huddled like a frightened rabbit in the crook of her mistress's arm. Lucienne turned her head to Trudy's ear. "You can say something, can't you, my dear?" she whispered. "You only need to venture a guess. There's an excellent chance you'll be right. Which is it?"

"I dun*no!*" poor Trudy cried, bursting into tears.

"No, of course you don't," Perry said gently.

Lucienne sighed. That had done it. She'd lost the game. Neither she nor Trudy had been capable of carrying through the deception. And what was most irritating of all was that Wittenden, knowing that he'd beaten her, was not crowing over his victory. He was being kind.

But she could not indulge in these thoughts now, not with Wittenden peering at her and Trudy sobbing. She turned her attention to her unhappy abigail. "There, there, Trud—Violet," she murmured consolingly, taking the weeping girl in her arms, "no need for tears. I told you it was only a . . ." She paused and met Perry's eyes bravely over Trudy's bent head. ". . . a pretense. This gentleman understands that you've been playing a role."

"Oh, Miss L-Lucy, I *knowed* no g-good would c-come o' this," Trudy sobbed into Lucienne's shoulder. " 'Ow cin I act a r-role when I ain't n-never even seen a *p-p-play?*"

Lucienne, wincing in embarrassment, nevertheless patted the maid's shoulder soothingly. "Never mind, my dear. The 'play' is over now. Let's go home."

"I'll call my man to see you to your carriage," Perry said as he pressed a handkerchief into the sobbing maid's hand.

"I'm right here, my lord," Magnus said, appearing as if from nowhere.

"Would you like a cup of tea or a drink of negus before you go?" his lordship offered the ladies kindly.

"That won't be necessary," Lucienne said curtly, turning Trudy toward the door. "I shall take care of her at home. I hope you're pleased with yourself, my lord. Not only have you succeeded in maligning me and refusing to make amends for it, but you've heartlessly reduced this poor girl to tears."

"Oh? *I've* reduced her to tears, have I?" Perry eyed her quizzically. "How is it, ma'am, that, innocent as I am, you always manage to find me guilty of some gross fault?"

"I don't know," she retorted over her shoulder as she led Trudy across the foyer to the doorway. "Perhaps fault-finding is a talent of mine, as writing verses is a talent of yours. I'm obviously not very good at my talent, but, if you ask me my opinion," she added nastily, "I think I'm better at it than you are at yours."

He laughed good-naturedly. "That's a facer, ma'am. Even if I thought highly enough of my poor verses to defend them, I realize that self-praise is the poorest recommendation. So you win that point, at least."

"Yes, but you won the major one," she admitted. At the door, she turned round to glare at him in sudden suspicion. "I'll wager you haven't a birthmark at all, have you?"

A grin lit his face. "Neither oval nor heart-shaped," he confessed.

"Dash it all, I should have guessed!" She expelled a furious breath. "Very well, my lord. The winning point *is* yours. But I warn you . . . if I ever find myself the subject of one of your literary efforts again, I shall institute a suit for slander against you that will cost you every cent you have in the world!" With that, she swept herself and her companion out of the door and slammed it behind her.

Perry stared at the shut door for a long moment. "What a very argumentative young lady that was, to be sure," he remarked.

"Yes, my lord, I quite agree," Magnus said, peering out of the door's glass inset to make sure the ladies were safely dispatched.

"Strange that such a pretty creature should have so irascible a temper. She was very lovely, though, didn't you think so, Magnus?"

"Oh, yes, my lord. Very lovely. Did you learn her name?

"No, come to think of it, I didn't. Her maid called her Lucy. I suppose I could inquire . . ." Perry continued to stare at the door thoughtfully for another moment. Then he shrugged. "But no, there's no point in it. Deuced provoking creature." He turned with sudden purposefulness and made for the stairs.

"I could make inquiries for you, my lord," Magnus offered.

"Don't bother," Perry said over his shoulder as he ran up two steps at a time. "She's not the sort I'd wish to know. If she ever comes calling again, Magnus,—" His voice died as he stopped abruptly in mid-climb.

"Yes, my lord? If she ever comes calling again—?" Magnus prompted.

"Never mind," Perry said, waving his arm before his eyes as if brushing away the whole troublesome subject. "She won't. That's one young lady we're not likely to see again."

Chapter Eight

Although Lucienne confided to Chloe nothing of her disastrous visit to Wittenden House, Chloe noticed that Lucienne's anger at Perry and his verses did not abate. Lucienne invariably flared up at the very mention of the Wittenden name. It soon became clear to Chloe that Lucienne would not forgive him. Therefore, she realized, she had to rescind her dinner invitation to him.

It was not a pleasant chore. She was terribly fond of Perry, and she had no wish to offend him, but how could he help but feel offended by a note which *un*invited him to dinner? What could one say in an *un*invitation: *Lady Chloe Gerard cordially invites you* not *to be present on the night of May fifteenth?*

To tell Perry the truth was, of course, out of the question. She couldn't admit to Perry that her niece detested him. That sort of honesty would never be acceptable in polite society. She tried long and hard to invent an excuse that would be both plausible and forgivable, but she could think of nothing. In the end, she merely wrote that "something unforeseen had come up," and that she "most sincerely regretted" being unable to entertain him that evening. She sealed the note, sent it off to Charles Street and, swallowing her disappointment that her favorite candidate for Lucienne's hand was no longer to be considered, tried to put the whole affair out of her mind.

As she dressed for a casual, at-home dinner on the evening of May fifteenth she couldn't help but think of Perry. If her plan had succeeded, she would now be donning her favorite plum-colored crepe gown, letting her dresser curl her hair and humming to herself in joyous anticipation of the evening. As

55

it was, however, she wasn't bothering to do her hair at all, and she'd chosen to wear an ordinary muslin round-gown that she'd always disliked because the shade was a too-brown puce, a color so dreary that it exactly suited her mood.

Her mood was mopishly glum. Although she usually didn't permit herself to indulge in ill humours, she felt that she could forgive herself for this one lapse. How else was she expected to feel, she asked herself, when all her hopes had been dashed? Just yesterday, Lucienne had written to her father that she'd accepted Sir Owen Tatlow's offer of marriage. The girl —now officially betrothed—was happily sporting the Tatlow family ring, a huge black pearl surrounded by diamonds. Chloe had no choice now but to accept the inevitable. She would have to spend the next few months helping Lucienne with her wedding plans, but she would take little pleasure in the preparations. Tonight was to be the first of many evenings in which she, Lucienne and Owen would be dining together and making plans. In the future, she would force herself to be cheerful, but was it so very dreadful to permit herself, for a short while, to indulge in the dismals?

The answer was yes, it was indeed dreadful. It wouldn't be kind to Lucy to be less than happy for her. Thus, when her toilette was completed, Chloe shook off her doldrums by sheer force of character and went downstairs. Kelby informed her that Miss Lucienne had not yet come down, but that Sir Owen had arrived and was awaiting his hostess in the drawing room. Chloe went to join him. She found him standing at the fireplace, comfortably leaning on the mantel and smoking a pipe. If she'd been in a different mood, she might have admired his appearance. In evening clothes, Owen's magnificent shoulders and trim hips were set off to perfection, and his stance with his pipe was so masculinely graceful that he might have been posing for a Reynolds portrait. But all Chloe felt was irritation. She very much disliked the smell of pipe smoke, and she disliked even more that he hadn't asked her permission before lighting up. Nevertheless, she forced a smile. "Ah, good evening, Owen. You've made yourself at home, I see."

"Lady Chloe, good evening. By saying that I've made myself at home, you're referring to my pipe, I suppose." With a complacent smile, he crossed the room and bowed over her hand. "Yes, I have made myself at home. I didn't think you'd mind my taking a few puffs before dinner."

Chloe would have liked to snap that she *did* mind, but her habitual good manners stilled her tongue. In a few years, she promised herself, when she became really old, she would permit herself to speak her mind and behave like an ill-tempered, crochety eccentric. Eccentricity in the elderly was considered charming, but she was still a few years too young to get away with it. Instead of telling him roundly that she didn't like her beautiful drawing room filled with his ill-smelling smoke, she merely removed her hand from his grasp and waved him to a chair. "Would you like some sherry before dinner, or is your pipe a sufficient *aperitif?*" she asked.

Owen's complacency was such that he completely missed the undertone of disapproval in her voice. He sat down in the armchair she'd indicated and continued to puff at his pipe. "A sherry would be delightful," he said.

Chloe was about to ring for Kelby, when the butler appeared as if by magic in the doorway. "Kelby!" Chloe said in surprise."You must have read my mind. I was just about to ring for you to bring in some sherry."

"Yes, your ladyship, at once. But I didn't read your mind." He threw her a worried look. "I came to announce the arrival of Lord Wittenden."

Chloe paled. "What?" she asked stupidly. "Did you say *Wittenden?*"

The butler, who was well aware that her ladyship had withdrawn her invitation to Lord Wittenden, gave an almost imperceptible and helpless shrug. "Yes, my lady. Lord Wittenden. He's here." And he stepped aside to admit the unexpected caller.

Perry, perfectly garbed in evening dress and bearing a bouquet of flowers, stepped into the room. "Good evening, Lady Chloe," he said with innocent warmth, holding out his bouquet. "I hope I haven't kept you waiting."

Chloe's mouth dropped open while her brain seemed to freeze. "Perry? What—?"

Her stupefied expression brought Perry to a standstill. "Have I made a mistake?" he asked, nonplussed. "Have I come at the wrong hour or mistaken the date?"

There was no answer from his hostess, who was stricken speechless. Owen slowly got to his feet but, not having met the new arrival and not knowing anything of the events that had transpired to bring this stranger into their midst, said nothing.

Perry peered from one to the other. "I *have* got the wrong date, is that it? I'd have sworn your invitation said the fifteenth. This is the fifteenth, is it not?"

"That much I can attest to," Owen offered. "I know it's the fifteenth because yesterday I attended my sister's birthday fete, and I'm quite certain she was born on the fourteenth."

Perry's lips twitched. "That does seem to settle the matter. If she was born on the fourteenth, and her birthday was yesterday, then—unless my talent at arithmetic is even weaker than my tutors used to claim it was—today must be the fifteenth. So it's the date of the *invitation* I've mistaken." He grinned at Chloe self-deprecatingly. "I'm the greatest clod in the world, Lady Chloe. But don't look so stricken. I'll take my departure at once and come back at the right time. No harm done. Please accept these flowers with my apology."

"Oh, *Perry!*" Chloe murmured tearfully, staring down at the blooms in her arms. "You're *not* mistaken. At least . . . Oh, dear me! I can't *imagine* what went wrong. Didn't you get my letter?"

"Letter? The invitation, you mean?"

"No, dear boy, the letter I sent afterwards."

"Did you send another letter?" His brow cleared at once. "Then that explains it. I've been out of town and haven't been home. I'm just back from Norfolk. This is the first stop I've made. I was so determined not to be late that I stopped off at an inn in Islington to change into my dinner clothes. The flowers are from Grandmama, by the way. She asked me to give you her best."

"Thank you, my dear," Chloe said, unable to meet his eyes. "I really am at a loss for words. This is so humiliating . . ."

"Nonsense, Lady Chloe. Don't take on. It's *my* blunder, not yours. I shall turn round at once, go home and *read my mail*, which, if I'd had a particle of sense, I would have done in the first place. So, if you'll forgive me, I'll take my leave without further—"

"I say, Aunt Chloe," came a voice from the hallway, "what's going on?" The door swung open and revealed Lucienne framed in the doorway. She looked quite magnificent in a ruby-colored lustring gown, her impressive appearance not in the least mitigated by the fact that she was carrying a tray on which was a decanter of sherry and several glasses. "Kelby was standing in the hall with the sherry as if he were afraid to come in. So I took the tray from him and sent him pack— *Good God!* It's—!"

Perry, who'd had his back to the door, had recognized something familiar in the voice and turned about. Startled at the sight of him, Lucienne made a movement of her arms, causing the tray to tip. The decanter and two of the glasses toppled over and slid to the floor. Her cry "It's . . . *Whittenden!*" was lost in the explosive crash of heavy crystal on hard wood.

"Oh, *Lucy*," Chloe moaned, staring at the shards of glass and the golden liquid seeping its way toward the magnificent Aubusson carpet which covered the center area of the floor.

"It's all *his* fault," Lucienne muttered defensively. "What's he doing here?"

Perry, having used the few seconds during which the crystal had crashed to recover from his own surprise, eyed the younger woman with a gleam of amusement. "Of course," he said with ironic gallantry. "My fault again."

"Are you acquainted with this gentleman, Lucienne?" Owen asked, his right eyebrow raised in mild curiosity.

"We've met," Lucienne answered curtly as she knelt down, picked up some of the larger shards of glass gingerly and deposited them on the tray.

"Once or twice," Perry added, also kneeling down and attempting to staunch the flow of sherry with his handkerchief. He threw the girl a wicked grin. "So your name is Lucienne. Is the surname Gerard? We *have* met once or twice, I believe, haven't we, Miss Gerard?"

"Perry . . . Lucy . . . don't do that," Chloe protested. "I'll get Kelby."

"I'm here, my lady," Kelby said from the doorway. "I

heard the crash." He entered, followed by two footmen and a housemaid, all carrying brooms, cloths and dustpans.

But Chloe wasn't paying any heed to her butler and his assistants as they set about clearing up the mess. She was staring at Perry with a puzzled frown. "Twice?" she asked. "Did you say you've met *twice?*"

Perry handed his sopping handkerchief to one of the footmen and helped Lucienne to stand erect. "Didn't I meet you twice?" he asked the girl pointedly.

"Never mind about that, my lord," Lucienne snapped, reddening in the memory of her brash and humiliating performance at their last meeting. She handed the tray to Kelby and tried to brush back a curl of hair that had come loose and fallen over her forehead. She paused for a moment until Kelby and his assistants had withdrawn, and then she faced Perry again. "What I'd like to know, my lord, is how you found me."

"Found you?" Perry threw Chloe a quick glance. "Purely by accident, I assure you."

"Accident? What sort of accident? And what do you want with me anyway? Don't tell me you've reconsidered and decided to publish a retraction!"

"No, I haven't reconsidered anything, ma'am," he said, gently firm. "There will be no retraction. You may as well reconcile yourself to that."

"Then what *do* you want with me?" she demanded, glowering at him.

"Really, Lucy, you can sometimes be the most provoking creature," her aunt cut in. "What makes you assume it's *you* he's come to see?"

Lucienne turned to her aunt in bewilderment. "What do you mean, Aunt Chloe?"

"I mean that, strange as it may seem to you, Perry has come to see *me*," her aunt declared with a touch of pride. "It's as simple as that."

"You?" Lucienne gaped at her. "But . . . why?"

"Because I asked him, that's why."

"*Asked* him?" The confused girl put a hand to her forehead and brushed back her curl again. "Why on earth would you do that when you knew that . . . that I . . . ?" She glanced over at Owen nervously.

Chloe, following her glance, sighed guiltily. "Well, you see, it was before . . . before the *West-Ender* appeared, you see . . ." she mumbled awkwardly.

"This time it *is* my fault, truly," Perry said, stepping in to assist Chloe in her explanation. "Your aunt had no intention of causing you embarrassment. The truth is that I didn't receive the note she sent me to rescind her invitation. I also had no idea that you were Chloe Gerard's niece. I'm terribly sorry that I barged in like this. And now, if you'll all excuse me, I'll take my leave at once."

"Hold on there," Owen objected. "Before you go, I'd be obliged if you'd take a moment to explain to *me* just what this is all about."

Perry peered at him through his spectacles. "Explain to you, sir? I'm afraid I've not had the pleasure—"

"I do beg your pardon, Perry," Chloe said hastily. "I should have made the introductions before. This is Sir Owen Tatlow, my niece's betrothed. Owen, Lord Wittenden."

Owen offered his hand. "To tell the truth, Wittenden, you aren't exactly unfamiliar to me. I've seen you at White's and heard you spoken of in quite admiring terms. How do you do? I'm glad to make your acquaintance at last."

"Thank you," Perry responded politely, shaking his hand. "Kind of you to say so. But if you'll excuse—"

Owen, however, was not willing to let Perry leave. "But you haven't explained anything yet," he persisted.

Perry's eyes, keenly observant behind his spectacles, swept over Tatlow. The fellow wanted information, but it was obvious that the girl—whose identity Perry now knew to be Lucienne Gerard, Chloe's niece—had not seen fit to tell her betrothed about the carriage accident or its aftermath. Then why was Tatlow mulishly insisting on learning the details? Any man with an iota of tact or a modicum of sense would refrain from pressing the point, but not this good-looking nodcock. Perry felt a wave of dislike for the fellow. He wondered why a young lady with the cleverness and spirit of Lucy Gerard would choose to attach herself to a peacocky stuffed shirt of Tatlow's ilk. Well, that was *her* affair, he told himself, and not any business of his. But as for him, he'd be dashed if Tatlow would learn anything from *his* lips. "Explain what, Tatlow?" he asked innocently.

"Why, *everything*. I haven't understood a word that's been exchanged among the three of you."

"Haven't you, old fellow?" Perry asked, giving him one of his crooked smiles. "I must admit that a great deal of it was over my head, too. My father warned me in my youth that Woman will ever be beyond Man's understanding. But now, if I may take my leave—"

"Wait, Wittenden," Tatlow ordered. "You didn't say how you came to be acquainted with Lucy without learning her name."

"An oversight, Tatlow, merely an oversight," Perry responded airily, crossing quickly to the door.

But Owen, being closer, stepped in front of it and barred the way. "Don't be in such a hurry, old man. It would be unthinkable for us to permit you to leave without offering you some dinner." Fatuously taking control of the situation, he turned to his hostess. "One of the things I fail to understand, Chloe, my dear, is why you found it necessary to rescind your invitation to this charming fellow."

Chloe ground her teeth in irritation. "I don't see why I should have to explain the matter to you, Owen. You may be *Lucy's* betrothed, but you're not mine."

"Then I'll ask Lucy. Tell me, my love, why does your aunt find it necessary to send this poor fellow out into the night without his dinner?"

"I have no idea," Lucienne answered coldly. "My aunt doesn't have to make explanations to me, any more than she does to you."

"Quite right," Chloe agreed.

Perry, uncomfortably aware of Tatlow's hypocrisy in insisting that he stay for dinner so that he could continue to pump him with questions, made another attempt to smooth over the waters and remove himself from the scene. "Don't give the matter of my dinner a second thought, Tatlow," he said blithely, turning to the door. "I'll do perfectly well at the club."

But Owen put an insistent arm about Perry's shoulder and

turned him about. "You'll do no such thing, Wittenden, if I have anything to say to it. And I'm sure Lady Chloe feels as I do, or she wouldn't have invited you in the first place. As near as I can determine, it is only Lucy who stands in the way. I don't know why she's taken you in dislike, but if she is willing to get over her pet—"

"Lucy is *not* willing," Lucienne said promptly. "Owen, you are behaving like a boor and embarrassing all of us. Step aside and let Lord Whistledown leave." Then, realizing what she'd said, she gave a little gasp. "I mean, Wittenden, of course."

"Whistledown? Did you say *Whistledown?*" Owen's heavy-lidded eyes widened in fascination. "Are *you* Whistledown? The fellow who writes that diary in the *West-Ender?* Well, well!"

He stared at Perry for a long moment, his right eyebrow lifted in astonishment. Meanwhile, Lucienne and Chloe exchanged helpless glances. Lucienne sank down on the nearest chair, dropped her head in her hands and groaned. But Owen took no notice. He continued to stare at Perry with something like awe. "I must say, that *is* a surprise."

"What is? My being Whistledown?" Perry asked, hoping to distract him so that he could get round him to the door. "Why so?"

Tatlow shrugged. "I thought Whistledown must be someone older."

"Did you?" Perry began to edge slowly round the fellow.

"Much older. Who'd expect a mere boy—how old *are* you, Wittenden, twenty-three? Twenty-four?—to write something as knowing as that last piece I read—the one about the shrew? Very amusing, that one. I laughed aloud, particularly at the place where that mysterious lady beat at you with her umbrel—" His eyes bulged out in sudden comprehension. "Good God, that's *it!* That's it, of *course!* It's *Lucy* in the poem!"

Lucy made a choking sound deep in her throat.

"*Really,* Owen!" Chloe snapped. "How *can* you—?"

"Of *course!*" Owen chortled, ignoring her. "Everything makes *sense* now—how you became acquainted with Lucy without learning her name, why Lady Chloe withdrew her invitation after she saw the *West-Ender*, why Lucy made that remark about your coming here to tell her you were going to print a retraction, everything! At last it all makes sense!" He threw back his head, crowing in self-satisfaction.

"Don't you think you might be jumping to conclusions, Tatlow?" Perry asked mildly.

"Not on your life," Tatlow declared, smiling broadly. He was completely sure of himself. "Who else but my Lucy would have driven her phaeton so wildly? Is there anyone else in all of London who would have run into a carriage and blamed the other driver? And who else would have made such a scene?"

"Who else indeed?" Lucy muttered between clenched teeth, looking up at him with her eyes flashing with suppressed rage. Her tone so icy that her aunt glanced at her worriedly.

"All your conjectures are nonsense, Tatlow," Perry said, pushing him firmly aside and pulling the door open. "The verse in the magazine was merely a *tale*—completely imaginary. A work of imagination from start to finish."

"Imaginary, eh? Don't think to fob *me* off, Wittenden. Do you take me for a moonling? Why would Lucy be so angry with you if the 'tale' was imaginary? And why did she ask if you were going to publish a retraction?"

"You'll have to ask her that. I can't speak for her. But I *can* speak for my verses, and I assure you that they are wholly fictional. And now, Lady Chloe, I shall offer my apologies to you once again for my unwarranted, troublesome intrusion, and beg your permission to take my leave."

"No reason to leave now, old man," Tatlow pointed out, "since everything's finally out in the open."

Perry shook his head. "Thank you, but—"

"That's a bit high-handed of you, isn't it, Owen?" Lucy asked, tight-lipped. "Don't you think that you might permit Aunt Chloe to do her own asking? Shouldn't she be free to choose whom she wishes to sit at her own table?"

"But I *would* like Perry to stay, dearest," Chloe said with unwonted timidity, torn between her loyalty to her niece and her affection for Perry, "now that everything's out. That is, if you no longer have any objections."

"Thank you," Perry repeated, "but—"

"Lucy can't have any objections," Owen stated with overweening finality. "Even though you may have teased her a bit in print, she owes you a debt of gratitude for it."

"Do I really?" Lucy asked with ominously exaggerated sweetness. "Debt of gratitude? Perhaps I should sit down and write him a letter of thanks."

"Perhaps you should," Owen agreed.

"Oh? Indeed?" Her ironic smile widened. "And what should I thank him *for,* may I ask?"

"Now, Lucy..." Chloe cautioned nervously, recognizing the tell-tale signs of the explosion to come.

"For showing you what I've been telling you for weeks— that your driving is nothing short of reckless."

Lucy stared at him, feeling inside her the inner explosion her aunt had been expecting. Was this the man to whom she'd given her hand, this self-important, conceited, top-lofty, insensitive clodpole? How could she ever have believed she cared for him? Why, even the irritating Perry Wittenden seemed modest and manly when compared to him! She leaped to her feet. "It wanted only that!" she said venomously. "That's the remark I've been waiting for. And dreading."

"Why, what do you mean?" Owen asked, so startled by the fury in her voice that he took a step backward.

"I mean," she retorted, pulling off her ring, "that I knew you would say it. That's why I never told you about the accident. I *knew* you would make some sort of prosy remark about my reckless driving." She grasped his hand, pulled it toward her, palm up, and thrust the ring into it.

"Lucy!" he gasped, gaping down at the ring in his palm. "You're not crying off!"

"I certainly am."

He didn't believe his ears. He was not the sort that females jilted. Not Owen Tatlow. Long sought after by husband-hunting young ladies, he was quite aware that they considered him one of the handsomest bachelors in town. One would have to be a fool not to have noticed how the girls simpered and blushed whenever he threw them a glance. Like many good-looking men, he overestimated the importance of a handsome face on a woman's heart. So great was his self-esteem that he couldn't believe anyone would reject him. "You must be joking!" he declared.

"You may take my word that I am not."

He blinked at her, trying to ascertain the depth of her sincerity. As usual, he misjudged it. She couldn't mean it, he decided. He shook his head, smiling in patient, paternal superiority. "But, my dear, you're just on your high ropes. Be sensible. You would not withdraw from our betrothal just because I criticized your driving! It's too ridiculous!"

"I suppose it must seem so to you. But it's quite clear to me now that the reason I tried so hard to keep you from saying those words was that I knew, deep inside, that if you *did* say them, I would have to recognize you for the self-righteous, pompous prig you are. Good-bye, Owen. Find yourself another girl. It shouldn't take you long. Choose a girl in Whistledown's other category: one of the shy ones—the sort who drives so slowly that it takes her a month of Sundays to cross the street. You should be very happy with her."

She turned on her heel and strode across the room, sweeping past her Aunt Chloe (who had quickly covered her mouth so that no one would see her relieved grin) and past the door where Perry still stood rooted to the spot from which he'd watched the entire scene in rapt fascination. She was two steps into the corridor when she came to an abrupt stop and wheeled about. She came back and confronted Perry with eyes still flashing. "And as for *you,* Peregrine Whistledown—!"

"I know," he said in his mild way. "*That* was my fault, too."

"It certainly was. I may be a virago and a shrew, but you, with your nauseatingly sweet disposition and relentless good humor, bring more turmoil and disaster in your wake than anyone I've ever known."

Perry's eyes twinkled. "Are you saying it was *I* who brought on this turmoil and disaster?" he asked.

"Exactly."

"Hmmmm." He regarded her with an expression of amused ruefulness. "Nauseatingly sweet, am I?"

"Yes, you are."

"And relentlessly good-humored?"

"Relentlessly."

"Good God!" He rubbed his chin dolefully. "You make me sound utterly repugnant. What do you think I should do about it, ma'am?"

"Do what you always do," she retorted, striding off down the corridor. "Put it in rhyme and print it!"

Chapter Nine

Within two days the name of Lucienne Gerard was on everyone's tongue. Not only had she been the first of the season's marriageable girls to have become betrothed, but she'd cried off even before the announcement had appeared in the *Times*. That information was titillating enough to set tongues wagging, but the added fact that both the betrothal and its dissolution had occurred during the very first month of the social season made the story even more delectable. Several of the girls who were still waiting for their first offers took satisfaction in quoting the old adage: *Hasty glory goes out in a snuff*. And several mothers warned their daughters, "There! You see? It's just as I've always said—'hasty climbers have sudden falls.'"

But if the gossips found a juicy bone to chew on in *that* news, the next day brought them a veritable feast, for word leaked out that it was Lucienne Gerard—yes, the very same Miss Gerard who'd jilted Tatlow!—who was the shrew in Whistledown's Diary! The word spread so rapidly that all of London was laughing over it before nightfall. The Ladies Haversleigh alone called at sixteen houses before tea-time.

Although the Haversleighs did not have the temerity to call on Lady Chloe, the talk was so widespread that even she heard the news that day. She'd stopped at her linen-draper and was waiting for the clerk to wrap some lace when she overheard two women, hiding themselves behind a bolt of cloth, giggling over it. She was so enraged that she stormed out of the shop without waiting for her parcel.

"It was that odious Tatlow who started the rumor, I'm certain of that," she exclaimed to Lucienne as soon as she stepped over the threshold of the girl's bedroom. "I could scratch his eyes out!"

Lucienne, who'd been in an inexplicably depressed state since the night she broke with Tatlow, was stretched out on a graceful gilt-and-velvet chaise, listlessly turning the pages of *Guy Mannering*. She looked up at her aunt with an air of dispassion. "Don't upset yourself, my love. It no longer matters to me that the world knows I'm Whistledown's shrew. I don't know why I was so concerned about it in the first place. Perhaps it was because I feared that Owen would disapprove. But now that I've placed the Owen episode behind me, the whole matter of those blasted verses leaves me quite indifferent."

"But it doesn't leave *me* indifferent," Chloe exclaimed. "The man's a worm! Only a worm would be so low as to malign a woman he professed to care for."

"Well, he certainly doesn't care for me any longer. Not after all those dreadful things I said to him."

"Those dreadful things were all true! He *is* a pompous, overweening prig. When I heard you say those things, I wanted to *cheer*."

Lucienne sat up and studied her aunt with interest. "Did you, Aunt Chloe? If that's how you felt about Owen, why did you not say anything before?"

Chloe shrugged. "I don't know. I didn't wish to hurt you. I thought you loved him too dearly. You see, I...I saw you with him one night. I didn't mean to be a snoop, Lucy. I came upon you quite accidentally. You were kissing him, you see ...in the morning room...in the moonlight. It was very romantic. You both looked so beautiful together, and you seemed to *melt* when he took you in his arms. So I crept away and held my tongue." She sat down beside her niece on the chaise and took her hand. "You've seemed very blue-deviled since you cried off, dearest. Are you regretting breaking off with him?"

"You're a dear to worry about me so," Lucy said, planting a fond kiss on her aunt's forehead, "but I'm not in the least blue-deviled over Owen. It was an infatuation, that was all. The fellow is so deucedly handsome that I failed to see the man beneath the facade. Do you know the strangest thing of all, Aunt Chloe? Once I realized what he was really like, he didn't even seem handsome anymore."

"I know just what you mean," Chloe said, nodding in sympathy. "After what he's done to your reputation, I find *everything* about him to be utterly repugnant."

"As to *that,* Aunt, I'm not at all sure I agree with you. He may be a pompous nodcock, but that doesn't mean he's the one who revealed my secret."

"Of course he's the one. Who else could it have been? No one else even *knew—*"

Lucienne gave her a pointed stare. "Someone else knew."

"You mean Perry. But I assure you, Lucy, that Perry would *never* do such a thing. It would be completely unlike him. I know you don't know Perry well, having met him only— Wait! I just remembered something. What did Perry mean the other day when he said he'd met you twice?"

"I don't know what he meant," Lucienne answered, instinctively defensive. But as she tried to meet Chloe's eye, she realized that she couldn't lie to her beloved aunt. She dropped her eyes to her hands that were still resting in Chloe's clasp. "No, that's not true," she admitted in a low voice. "The truth is that I'm ashamed to tell you about the second time we met."

Chloe stared at her bent head in surprise. "Then you did meet again after the accident?"

"Yes. I did a very brazen, dreadful thing. Don't ask me to tell you the details, for they would only shock you. I'll say only that I called on him—with Trudy as a chaperone, so you needn't worry on that score—to try to force him to print a retraction of his blasted poem. The visit was disastrous. He, in his irritatingly mild-mannered way, managed to make a complete fool of me."

"Oh, dear," Chloe murmured, trying to imagine what took place. "I hope you . . . he . . . that there wasn't a dreadful scene."

"No. He was *un parfait gentilhomme*. He made me feel foolish in the most polite way."

"I see. But Lucy, if you're saying that he behaved like a perfect gentleman in spite of your being brazen and dreadful, then doesn't that prove what I was saying before? You know something more of Perry's character now. Do you honestly think he's the sort who would reveal your name for the gossips of London to smirk over?"

"Honestly?" Lucienne wrinkled her brow in thought for a moment and then sighed. "No, to be honest, I don't. It wouldn't be like him at all. He's too . . . too . . ."

"Too relentlessly good-natured?" Chloe teased.

"Yes," Lucienne admitted, coloring.

Chloe got up and smiled at her niece. "Do you know what I think, Lucy, my love? I think you're blue-deviled over *Perry*."

"Don't be ridiculous!" Lucy gave a dismissive wave of her hand. "Why would I be blue-deviled over *him?*"

"For the very reasons you yourself stated—that he's good-natured and sweet."

"*Nauseatingly* sweet," her niece corrected, stretching out on the chaise again and picking up her book. "You may also remember that I called him gawky and sanctimonious."

"You may call him whatever you wish, Lucy, but it seems to me that your sudden awareness of the flaws in Owen Tatlow's character occurred only after you became acquainted with Perry and were able to compare his quite admirable character with Tatlow's shallow one."

"What humbug!" Lucienne laughed. "If you're still hoping to make a match between us, Aunt, you're fair and far off. I'm sure Peregrine Whistledown finds me quite as detestable as I find him."

"Detestable?" Chloe drew herself up in offense. "How could he possibly find you detestable?"

"Very easily, my love. Now that I think of it, I realize that I've behaved in an utterly detestable manner every time we've met. The first time he met me he labeled me a shrew, did he not? The second time even *I* must admit that I behaved like a vulgar harridan. And I certainly failed to acquit myself with distinction at our third meeting. You were a witness to that encounter yourself. Wouldn't you call my behavior detestable?"

"Well, not detestable, exactly," her aunt said loyally. "Overwrought, perhaps. A little impetuous—"

"*Impetuous?*" Lucienne gave a mirthless, self-mocking laugh and shook her head. "Do you think impetuous is the word for me? I broke your lovely crystal glasses, I embarrassed you before a guest whose invitation to dinner you'd had to retract because of me, I made the brash and egotistical assumption that your guest had come to see *me*, I broke with my betrothed on a sudden whim and handed him back his ring before the eyes of a stranger, I called Owen a prig and Perry nauseating—and all this in less than ten minutes' time, mind you!—and you call it a *little impetuous?*" She turned her eyes to her book with a sigh. "If he doesn't find me detestable, he's a greater fool than I think he is."

Chloe looked at her lovely niece for a moment without speaking. The girl *was* blue-deviled, that was certain. She'd hardly left her room for days. Her cheeks were pale, her gestures listless and her eyes sad. But Chloe could scarcely blame her. It was not pleasant to be turned overnight from one of society's most admired beauties to a laughingstock.

But this spell of the dismals had begun *before* the gossip started. That meant that there had to be another reason for Lucienne's depression. It seemed to Chloe that the cause was revealed in the little speech the girl had just made. *She was ashamed of herself!* She had been used to seeing herself, all these years, through the admiring eyes of her father. Now, for the first time, she was seeing herself through eyes that were not so admiring, and the possibility had suddenly occurred to her that some people might even find her detestable. What a shock it must have been to the poor girl to discover that (1) she was not universally adored, and (2) that her character was not perfect! No wonder she was blue-deviled!

Chloe bit her lip to keep herself from shedding a flood of sympathetic tears. Wordlessly, she went to the door, but as soon as her hand touched the knob she paused. She couldn't go without offering the girl a bit of comfort. "*I* didn't find you detestable, my love, and I'm not a fool, am I?" she asked gently.

"No, but you're my loving aunt, so you don't count," Lucienne answered in a small voice, keeping her eyes on her book.

"Yes, I'm your loving aunt, so I know you won't believe me, dearest, when I say that no one else finds you detestable either. You are not faultless, but there are degrees between being perfect and being detestable. I think an objective observer would place you closer to the former than the latter."

"Would he?" Lucienne peeped up at her aunt, a tiny smile appearing at the corners of her mouth. "And where would Wittenden place me, do you suppose?"

Chloe felt an inward lift of her spirits. That question certainly proved that Lucy was much more interested in Perry than she'd admitted. But outwardly the aunt merely shrugged. "I have no idea. But you can wager your fortune that I'll ask him at my very first opportunity."

"*Ask* him?" Lucienne's eyes widened in horror. She sat up abruptly, crying, "Aunt Chloe, don't you *dare!*"

But Chloe had whisked herself out the door and was gone.

Chapter Ten

Lucienne needn't have worried, for her Aunt Chloe was not to be given an opportunity to question Perry about his evaluation of her niece's character. Fate stepped in to prevent it: shortly after the ill-fated evening at Chloe's, Perry received word that his grandmother's health had taken a turn for the worse, and he returned to Norfolk for an extended stay. His monthly columns in the *West-Ender* were all that London society heard of him for the next few months.

Meanwhile, Lucienne was having a very difficult time of it. The gossip proved more destructive than Chloe had anticipated, for the number of her invitations fell off sharply, and those friends, like Lady Rutherford, who remained loyal to Chloe and who continued to request her presence and that of her niece at their tables and in their ballrooms could not prevent their other guests from making slurs or whispering behind their fans. "One can't really blame them," Lady Rutherford said to Chloe. "A girl who jilts a 'catch' like Tatlow, and is known as a shrew as well, must expect her reputation to be ripped to shreds."

For Chloe as much as for Lucienne, going out was unpleasant, and staying at home was depressing. After enduring a fortnight of gloomy evenings, Lucienne announced to her aunt that she'd had enough. She was going home to Yorkshire.

Chloe did not argue. It was clear that the season was ruined for the girl. It would be better for her future if she disappeared from the scene. Once she was gone, the gossips would soon be wagging their tongues about someone else, and Lucienne Gerard would be forgotten. Then, next year, she could reappear without ill effect. Even if a few troublemakers tried to revive the gossip, it would all be stale news by then. Lucienne would have a new start in a new season.

Chloe would not let Lucienne go until the girl had given her word that she would return to London the following spring. Lucienne was reluctant to agree, convinced that, as far as the *ton* was concerned, her name was sullied forever. It took all of Chloe's powers of persuasion to convince the girl that everything would be forgotten by next season. Last year's gossip, she swore, was as valueless as last year's bonnet. "By next season, the gossip about you will be as outmoded and commonplace as Evaline Haversleigh's striped hat, and Evaline is as unlikely to be talking about the one as wearing the other," Chloe assured Lucy earnestly. "Believe me, my love, next season will find her spreading rumors as fashionably new as the fashionable new monstrosity she'll be sporting on her head."

Lucienne eventually gave her word, and, with tears and embraces, aunt and niece parted. Lucienne returned to Yorkshire, after only two months in town, a great deal more humble and subdued than when she'd left.

The summer in Yorkshire was quiet and dull after the excitement of London, but Lucienne did not complain. She relished the peace and the privacy. The company of her adoring father was soothing; she spent the mornings with him, discussing the business of the estate, reading the newspapers sent up from town, or sitting quietly on the terrace overlooking the south lawn, enjoying fragrance that the breeze wafted up to them from the rose-garden below. During the long afternoons, when her father napped, she took to walking. In town, a girl would not be permitted to walk unchaperoned, but here in the quiet of the Yorkshire countryside there was no danger to a solitary female. Her father made no objection to her lonely walks, and they became, for Lucienne, the highlights of her days.

Summer is Yorkshire's most benign season, during which the winds are at their gentlest and the sun makes its most frequent appearances. Thus, with the blessing of delightful weather, the girl was able to enjoy long rambles along the banks of the rivulet that flowed through the grounds of her

father's extensive acreage or along the footpath that wound
through green fields, over styles and across brooks until it
joined, like a tributary to a great river, the wide, paved road to
Harrogate and Leeds. But Lucienne never walked down that
highway. It led to towns, and she had had enough of towns for
a while.

During her rambles, she often reviewed in her mind the
events of her London season. It was painful to think of them at
first, for she couldn't bear remembering her own conduct. But
she made herself relive those memories over and over until at
last she was able to face them without the painful clutch of
humiliation in her chest. In the ameliorative glow of the Yorkshire summer and her father's affection, she began to recover
her self-confidence. Perhaps she hadn't actually been *detestable,* she told herself. Though she couldn't deny that she'd
been headstrong and impulsive, had acted without caution and
spoken without thinking, she began to believe she would do
better next time.

Chloe sent long letters every few weeks—closely written
in an elaborately curlicued scrawl and peppered with capital
letters which conformed to no recognizable rules of either
logic or grammar—in which she informed Lucienne about all
that was happening in town. Each letter contained fascinating
tidbits, and Lucienne perused them all with eager eyes. One
missive was filled with the details of a spectacular gala that
the Regent had held at Brighton to which Chloe had been
invited; the Pavilion was opulent beyond belief, she wrote, but
it had been so hot and steamy in every room that she'd almost
fainted. Another letter, written in late July, gave a full account
of the funeral of Richard Brinsley Sheridan, whose delightful
play *The School For Scandal* Chloe had taken Lucienne to see
when it was revived at Drury Lane. Chloe wrote that although
Sheridan hadn't written a successful play in years and had
quarreled bitterly with the Prince, he'd been buried with great
pomp in Westminster Abbey. Her account of the ceremony
was so full of mesmerizing details—who was there, what they
wore, what they said—that Lucienne read the letter aloud to
her father.

In each letter Chloe reported at least one new betrothal.

One by one, the young ladies with whom Lucienne had become acquainted in London were becoming betrothed. The most interesting betrothal-news came in August, when Chloe wrote that Owen Tatlow had got himself leg-shackled again. His choice, this time, was a Miss Cora Trevellick, daughter of Sir Henry Trevellick of Cornwall and cousin to Chloe's friend, Jenny Rutherford, who was again instrumental in bringing the pair together. *Miss Trevellick would be considered a pretty little Chit,* Chloe wrote, *except for a pair of large, rabbity front Teeth which, because she smiles at every Remark even if it is not Remotely Amusing, becomes the Feature one notices first. What I find Ironical about Tatlow's choice, Lucy, my love, is that Miss Trevellick is so Biddable. She agrees with Everything Tatlow says and hangs on his arm like an adoring Poodle. It was to be expected, I suppose, that he would shy away from tying himself to another Girl of Spirit such as you for fear that she might Find him Out and toss him aside as you did.*

Chloe's letters were a welcome diversion. But more than that, they brought the distant London scene to life and kept unbroken that tenuous thread that connected Lucienne to her past. However, there was one omission in the letters that Lucienne couldn't help noticing: Perry Whittenden was never mentioned. Nor was there ever a word about the Whistledown Diaries. It was as if Chloe had forgotten Wittenden's very existence. Lucienne didn't like to admit to herself that she searched eagerly through her aunt's closely written pages for some word of him, but somewhere deep inside she was uncomfortably aware of it. She told herself that her interest in him was merely curiosity, and she pushed her pangs of disappointment—a small emptiness that opened inside her when she came to the end of each letter that had no word of him—to the back of her mind.

In the late fall, however, she received a letter which brought her so great a thrill of pleasure that it made up for all the previous disappointments. It was not much longer than a note, really, but it was full of him: *You will undoubtedly be interested to learn,* Chloe wrote, *that Perry Wittenden has returned to Town after a five-month Absence. His Grand-*

mother suffered a Long illness, and he stayed at her Side through it all. She died last Month. I didn't learn any of this from Perry himself, for he hasn't yet paid a Call on me, but I heard of his return to Town from several of my Cronies. Although he has not shown himself about a great deal, being still in Mourning, his return has caused a Stir. I didn't realize how very Popular the boy is. I hope he'll pay a Call on me as soon as he's put off the Black Gloves.

Meanwhile, however, his Diary entries continue to appear monthly. I have not sent you any of his Writings before this for fear of being Accused of Pushing him at you. I assure you, Lucy, my dear, that I have given up all Thoughts of Matchmaking between the two of you. If you say you Detest him (though how you can Detest so Lovable a young man is quite beyond me), I have no Choice but to accept your Judgment. I realize perfectly well that just because Perry would have suited Me at your age (or at any age, if it comes to that, for if I were Thirty Years Younger I would pursue the boy for myself!) it doesn't follow that he'd Suit you.

That being said, I now Admit that I'm enclosing this month's Whistledown Diary because I can't Resist sending it. If you put aside your Prejudice, I think you will find it of Particular interest. Please read it at Once.

Lucienne hastily complied, pulling the folded clipping out of the envelope with eager fingers. Her eyes scanned the words, quickly at first and then slowed down by the meter of the verse itself. But the words seemed too complicated to grasp in a hasty reading. She slipped the clipping in the bosom of her dress and ran outdoors. She made for the bottom of the south lawn, to her favorite summer reading place—a spreading elm in whose shade she loved to sit on sunny afternoons. She sat down on the grass and, resting her shoulder against the tree trunk, withdrew the folded clipping and opened it. There was the familiar Whistledown Diary heading and, beneath it, a one-word title—VILLANELLE. She wasn't sure what it meant, but she guessed it merely referred to the poem's form, a rather odd combination of three-line stanzas. Then, with a slow intake of breath, she read the lines aloud:

I wrote her name upon the sand one day,
A sweet and gentle girl I've now forgot;
From sand and memory she's washed away.

Another girl who never said me nay,
Who never quarreled and who irked me not,—
I wrote her name upon the sand one day;

Her purpose but to love and to obey,
No kinder creature ever was begot;
From sand and memory she's washed away.

A third, a proper lass who loved to pray,
Who followed every rule to the last dot,—
I wrote her name upon the sand one day.

I can't remember them, to my dismay,
The kind, the sweet, the proper ones—the lot!
From sand and memory they're washed away.

But one, with scornful eyes and smile at play,
Who argued, mocked, riposted like a shot,—
I wrote her name upon the sand one day
That years of stormy waves won't wash away.

Her mind remained stubbornly blank at first, but when she finished reading, she found her heart beating strangely. What did he mean? He was obviously writing about girls he'd loved. Why didn't he remember them? And the last stanza— the one that had caused her pulse to race—what was he saying *there*?

At that moment she noticed a little scrawl in the margin near the last stanza. Her aunt had written a comment in a tiny hand. Lucienne had to hold the paper close to make out the words. When she deciphered them, they made her hand shake. Her aunt had written: *Do you know what I think, my love? I think he means you!*

Chapter Eleven

November in Yorkshire is not benign. The sun stays mostly in hiding, the air is wet and chill, and the winds are cruel. Lucienne was forced, on most days, to give up her rambles and stay indoors. She was lonely and bored, finding little pleasure in anything except the company of her father in the morning, an hour or so at her pianoforte in the afternoon (playing the piano having given her much joy since her childhood, although she would be the first to admit that she played with more passion than technique), and, at night, an occasional rereading (for reasons she couldn't explain to herself) of a bit of verse that she kept tucked away in a little box in her nightstand.

The days passed well enough, but the nights came early and seemed endless and empty. The winter loomed up ahead as if it were a cavernous passage—cold, dark and *long*—which had to be traversed with teeth-gritting strength in order to reach springtime. There was little to look forward to in a Yorkshire winter: only an occasional Assembly at Harrogate (if an unexpected snowstorm didn't block the roads), or a rare visit from a not-too-distant friend whom boredom had driven from home. Thus the letter from Chloe, in which was enclosed an affectionately worded invitation from Chloe's friend, Lady Rutherford, asking her to join them for a fortnight's stay at Rutherford Grange, the Rutherford's country place in Mendlesham, Suffolk, was very eagerly welcomed.

Chloe's letter bubbled. *This is just the sort of Opportunity we need*, she wrote, *to Reinstate you in Society. Do say you'll come! The Guests will number no more than a dozen, and they're certain to be Friendly, for by this time the gossip about you is old Hat. Now that Tatlow is betrothed, the gossips have Nothing more to say on that head, and the Whistledown business is quite forgotten. (The latest on-dits are all about Sybil Sturtevant, who has gotten herself Buckled to a French Count twenty-five years her Senior. Since this is her fifth Betrothal, they are taking odds at the Clubs that she will cry off within a Month. So you see, you've been superceded. As I told you, Notoriety is short-lived.)*

I must warn you, however, that since Miss Trevellick (who, you may remember, is Tatlow's intended) is Jenny Rutherford's cousin, she will be among the guests. Jenny tells me that Tatlow will not be joining us for the first week but intends to come for the second. Their presence should in no way embarrass you, but if you still have any residual feelings for Tatlow and wish to avoid facing him or his bride-to-be, I shall certainly understand.

I hope, however, that you will not let yourself be Deterred by fear of embarrassment. Tatlow is not worth a second Thought. What you should think of is the Pleasure you'll have at a large, lively Party. The Rutherfords call their estate the Grange, but the appellation is too modest. The Manorhouse is quite luxurious, Jenny is a generous—no, a Lavish—hostess, and the entire fortnight promises to be a most entertaining Diversion. Pack up your prettiest Gowns and your Dancing Shoes, for she plans to have several evenings of Music and Dancing. Incidentally, you needn't Worry about bringing along an abigail, because I shall send Trudy to you. She has Missed you dreadfully, you know. When I told her you might join me at Rutherford, and that she might accompany you, she was in Transports.

Lucienne hesitated to accept the invitation, but not for the reason suggested in her aunt's letter. (In fact, her aunt's suggestion that she might have residual feelings for Owen made her laugh. She'd given Sir Owen Tatlow not a thought all summer long, and even when she'd read the news of his betrothal she'd not felt the slightest regret. The only thing she'd felt was a twinge of pity for the biddable girl with rabbity front teeth who'd overestimated the value of a handsome face.) Her hesitation was caused by a reluctance to leave her father alone during the icy gloom of a Yorkshire winter. "But it's only for a fortnight," he said, waving her objections away with a flip of his arm. He insisted with stern finality that she write her acceptance at once. "If you think I cannot get along without you for a fortnight, you are grossly underestimating me," he declared.

Thus, in early December, on a cold, misty morning that showed no hint of sunshine, the family carriage was brought to the door, two trunks and five bandboxes of assorted shapes and sizes were loaded aboard, the coachman climbed up on the box, and Lucienne, wrapped in a fur-trimmed, hooded cloak, carrying an enormous muff, and followed by an excited Trudy (who'd arrived from London only two days before), was helped up the steps. She waved good-bye to her father who stood watching in the doorway and, with an ambivalence that was compounded by equal parts of trepidation and antici-pation, set off on her second attempt to make her mark in polite society.

Chapter Twelve

Lucienne had hoped to make the trip to Suffolk in two days, but travel on the second day was so dreadful—an icy, driving rain seemed determined to accompany them all the way south —that she decided to rack up early at the first presentable hostelry they encountered and finish the journey the following morning. The first inn they came upon, a few miles south of Newmarket, appeared to be adequate to their needs. There was no need to ask the name of the neat little place, for the crudely painted sign above the door pictured a black boar with two enormous teeth curving from each corner of its evil mouth. The Black Boar Inn was a squat, beam-and-plaster building in the Tudor style, with a pair of dormers whose fan-shaped windows peeped from under its thatched roof like half-round eyes. But despite its forbidding name and hideous signboard, the inn looked inviting enough. The place was clean, the grounds well kept, and a pleasant light filtered through the rain from the large, mullioned windows on either side of the doorway.

While the coachman unharnessed the horses and led them to the stables, Lucienne and Trudy climbed down from the carriage and ran through the rain across the innyard. Inside the inn they were greeted by the innkeeper's wife, a large, ruddy-faced woman who contained her bulk neatly in a black bombazine dress covered by an immaculate apron. She introduced herself as Mrs. Dymock, clucked with dismay over the wet-ness of their cloaks, bustled them into the private parlor and settled them beside the fire. But when Lucienne requested a bedroom for herself and her abigail, the woman looked troubled. "I cin take care o' yer 'orses and yer coachman well enough in the stables, Miss Gerard, but as fer a proper bedroom fer yersel's, well . . . I'll 'ave t' speak t' Mr. Dymock."

Mrs. Dymock left them warming themselves at the fire and went to look for her husband, but he was nowhere about. He'd probably gone to the stables to help Miss Gerard's coachman with his horses. Should she go after him and get her newly pressed bombazine soaking wet, she asked herself, or should she decide for herself about the bedroom? They *did* have one bedroom vacant (the second one having already been bespoken by the nice red-headed gentleman who'd arrived earlier that afternoon), but the problem was that they'd had a letter from Lord Applegarth, a most frequent and favored guest, informing them that he expected to be stopping there either this evening or the next and that he wished to reserve his usual room and his usual supper. Lord Applegarth, a man who liked his comfort, traveled from London to Scotland two or three times a year, and he always spent the first night of his journey at the Black Boar. Mr. Dymock would not wish Lord Applegarth to be disappointed, which was why he was keeping his lordship's "usual" room vacant.

But there was this new visitor to consider. The pretty Miss Gerard was not the sort Mr. Dymock would like to turn aside, especially on such a horrid night as this. And where would they send her? The nearest inn was ten miles distant, and it was already dark. Mr. Dymock would certainly agree that it wouldn't be right to turn the pretty creature out and force her to travel ten miles in the cold, wet dark. Besides, Lord Applegarth didn't say he'd surely be here today. "Either Wednesday or Thursday," he'd written.

Mrs. Dymock twisted her fingers in an agony of indecision. Should she give Miss Gerard the room being saved for Lord Applegarth or shouldn't she? Was his lordship coming or wasn't he? It was unlikely that he was, for it was already after six and he always arrived before five. He'd probably decided, because of the downpour, to put the trip off until tomorrow. There were not many who were venturing out in this weather; the usually busy taproom had only one customer this evening. It made no sense, the woman told herself, to keep the room empty for someone who wasn't going to come, when there was a lady right here on the premises who had such need of it. "First come, first served,' she muttered under her breath.

The decision thus made, Mrs. Dymock marched herself back to the parlor and informed Miss Gerard that her room was ready. "It's the door t' the right o' the stairs," she said to the relieved guest. "Our very nicest room."

Lucienne smiled gratefully. "Thank you, Mrs. Dymock, I'm certain it will please us." She rose from the rocking chair and rubbed her still-frozen hands together. "We'll go up right now, if you don't mind, and get out of these damp clothes. Please have someone bring up my small trunk. And if you can arrange to serve us some supper in about an hour, I'd be most grateful."

"Yes, Miss, I can an' I will, if barley soup an' mutton stew'll suit ye."

"It will suit us very well," Lucienne assured her as she urged the shivering Trudy out the door. "Come Trudy. Let's get out of these things before we contract an inflammation of the lungs."

Mrs. Dymock called to her son, who was serving ale to the lone customer in the taproom, to fetch the lady's trunk—"The small one, mind!"—and hurried into the kitchen to ready the supper. She was soon bent over a steaming pot, stirring extra beef stock into her barley soup. (She wanted to be sure there'd be enough, for the red-headed gentleman in the second bedroom would surely want some, too.) That was why she didn't hear the crunch of gravel that announced the arrival of another carriage at their door.

But her husband, who hadn't been to the stables at all but down in the cellar searching for a special bottle of port for the gentleman in the second bedroom, came up in time to greet the new arrival at the door. "Ah, Lord Applegarth," he beamed, bowing in welcome. "Come in, m' lord, come in and le' me take yer wet beaver."

His lordship, a portly gentleman of more than forty years whose veined nose and gouty walk already showed the ravages of too much drink, handed the innkeeper his hat. "Good evening, Dymock," he said, leaning heavily on his cane. His hearty manner was in strange conflict with his croaking, whiskey-hoarsened voice. "Terrible night out there, ain't it? Damme if I ain't glad to be out of that wind!"

"Worse night we've 'ad this year," the innkeeper agreed. "Come into the taproom an' le' me fix ye a mug o' mulled wine."

"Later, Dymock, later," his lordship said, hobbling to the stairway. "Let me change my coat first. When my man comes in with the bags, tell him I've gone upstairs."

"Very good, m' lord," the innkeeper said, "but don't ye wish me t' show you up?"

"Show me up? Whatever for?" Applegarth, without looking round, gave the innkeeper a dismissive wave of his fingers. "I know my way as well as you do."

Upstairs, in the "nicest" bedroom—a small, low-ceilinged room with a window-seat in the dormer, a small fireplace in which a fire was burning that gave out more smoke than heat, a featherbed on a rough-hewn wooden frame wide enough for only one (Trudy would be supplied later with a cot), a well-worn dresser topped by a mirror from which so much of the silver had peeled that one could barely see one's face in it, and a huge, carved wardrobe that occupied fully one third of the floor space—Trudy was unhooking the back of Lucienne's travel dress. She herself, at Lucienne's insistence, had already taken off her damp clothes and, wrapped in Lucienne's warmest dressing gown, had stopped shivering. She had just undone her mistress' last hook, and the dress had slipped from Lucienne's shoulders to the floor, when the door was pushed open. Lucienne wheeled about to face it, gasping, while Trudy let out a frightened little scream.

Lord Applegarth stood in the doorway, blinking in surprise, his mouth agape. "Who—?"

"Would you please *shut my door?*" Lucienne demanded, bending down hastily and reaching for her gown.

Applegarth stiffened. *"Your* door? Whatever do you mean? This is *my* room," he croaked angrily.

"How can it be your room," Lucienne snapped, holding the soggy dress up in front of her in an attempt at modesty, "when it is obviously occupied by someone else? Go away at once!"

"I shall *not* go away! This is *my* room. It has always *been* my room when I stop here, and it will always *be* my room. What are you doing here?"

"I am *trying* to dress for dinner, but I can't do it while you stand gaping in the doorway."

"I am not gaping, young woman. I do not gape at unclad females."

"Then close the door and *go away!*" Lucienne snarled between clenched teeth. Then she turned her head to Trudy, who was cowering behind her. "Trudy, there's no reason for you to hide like a rabbit. It's I who's undressed, not you. Now, go and close the door."

Trudy made a brave approach, but a glare from Lord Applegarth undid her, and she retreated. Applegarth, determined not to be dislodged, moved his huge bulk forward and wedged his foot and shoulder against the door. "I won't go away," Applegarth said stubbornly, sticking out his chin. "This is my room."

"If you don't close that door at once, I shall shout for the innkeeper!" Lucienne threatened.

"Don't bother, I'll do it myself! *Dymock! Dymock,* you clodcrusher, come up here at once."

"I say, Applegarth, is that you?" asked a voice from down the corridor. "What on earth is going on there?"

Lord Applegarth peered down the narrow, unlit hallway. "Who's that there? Someone I know? I wish you'd come here into the light and tell this young woman that she's usurped my room."

"My good man," exclaimed Lucienne in horror, "are you inviting someone *else* to gape at me? Permit my abigail to close the door or I'll scream!"

"Usurped your room? How can that be?" asked the man in the corridor, his voice getting closer. "I'm sure it's nothing but a small misunder—Good God! Miss *Gerard!*"

Lucienne whitened. The new figure in the doorway was Perry Wittenden.

"Wittenden?" Lord Applegarth beamed at Perry, whom he took to be an ally in his cause. "What luck to run into you this way! Good to see you, old chap. Do you *know* this lady?"

But Perry scarcely heard him. He was staring at Lucienne as if he'd never seen her before. And indeed, in her state of partial undress, with only the straps of her chemise showing on her deliciously bare shoulders and damp ringlets of hair dripping on her face and neck, she *was* unlike any girl he'd seen before. The skin on her soft shoulders glowed, her neck was slender perfection, her face surpassingly lovely in its pristine lack of cosmetic adornment, and, though the rest of her was covered by the dress she still clutched to her chest, one leg was extended beyond the damp emergency drapery and revealed an appetizing glimpse of a shapely ankle and a bare foot. In short, she looked to him like Aphrodite rising from the sea. "*Miss Gerard!*" he repeated breathlessly.

But neither Applegarth nor Lucienne noticed the breathlessness. Lucienne, more embarrassed and humiliated than she'd ever been in her life, was conscious only of a wish to die. Of all the ways imaginable for her to meet him again, this was the worst. Here she stood, wishing to sink into the ground, but to her eyes *he* was quite unaffected by these circumstances. It seemed to her that he was merely smiling that irritating little half-smile of his and revealing her name to that boor in the doorway. "Lord Wittenden," she said icily, "do you think this is the proper time to make introductions?"

"Introductions?" he echoed stupidly, trying to catch his breath.

"I am standing here in a state of *undress,* my lord, while this . . . this . . . *friend* of yours holds open the door! It hardly seems the appropriate time or place to tell him my *name.*"

"I wasn't . . ." Perry stammered awkwardly. "I didn't mean—"

"Of course you didn't. How uncharitable of me! What you *meant* to do is stand there and *observe* it all, so that you can write about this in your diary later!"

Her anger, so readily re-directed at him in spite of the accidental nature of his presence on her doorstep, cured him of his temporary embarrassment. His eyes brightened in amusement. "Perhaps you should go one step further, Miss Gerard, and accuse me of *arranging* this *contretemps* myself, just to get new material for my diary."

She lifted her chin. "I wouldn't believe it to be impossible."

He laughed. "I should have guessed, the moment I saw

you, that you would sooner or later find a way to make this my fault."

"I admit that you are not to blame for this, Lord Wittenden, but you're not helping matters either," she pointed out coldly. "If this gentleman is a friend of yours, will you be good enough to ask him to *close the door?*"

"No use in his asking," Applegarth said flatly. "Friend or no friend, he can't make me—"

A heavy step behind them made the two men turn. "Lord Applegarth," said the innkeeper, arriving hurriedly at the top of the stairs, "I 'eard ye call. Is somethin' amiss?"

"Amiss? I should say so, yes," Applegarth barked. "Something is *very* amiss. There's a . . . a *person* in my room!"

"A *person?*" Dymock peered over Applegarth's shoulder into the room. "Blimmey!" he exclaimed. "An' 'oo might *you* be?"

"Ask your wife," Lucienne snapped. "*After* you close the door!"

"Are ye saying my wife gave ye this room?" the innkeeper asked, frowning. "She never did! We were keepin' it fer 'is lordship."

"Come now, Dymock," Perry said quietly, "you can't accuse Miss Gerard of lying. Besides, it's quite obvious that she couldn't—and *wouldn't*—have stolen into the room behind everyone's back. Mrs. Dymock *must* have put her here."

Dymock rubbed his chin as the reasonableness of Perry's remarks sank into his brain. Then he turned to the stairway. *"Martha!"* he shouted down the stairs in a mighty roar.

"This is a great storm in a teacup, Applegarth," Perry murmured to the man in the doorway. "There's no need to raise a dust. You can have—"

"Martha!" the innkeeper shouted even louder. "Did ye let Lord Applegarth's room?"

There was the sound of a crash of crockery from down below, followed by the clatter of wooden-heeled shoes running toward the stairs. "Yer not tellin' me 'e's *come!*" Mrs. Dymock cried. "Don' give 'im the room, Peter! There's a *girl* in there!"

"Ye don' say," her husband muttered as his wife lumbered up the stairs to the landing.

"As I said, Applegarth," Perry began again, "you can have—"

"Mrs. Dymock," Lucienne said, catching a glimpse of her, "will you *please* tell this nodcock to *close this door?*"

"Mrs. Dymock," said her husband, "will ye *please* tell *me* 'ow you come to *let 'is lordship's room?*"

The innkeeper's wife wrung her hands. "It were so late, y' see, Peter. After six it were. I didn't think 'e was comin' no more. It didn't make sense t' keep the room empty—"

"But if I hadn't come, I'd have paid the shot for the room anyway, you know that," Applegarth said disgustedly.

"It weren't the m-money, yer lordship," the woman said, beginning to cry with deep, blubbery sobs. "It was the young m-miss, y' see. I didn't wish t' send 'er out in all that weather. And so d-dark it were, too."

"Mrs. Dymock," Lucienne reminded her exasperatedly, "the *door!*"

"It's all right, Martha," the innkeeper muttered, putting a comforting arm about his wife, "no need to turn on the water-works."

"It's *not* all right!" Applegarth shouted, turning a deep, furious red. "This chit is *in my room!* What are you going to *do* about it?"

"I've been trying to tell you," Perry put in soothingly, "that you may have *my* room. It's almost the same as this one, you know."

Perry's calmness took some of the wind from Applegarth's sails. "But I like *my* room," he pouted, a bit chastened. "I've had that room for *years.*"

"I know, old fellow, I know. But just this once—" Perry took his arm and attempted to dislodge him from the doorway where he seemed to have taken root.

Applegarth resisted. "And where will *you* go, if I take your room? We can't share it, you know. I can't abide sharing a room with anyone."

"Don't worry about it," Perry assured him. "I'll find somewhere to bed down. I can double up with my man in the servants' quarters, if need be."

"Thank ye, Lord Wittenden," the innkeeper said gratefully. "Ye're a great gun t' do this. With yer permission, I'll go along right now an' pack up yer things." And he hurried down the hall.

"Bless ye, me lord," Martha Dymock seconded, sniffling in gratitude. "I'll see to it that there's a comfortable place fer ye. An' Lord Applegarth, I'll fix up t'other room just as ye like it, with hot bricks t' warm the sheets 'n' everything." And with a bob to both of the gentlemen, she followed her husband down the hall.

"May we close the door *now?*" Lucienne inquired icily.

"I suppose so," muttered the still-irascible Applegarth, stepping back from the doorway at last. "But I must say, ma'am, that I find you a most selfish and perverse young woman! Good day to you." And he hobbled away down the hall.

"*Selfish!*" Lucienne gasped, staring after him. "Did he expect me to go out in the rain in my underclothes just so that he might have the bedroom he's accustomed to?"

"Don't pay him any mind, Miss Gerard," Perry soothed. "Lord Applegarth is very set in his ways. And must always have the last word, too. They joke about that at the club. I once wrote about it in my—" He caught himself up and reddened.

"In your diary?" she finished for him drily. "Yes, I should have known. I suppose that next month I'll find *myself* back there again, not only shrewish but selfish and perverse."

"No danger of that, ma'am," he said, smiling his half-smile. "I told you before that I write about fictional characters only."

She threw him a withering look as she crossed to the door. "Oh, yes, quite. I'm very well aware of how fictional they are." She pulled the door almost closed but stopped while it was still a few inches ajar. "I suppose I ought to thank you for giving up your room."

He grinned. "No, don't bother. It was just another manifestation of my nauseating good nature."

"Then nothing more need be said," she said, shutting the door with a bang. But before he turned away, she opened it again. "Your good nature won't save you, you know, if you write a *word* about this incident," she warned, glaring at him through the three-inch opening.

"Won't it?" he asked innocently. "What will you do to me?"

"I don't know. But you can be sure that it will be a better scheme than my last one." And she gave the door a final slam.

Inside, she stood staring at the door for so long that Trudy took notice. "Is anything the matter, Miss Lucy?" she asked timidly.

Lucienne shuddered, drew in a choked breath that was very much like a sob and lowered her head until her forehead fell against the door. "Oh, Trudy," she groaned, "why is it that whenever that man is anywhere in my vicinity I behave like a shrew?"

Chapter Thirteen

Lucienne ate her barley soup and mutton stew in her room, having no wish to encounter either Wittenden or his choleric friend Applegarth downstairs. And the next morning she kept to her room until nine. By nine, she estimated, all the other guests of the inn would have gone on their way.

But one of the other guests had not gone on his way. Perry Wittenden was still on the premises. The fellow had had a difficult night. The innkeeper had given him his son's room for the night, and the boy's bed had been deucedly uncomfortable—a lumpy mattress pad on a flat board. Perry had spent the entire night shifting from side to side in a futile attempt to find a comfortable niche between the lumps. Finally, in the wee hours of the morning, he'd given up and gotten out of bed. He'd paced about the tiny room, thinking of—of all things!—the way Miss Gerard had looked in her *deshabille*. Never had he seen so lovely a vision. The girl had completely taken his breath away.

It was strange, he thought, how the memory of that girl lingered in his mind. From the first, when she'd run into his carriage, he'd been fascinated by her. It was too bad they'd met the way they had. They'd started off on an entirely wrong footing. Then, of course, he'd completely offended her by writing that idiotic verse about the shrew. It seemed that she would never forgive him for that. But even if he hadn't written it, she'd have undoubtedly held him in distaste. She thought of him as "nauseatingly" good-natured. He'd laughed at the epithet at first, but now it seemed to him a devastating rejection. What, he wondered, was so nauseating about being good-natured?

He thought about the question from every side, but the only answer that made sense was that there was absolutely *nothing* wrong with being good-natured. The problem wasn't with him, but with her. She was obviously the sort of female who admired those big, brutish men who behaved like louts and knocked their women about. The Petruchios of this world.

He lit a candle, put on his spectacles and stared at his face in young Dymock's tiny mirror. It was definitely a good-natured face, with unruly red hair tumbling over a broad forehead, gentle eyes hidden behind schoolboy spectacles, a nose strewn with freckles, and a mouth permanently curved in that deuced half-smile. It was a pleasant-enough face, he supposed. Kind. Humorous. Even appealing, perhaps, in a boyish way. But not a Petruchio. To win a girl like Lucienne Gerard, a man had to be swarthy, with dark hair, keen, cold eyes and a thick-lipped mouth curved in a permanent sneer.

He'd tried, as a clock somewhere far away struck four, to twist his mouth into a proper sneer and then laughed at the ludicrousness of it. No, he could never turn himself into a brute. He was what he was, an amiable, easy-going, good-natured fellow, and if a certain female found him nauseating, well, so be it. There were other fish in the sea.

But this attitude of philosophical resignation did not last. The dark hour before dawn is not conducive to philosophical resignation. At four in the morning one is much more likely to feel anger or despair, and it was anger that soon overwhelmed Perry. He'd been much too generous to the self-centered Miss Gerard, he told himself. From simple goodness of heart, he'd accepted the blame for all sorts of misdeeds for which he had not an iota of guilt. And instead of gratitude, all he'd ever received from her was scorn. Well, he was quite finished with behaving in *that* way. He might not be capable of making himself a brute for her, but that didn't mean he had to be her *doormat* either. From now on he'd be different. He didn't know if he'd ever see her again, but if he did, he'd be damned if he'd show her a smiling face. If his good nature was so nauseating, then she'd seen the last of it!

With this angry mood wrapped round him like a blanket,

he threw himself down on the bed again and, as a pale sun rose, he fell sound asleep. When he awoke, it was almost eight. His earlier anger, like the morning fog, refused to dissipate. In this mood he dressed himself and packed his bag, and in this mood he bespoke the private dining room for an uncheerful breakfast of porridge and coffee, his pleasant face showing more of a glower than he would have thought possible when he'd studied it the night before.

The taproom clock was just striking nine when Lucienne and Trudy came down the stairs, warmly dressed to face the icy fog and looking forward to a hot breakfast before taking their departure. Trudy went to look for Mrs. Dymock to relay their breakfast order, while Lucienne made her way to the small, private parlor at the front of the house. To her surprise, she found Wittenden at the table, still lingering over his coffee and the morning newspaper. "Oh, I beg your pardon," she mumbled, backing to the door. "I didn't know anyone was here."

He got to his feet. "Good morning, ma'am," he said politely. "Do come in."

She shook her head. "I have no wish to intrude."

"It is no intrusion. This is the only private dining room. Besides, I've finished all but my coffee. I merely await word that my carriage is ready."

"Very well, then, if I'm not disturbing you, I shall come in. Thank you, my lord."

He held a chair for her. "I trust you slept well, Miss Gerard."

She nodded, feeling awkward and nervous because of his withdrawn manner and because of coming upon him so unexpectedly. Now that she thought about it, she was *always* coming upon him unexpectedly. Perhaps that was why she always behaved so badly when they met. She'd make a much better impression, she was sure, if they could, just once, meet by design, when she'd have time to prepare herself.

Clenching her fingers in determination not to do or say a thing this morning that could possibly be construed as selfish or shrewish, she smiled at him brightly. "I probably slept better than you did, my lord. What sort of sleeping place did our landlord find for you? A haystack in the barn?"

"No such luck," he said, showing no sign of a responding smile. "He gave me his son's bed. A torture rack couldn't have been more riddled with lumps. A haystack would have been far better. I wish I'd thought of it."

"I am sorry," she said, seating herself. "I suppose you must blame me for having to give up your room."

"No, I am unlike you in that regard," he retorted, returning to his place at the table and taking his seat. "I don't toss blame about like a ball to be caught by the nearest bystander."

She glanced over at him in surprise, taken aback by the slight tinge of bitterness in his voice. "Is that what I do? Toss blame to the nearest bystander?"

"Yes, so it seems to me," he said with unwonted coldness. "Or at least you do it when *I'm* near enough to catch it."

She found herself stiffening. He'd always spoken to her in a bantering tone before, but this time there was no hint of playfulness about him. A sharp retort sprang to her lips, but she remembered her pledge to herself, made only a moment ago, and she held her tongue. Perhaps he didn't mean to be short with her. Perhaps he was the sort—not unusual with these agreeable types—who was grumpish in the morning. "Are you scolding me, my lord?" she asked archly, hoping to charm him into his usual cheerfulness. "It's a bit early in the day for scolds, isn't that so? I find that my digestion is so much better when I see a few smiles before breakfast."

"Do you indeed?" he muttered, colder still. "Then perhaps your abigail can oblige when she comes in." And, without so much as a by-your-leave, he picked up his newspaper and resumed reading.

Lucienne froze. His remark was certainly a set-down, and his picking up his paper was positively rude. How *dared* he treat her that way! Was *this* her reward for being sweet-tempered with him? She glared at the newspaper that he held up between them, drumming her fingers furiously on the table as she tried to think of a withering remark to set *him* down as he had her.

After enduring the irritating drumming for a few moments, Perry lowered the paper and frowned at her. "Is something wrong, ma'am? You seem disturbed."

"I am not disturbed, my lord. I am only surprised."

"Surprised? What has so suddenly surprised you?"

"You, my lord."

"I? I surprised you? In what way, ma'am?"

"I had previously thought of you as a man who was invariably gentle-natured—"

"Nauseatingly so, I think you said," he put in drily.

She ignored the interruption. "—and now I find it to have been a facade. I had not expected to discover that behind that facade was a *rudesby.*"

"Oh? Am I a rudesby now? But why should that disturb you, Miss Gerard? I'd have guessed that my being a rudesby would be preferable to you to my being nauseatingly good-natured."

"I may not find it preferable, but I certainly find it logical. It's the rudesby who's the *real* man, isn't that so, my lord?" she asked nastily. "The one who writes the Diary?"

"There is *nothing rude* about the Diary," he declared, re-opening his paper with an angry snap and turning away from her.

"So you say! *You* haven't been a victim of it."

"Damnation, that's enough!" He threw the paper angrily on the table and jumped to his feet. "Let's have done with this nonsense about the Diary! You were not a 'victim' of my diary in any sense of the word. And what is more, you know it!"

"Please do not curse at me!" she said, rising like the goddess Juno in offended dignity. "This is not your club, and I am not your friend Applegarth! Or have you forgotten how to act the gentleman in the presence of a lady?"

He threw up his hands in disgust. "Arguing with you is like arguing with an eel! Do not think you can use the *argumentum ad hominem* against me again, ma'am, though I admit you have mastered its techniques quite well."

"I don't see how I can master a technique that I don't even know the meaning of," she muttered.

"It's a way of squirming out of an argument when you're in a tight corner by throwing in an irrelevant accusation against the character of your opponent. You did it the first time we met, and you did it again just now. You see, you only attacked my lack of gentlemanly behavior because you had no satisfactory reply to my declaration that you were not victimized by my verses."

"Are you saying," she demanded, placing her hands flat on the table and leaning toward him aggressively, "that I had no right to object to your using an improper word in my presence?"

He positioned himself against the table in the very same way, so that they were almost head to head. "I am saying, ma'am, that your objection to what was only a slip of the tongue is irrelevant to the question under discussion."

"Oh, it is, is it? I was not aware that we were having a formal debate that required a knowledge of the rules of forensics."

"One needn't have a knowledge of the rules of forensics to understand that any logical argument requires that the responses be relevant to the subject under discussion. And the subject under discussion was *your obsession with my verses!*"

"Then I'll make my objection relevant, my lord, by pointing out that your so-called slip of the tongue *proves* you are *no gentleman,* either with the *spoken* word or with the *written* one, so there!"

"And you, ma'am," he retorted, "are a lady *only* until someone dares imply that there is something in your character that is less than perfect! As soon as you detect the slightest hint of criticism, your ladylike qualities seem to fly right out the win—"

"Ahem!" The cough came from the throat of Mr. Dymock, who stood framed in the doorway, a greatcoat over his arm and a high beaver in his hand. Behind him, peering pop-eyed over his shoulder, were Trudy and Mrs. Dymock. How long they'd been standing there was a question neither Lucienne nor Perry could have answered, but it was plain they'd heard more than they should.

Perry, unaccustomed to being caught playing the role of loutish brute, colored to the ears. "Hang it, Dymock," he demanded brusquely, "did no one teach you how to knock?"

"I knocked, m'lord. Three times. Beggin' yer pardon, m'lord, I on'y wanted t' tell ye yer carriage is waitin'."

"And did you need the women behind you to assist with that message?"

"No, m'lord. They was on'y waitin' t' bring in Miss Gerard's breakfast. They didn' wish t' interrupt—"

"Yes, yes, very well, have them come in. Tell Magnus I'm ready to go."

"Yes, m'lord. May I 'elp ye with yer greatcoat, m'lord?" He came up behind Perry with the coat, while his wife and Trudy scurried past him with their trays and began to set out the breakfast things. As the innkeeper held the coat up he remembered a message he'd been asked to relay. "Oh, yes, m'lord. One thing more. Mr. Magnus said t' tell ye that 'e reckons ye can reach Mendlesham in three hours."

Lucienne, who'd turned her back on all of them, wheeled about. "Mendlesham?" she gasped. "Did he say *Mendleshan?*"

Perry, with one arm in the coat, peered up at her. "Yes, he did. Why?"

"You're not . . . it can't be that you're on your way to . . . to *Rutherford Grange!*"

Perry's eyebrows rose. "Yes, I am. How did you . . . ? Oh, *no!*"

"Yes," she said, shutting her eyes in dismay. "Oh, *yes.*"

Perry stood stock still for a moment before thrusting his other arm into his coat. Then he snatched his hat from the innkeeper's grasp. "What a delightful fortnight *this* promises to be," he muttered as he clapped it on his head and strode out to his carriage.

Chapter Fourteen

Lucienne's first reaction to the news that Wittenden was to be a guest at Rutherford Grange was to decide to turn right about and go home. What was the point of continuing her journey to the Grange, she asked herself, when all hope of enjoying it was now destroyed? Better not to go at all than to spend the fortnight being miserable. And with Wittenden there, how could she help but be miserable? After the fiasco this morning, how could she even face him in the company of others? In order to behave with proper civility, she would have but two choices, one worse than the other: either to spend each day trying to avoid him, or remain in his company and *pretend* that she felt cordial toward him. *No,* she told herself, *it would be impossible either way.*

She promptly ordered the coachman to turn north toward Yorkshire instead of east toward Mendlesham. But as they trundled along, second thoughts beset her. What would Aunt Chloe say? Would she accuse her niece of breaking her word? Would she not feel deserted or betrayed? And would not Lady Rutherford be offended? And as for the gossips who'd had such a fine time for themselves on the subject of "Whistle-down's Shrew"—wouldn't they be delighted to spread this latest on-dit? She could hear them now: "Haven't you *heard,* my dear, about Lucienne Gerard running off from the doings at Rutherford Grange because she'd been unable to face Wittenden again? Yes, it's absolutely true... the silly creature scurried home like a fainthearted rabbit!"

It was the realization that she was being cowardly—for, in truth, she *was* running off like a fainthearted rabbit—that changed her mind. As much as she would dislike the fortnight at the Grange, she had to go on with it, if only to keep tongues from wagging about her again. It had been hard enough to bear being called a shrew, but to be called fainthearted was not to be borne. She was many things that were not admirable, but a milksop she was not!

So the carriage was turned about again, and Lucienne continued her journey to Mendlesham. And she promised herself that no matter how low her spirits fell during her stay, she would make sure that no one, not even her loving aunt, would be able to tell.

She arrived in late afternoon. The fog was still thick, making it difficult to see more than a few feet ahead. She didn't even realize she'd arrived until the carriage came to a stop. But her hosts were evidently watching for her, for she'd barely climbed down from the carriage when she was surrounded by a trio of welcomers, her aunt and the Rutherfords. "Is this not a magnificent *pied-à-terre?*" Chloe whispered into her right ear as Jenny Rutherford kissed her left cheek and Lord Rutherford pumped her hand. But it was not until the Rutherfords turned their attention to directing the servants in the removal and disposition of her baggage that Lucienne was able to look about her. The house was indeed impressive, even as seen through the mist. As Chloe had said in her letter, the word Grange was much too modest for such an imposing country house. It was a square building made of grey stone, with a double-arched stairway leading to the front door. The square shape made the building seem stolid and ponderous, and even the softening effect of the fog did not mask its impressive solidity. Although the door and the center window above it on the second floor were both topped by beautifully shaped fanlights, giving the facade a touch of grace, the overall effect was of sturdy British substantiality. If this "grange" had ever truly been a farmhouse, there was no sign of such modesty left.

The large-bosomed Lady Rutherford and her stocky husband, Spencer (who looked more like a plump, ale-swilling farmer than the influential peer that he was), did not permit Lucienne to spend much time in studying her surroundings. As soon as the orders concerning the baggage had been given, they ushered her up the stone steps, across the large, light-filled foyer and into the drawing room where all the other guests were already assembled. Spencer Rutherford took her forcibly by the elbow and brought her round the room to greet the others. He introduced her first to his closest friend, Admiral Rodney Dawes, and his wife, Lily. The Admiral, now retired, was not in uniform, but though he stood only five feet three and was garbed in civilian dress, he seemed commanding. His posture was stiff and his manner gruff, but he had bright eyes and an easy laugh. His wife, dressed and coiffed in a fashion that could only be called eccentric, stood a head taller than her husband, but she had the same alert expression in her eyes. "So *you* are Whistledown's shrew," Lily Dawes remarked with a twinkle as soon as they were introduced. "The moment I read about how you defended your honor with your umbrella, I knew I would like you."

Her husband snorted with laughter. "You mustn't mind Lily, my dear," he said. "She means no offense. A sailor's wife, y'see. Frank to a fault."

"You needn't apologize for me, Rodney," his wife cut in promptly. "It is my opinion that to call someone a shrew is no insult. It merely indicates that the girl has spirit. I'm a shrew myself."

"Ha! You certainly are," her husband agreed, chortling.

Before Lucienne could assure the Admiral that she'd taken no offense, Lord Rutherford pulled her on. "Now you must meet the Trevellicks," he informed her. "All four of them. There would have been five, but Lord Trevellick could not be persuaded to leave Cornwall. He's so difficult to budge that his wife says she'll have difficulty getting him to come to town for his daughter's wedding." Laughing a booming laugh, he drew her to a small group of three women sitting together on a sofa near the fire. The fourth member of the party was a dark-haired, dark-moustached young man who'd perched on the sofa's back and was watching Lucienne's approach with interest. "This is Lady Trevellick, of course," Lord Rutherford said, indicating the apple-cheeked matron seated between two young girls who were obviously her daughters. "Lady Trevellick, this is Lucienne Gerard, Chloe's niece."

" 'Ow do 'ee do?" Lady Trevellick said in a heavy Cornish

accent. "Atween Owen an' yer auntie Chloe, Miss Gerard, I've 'eard a dale about 'ee."

"I've heard a great deal about you, too," said one of the girls. "I'm Cora Trevellick, Miss Gerard."

Lucienne had already guessed her identity. The rabbity front teeth made her instantly recognizable. But it was the other sister who drew her gaze. As Lord Rutherford introduced Mabyn Trevellick, the youngest of the family, Lucienne noticed that, while all the Trevellick women were pleasing in appearance, this one was a beauty. She did not seem to wish to make a show of it, however, for her silky, red-gold hair was braided tightly and twisted at the nape of her neck in a modest bun, her eyes—breathtakingly green—were hidden behind a pair of spectacles, and her form—not tall but perfectly proportioned—was covered by a modest gown of grey poplin with a white tucker at the neck. To add to the impression of prudish restraint, the girl had an open book on her lap. Lucienne couldn't help wondering why a young woman as lovely as this one made herself look like a governess, while her sister was dressed with as much style and elegance as any London belle. Lucienne smiled inwardly as she realized why Owen, whose powers of observation were obviously as shallow as his character, had chosen the more ostentatious sister to wed.

Meanwhile, their brother had come round the sofa and was tugging at Rutherford's elbow. "You're not going to forget me, are you, Rutherford?" he asked impatiently. "Am I not to be made known to this charming young lady?" He turned and beamed down at Lucienne from a height almost as tall as Owen's. "I'm Colin, the black sheep of the family."

"Don't 'ee listen to 'im, Miss Gerard," his mother warned. " 'Ee likes to talk fal-the-ral."

"Mama thinks any slur on one of us is fal-the-ral," the beautiful Mabyn said, patting her mother's hand fondly.

"But what *is* fal-the-ral?" Lucienne asked, charmed by the soft sound of the mother's accent.

"It means nonsense in the 'auld tongue'," Colin explained. "Fol-de-rol, you know."

"Oh, of course. I should have guessed."

"You'll get used to Mama's way of speaking," Mabyn said. "It's not too hard to learn."

"It's not too hard to *un*learn, either," Cora said with a touch of asperity, "but Mama says she can't do it, and that the only reason *we* managed it is because we all went away to school, but I think Mama doesn't *want* to unlearn it."

"An' why, I ax 'ee, should I want to unlearn it?" the mother said placidly. "A right lovely tongue the auld tongue is."

"Yes, I think you're quite right," Lucienne agreed.

"Thank 'ee, my dear," the mother said, moving closer to Cora to make room on the sofa. "Set 'ee down a crum."

"Yes, do sit down, Miss Gerard," Colin urged. "We all want to know the young lady who gave Owen the jilt."

Mabyn winced, and Cora glared at him. But their mother only sighed. "Colin, don't 'ee be an ass-neger!"

"That, Miss Gerard," Mabyn explained, "means a silly fool, which describes my brother to the core."

"Not a silly fool at all," Colin said calmly. "Merely honest. Well, Miss Gerard, will you join us?"

"She can't," Lord Rutherford said, pulling at her arm again. "She hasn't yet completed the rounds." And without further ado, he led her off toward the side of the room where a row of glass doors leading to a balustraded terrace were now tightly shut against the fog. Standing in the glow of the misty light were Lady Rutherford and Chloe, engaged in animated conversation with Perry. "I say, Wittenden," Lord Rutherford exclaimed jovially, "come and meet Miss Gerard."

Perry turned, his smile fading from his face. "Miss Gerard and I have already met," he said tightly.

"Yes, once or twice," Lucienne said, putting out her hand. "How do you do, my lord?"

Their eyes locked for a moment with tense antagonism. Lucienne, in offering him her hand, was indicating that she was willing to ignore their quarrel and put a good face on things, but the look in her eye told him clearly that, should he not take her peace offering, she was perfectly capable of returning his fire.

He hesitated only a moment before lifting her hand to his lips. "Miss Gerard," he murmured, "how nice to see you again."

"Well, well, old friends, eh?" Rutherford said heartily,

slapping Perry on the back. "Then I need feel no compunction, Wittenden, if I go off to see to the housing of the horses and leave Miss Gerard in your hands."

Perry and Lucienne watched in silence until their host was out of earshot. Then Perry turned to her. "You did not leave the Black Boar immediately after I did, did you, Miss Gerard? You took so long in arriving that I began to fear I'd frightened you off."

"You flatter yourself, my lord," Lucienne said grandly. "In the first place, I am not easily frightened. And in the second place, I do not take *you* into consideration in any plans I make. Your presence here is a matter of complete indifference to me."

"Is it?" Perry's irrepressible smile made a brief appearance. "Then I need not bother to make the apology I'd prepared."

"Apology, my lord?"

"For my behavior this morning. I don't often act the rudesby, but I'd had a sleepless night, you know. You judged it to be my real character, but I assure you that my behavior is usually more even-tempered. Nauseatingly good-natured, as you so poetically described it."

"Than you admit to being disgustingly rude this morning?"

"I admit it, although I must voice a small objection to the descriptive words you so invariably apply to me, like nauseating and disgusting. I admit to rudeness, but I will *not* accept disgusting."

"Since you so magnanimously admit the rudeness, my lord, I shall withdraw the disgusting."

"Thank you, ma'am," he said, making a small, ironic bow. "Does this mean we've arrived at a truce?"

"I suppose we have." Something inside her sighed in relief as she held out a hand. "A truce, at least for the time being. Here's my hand on it."

But before he was able to seal the bargain by taking her hand in his, their attention was distracted by Mabyn Trevellick, who appeared suddenly at Perry's side, her book clutched in her hand. "Excuse me, Lord Wittenden," she said. "I hope I'm not interrupting a private conversation between you and Miss Gerard . . ."

"Not at all, Miss Trevellick," Perry assured her promptly.

Perhaps too promptly, Lucienne thought, aware of a twinge of irritation at the girl's invasion. However, she forced herself to smile. "We were merely agreeing with each other," she said to the younger girl, throwing Perry a challenging glance, "and agreement, as you know, is so boring that an interruption is welcome."

"Nothing you say could ever be boring, Miss Gerard," the girl said sweetly, making Lucienne feel three inches tall for having had uncharitable feelings about her. "But I've just heard from Cora that Lord Wittenden is the poet who writes the Whistledown Diary, and I wanted to know if it's true."

"I couldn't say," Lucienne responded, turning to Perry with an expression of bland innocence. *"Are* you the poet who writes the Whistledown Diary?"

Perry glared at her before turning to the questioner. "Miss Gerard knows perfectly well that I'm Whistledown, but she'd be the first to tell you that I'm no poet, Miss Trevellick."

"Oh, but you *are!"* the girl breathed, smiling up at him admiringly. (Lucienne couldn't help but notice that Mabyn was the perfect height for Perry, her head coming up only as high as his shoulder. Lucienne, being almost as tall as he, could never turn her eyes up to his in that adoring way.) "I've read the diary every month since I discovered it, and I believe that you have a way of turning a phrase and a . . . a special way of seeing that only a true poet has."

"Do you really?" Perry threw Lucienne a twinkling glance before turning back to his admirer. "You don't find the writing nauseatingly good-natured?"

"Good heavens, no!" the girl exclaimed, appalled. "What makes you ask so silly a question?"

"Even poets can ask silly questions sometimes," Lucienne murmured drily.

"But I didn't approach you merely to tell you that I'm an admirer," Mabyn went on, showing no sign of having heard Lucienne's remark. "I've come to ask for your help. Since you write poetry—"

"I write verse, Miss Trevellick, verse. It is a very different thing."

"I will not argue the point with you, my lord. Poetry or verse. I'm sure you can help me to understand what I've been reading. It's this Ode of Mr. Wordsworth's, and—"

"Now, *there*, Miss Trevellick, is a poet worth reading," Perry said frankly. "Much more worth your time than a versifier like me. Are you speaking of his magnificent "Intimations of Immortality"? What did you wish to say about it?"

"Well, you see, although I sense that it is very beautiful, I find that the meaning of it often eludes me. Here, for instance . . ." She sat down on a nearby chair and rifled through the pages of her book for her place. When she found it, she held it up for him to see. "Here, where he says we are born trailing clouds of glory . . . and here, where he says the homely Nurse does all she can to make him forget the glories he had known . . ."

Perry leaned over her shoulder to see. "Ah, yes," he murmured. "Wonderful lines. You see, Mr. Wordsworth expresses here a feeling that a child is born with memories of a prior—and splendid—state of existence . . ."

Lucienne looked at them with their heads bent over the book, both completely absorbed in the poem. Perry's cheek was just touching Mabyn's hair. They made a charming pair, Lucienne admitted to herself sourly—she with her Titian hair, he with his darker red curls, and both looking so scholarly and appealing behind their spectacles. They might have been made for each other.

But they seemed to have forgotten *her* "state of existence." Lucienne's irritation with the intrusion of Mabyn Trevellick into her tête-à-tête with Perry blossomed into a very pronounced feeling of jealousy. She stared at them for a moment, wondering what was happening to her. Jealousy was not an emotion she'd felt before. What was the matter with her? And what was there to be jealous *of*? If the nauseating Lord Wittenden and the beauteous Miss Trevellick fixed their affections on each other, it would be much easier for her, Lucienne, to enjoy the rest of the visit. He would be too preoccupied to have anything to do with her, and thus *she* would not be forced to avoid him or to pretend to a civility she did not feel. With his attention focused in another direction, she would be free to follow her own inclinations. The moustachioed Colin, for example, might make an amusing swain. If Wittenden was táken with Mabyn, then Lucienne was *glad* of it!

That settled, she turned on her heel and went off to find her aunt. But after she'd taken a dozen steps, she wondered if her departure from the poetic couple had been too abrupt. Perhaps she should have taken proper leave of them. She glanced back over her shoulder. They were just as she'd left them, their heads charmingly close together and their eyes on the book. They hadn't even noticed that she'd gone.

Chapter Fifteen

Intimacy develops quickly at a house-party where everyone realizes that they will have to endure each other's companionship—and no other—for an entire fortnight. By the time the guests sat down to the first dinner, everyone had already learned all sorts of secrets: that Lady Trevellick was likely to fall asleep in her chair at any time, for example, or that the Admiral could not sit down to a meal without stealing outdoors first to "blow a cloud" with his cigar. During dinner, Cora revealed to half the table that the reason her betrothed, Sir Owen Tatlow, hadn't come with the others was that he'd gone to Derbyshire to pay his respects to an uncle who had promised to write him into his will as soon as his nephew was wedded. And by the time dinner was over, Lily Dawes and Chloe (who had not met before) had already become fast friends, Colin has asked Lucienne to ride with him the next morning, and Mabyn and Perry were addressing each other by their first names.

Lady Rutherford had made only simple plans for her guests' first evening at the Grange in order that they all, weary from their travels, might retire early. After the men had had their brandies, the party assembled in the music room where, Lady Rutherford announced, they would make their own entertainment for an hour or so. After a few moments of desultory conversation, Lily Dawes suggested opening the pianoforte. The hostess grasped at the idea as a drowning swimmer might at a lifeline, and she turned at once to Lucienne, whose reputation as a talented performer was well known to her. Lucienne, not the sort to be coy, was soon prevailed upon to play for them.

She chose a sonata by Haydn which had to be played *con brio*. *Con brio* was the style Lucienne loved best, and she executed the charming, lively piece with vivacious brilliance. The runs and trills flew under her fingers, and she struck the chords with enough passion to make the old pianoforte vibrate with sound. The audience was enraptured, not only by Lucienne's musical talent but by her loveliness. At the keyboard, with the glow of a huge branch of candles lighting her face, Lucienne—in a Persian-red velvet gown cut low across the bosom and her dark hair brushed casually back from her forehead, caught at the nape of her neck by an exquisite diamond clip and brought down over her bare shoulder in one thick curl—was ravishing. When her strong fingers had hammered out the last chord, the audience broke into loud, prolonged applause.

Lady Trevellick, who'd been dozing in her chair, awoke with a shudder. She recovered at once and joined in the applause. "My Mabyn plays the pianoforte, too," she announced as soon as she could be heard. "Come, Mabyn, love, why'nt 'ee set down an' play a crum? Don't be timmersome."

"Yes, do play for us," the hostess seconded.

Other voices joined in to urge the girl until, with a sweet, self-effacing smile, she rose and went to the instrument. She flexed her fingers and stiffened her shoulders, as if to steel herself, and then, removing her spectacles and placing them gently on the ledge above the keyboard, she put her fingers on the keys, threw her head back, shut her eyes and began to play. It was the Mozart Sonata No. 9, which begins with a graceful *andante* and moves through several variations until it ends with an *allegro* of great intricacy and charm. Lucienne, listening, could barely breathe. Almost from the first notes the girl struck, Lucienne knew she'd met her match. Mabyn played with such sensitivity and feeling, such gentle sureness in her fingers and such easy adjustment to the changing moods of the variations that Lucienne was amazed. By the time the sonata was concluded, Lucienne had surreptitiously brushed away a number of salty tears. But whether she'd been crying over the beauty of the music or her own inadequacy, she didn't know.

For the rest of the audience, however, the experience was less shattering. They were all moved by the playing, but most of them were neither capable of, nor interested in, making fine distinctions between two talented musicians. They felt fortunate that they had *two* such gifted musicians among them—two girls who were as pleasing to see as to hear. For Mabyn, too, was a joy to behold in the candlelight. Her hair, not as severely braided as it had been earlier, made a soft golden frame about her pale face; her head, tilted back in trancelike concentration, seemed sculpted in marble; and her neck, stretched taut, was as lovely as a swan's. Her gown, modestly understated, was made of lustring in a pale lilac color, which added to the overall impression of a vision in pastels. Lucienne had also been a vision, but in vibrant oils.

When the concert was over, everyone milled about the room, congratulating one and then the other pianist with equal enthusiasm. Lucienne accepted the compliments with a gracious smile, but she felt little pleasure in the kind words. Even Perry Wittenden's praise did not cheer her, for she'd noticed that he'd approached Mabyn first. She felt nothing but relief when the party began to say their good-nights.

At the foot of the stairway, Chloe and Lucienne found themselves alone. Chloe put an arm about her niece and kissed her cheek. "You played beautifully tonight, my love," she whispered. "I was so proud of you!"

"Nonsense, Aunt Chloe," Lucienne said frankly. "Mabyn Trevellick put me to shame."

Chloe's eyes widened in sincere surprise. "How can you say that?" she demanded. "Miss Trevellick played well, I admit, but I failed to find any difference between her talent and yours."

"There was a difference," Lucienne muttered as she started up the stairs. "A very great difference."

"What sort of difference?" her aunt persisted, following her. "Explain it to me. I want to understand you."

Lucienne paused, her brow knit thoughtfully. "It's hard to explain the difference, Aunt Chloe, but it's very real. It's like

... It's like ..." Her brow cleared as an explanation occurred to her, but her eyes clouded. She turned to her aunt and sighed. "It's like the difference between a verse and a poem," she said.

Chapter Sixteen

As they'd agreed the night before, Colin and Lucienne met in the foyer before breakfast, dressed for riding. Although the morning was overcast and icy cold, they decided to brave the elements and ride as planned. They made their way to the stables where Lord Rutherford's stableman provided them with two spirited roans, and they set off across the south field to explore their hosts' grounds.

They proceeded at a moderate trot through a series of open fields, keeping apace of each other so that they could converse. Colin told her about the Trevellick castle in Cornwall, describing its magnificent situation near the sea and the ruined abbey on its grounds in which he'd played as a boy.

Lucienne, in her turn, recounted anecdotes of her childhood in Yorkshire, depicting in great detail an account of the first time she'd galloped a horse, when she was only nine. The horse had really run away with her, she confessed, but she would not admit to her father and her riding master, who'd been watching the scene in great alarm, that she'd lost control of the animal. "I pretended to them that I'd spurred the animal on purpose, that I'd not been frightened in the least, and that I intended to do nothing but gallop from then on."

Colin, bright-eyed and red-cheeked from the cold, laughed appreciatively. "You were a game little tyke, at nine, Miss Gerard, I must say."

"You may call me Lucienne, Mr. Trevellick. Or Lucy, if you prefer. Familiarity seems to be the style here. Yes, I suppose you might say I was *game*."

"Are you just as game now?"

"Game for what?" she asked suspiciously.

"To go galloping, Lucy, my girl. To race like the wind. It's too cold to keep ambling along at this snail's pace. Are you game to race over that next rise?"

"It's a bit reckless, is it not, Mr. Trevellick, to go galloping over ground with which we're not familiar?"

Colin made a moue. "In the first place, if I'm to call you Lucy, you must call me Colin. Trevellick is a dreadful mouthful, is it not? And in the second place, I'm the reckless sort. Didn't you heed my warning yesterday, when I told you I'm the black sheep of the family? I have a well-deserved reputation for being wild and reckless."

"I think, Colin, my lad, that you're trying to paint yourself black because you think it captivates the females."

"Not at all. I'm nothing if not honest. Ask my sisters. They'd be the first to warn you about me. And, by the way, you sound just like them, which is something I didn't expect. I expected you to be different. More spirited."

"Really?" Lucienne asked curiously. "Why?"

"Because you had the spirit to jilt Tatlow, that's why."

"That's a strange thing to say, when your own sister is to wed him. Don't you like him?"

Colin shrugged. "He's all right. A *catch*, Mama says, though I don't see why. I know that you ladies consider him a handsome devil, and he's plump in the pocket, with more blunt coming in when his uncle passes on, and all that. But I find him a bit stuffy. However, *I'm* not marrying him, so I don't much care. And I suppose he and Cora will suit well enough."

"Then why did you think me spirited for giving him the jilt?"

He smiled at her broadly, his moustache twitching with the movement of his mouth. "Because, Lovely Lucy, it's a rare young lady who tosses away a 'catch'."

"Ah, but you've changed your mind about me, isn't that right? You said that I sound like your sisters after all."

"Yes, because you made that cautious remark about worrying about unfamiliar ground."

She tossed her head defiantly. "It was a very sensible remark. It is rash to go galloping over unfamiliar ground."

"If you ask me, all ground is very much alike. Is a rut more dangerous on unknown ground than on familiar?"

"Of course it is. On familiar ground you know it's there."

"Rubbish! Wherever you ride, you look ahead of you, don't you? And a good rider can maneuver over a rut wherever he finds it. Even on familiar ground, one comes upon ruts unexpectedly, isn't that so?"

"Yes, I suppose so."

"There, then." He looked over at her eagerly, but getting no response, he sighed. "Oh, well, I didn't really expect you to race with me. All you women lack the courage to adventure into the unknown that we men possess."

"We women have courage, too, I assure you." She threw him a sidelong, interested glance. "Were you implying, a moment ago, that your sisters don't race with you?"

"Race? *My* sisters? Don't be absurd. Oh, they ride well enough, for females, but always at a sedate pace like this. I don't call this sort of canter a real ride."

"Nor do I," Lucienne agreed, feeling a sudden, rash impulse to take his absurd challenge. Galloping a horse was second nature to her, and there was nothing she would rather do at this moment than race with him. And though she realized that it was a petty, small-minded impulse, inspired by the knowledge that Mabyn wouldn't have been able to do it, she succumbed to it. Here was one talent, at least, in which she had some superiority over the girl toward whom she felt such inexplicable rivalry, and she intended to show that talent off.

Colin could hardly believe what he'd heard. "Do you mean you *will?*" he asked eagerly. "You'll *race* me?"

"Yes, of course. As soon as you're ready."

They spurred their horses and set off toward the rise, Lucienne taking the lead almost at once. The cold wind whipped by her face and set her scarf flapping wildly behind her, making her feel more stirred and invigorated than she'd felt in months. She kept the lead over most of the stretch, but when they approached the rise, an instinct made her pull back on the reins. Colin thundered past her and over the rise. Almost immediately after he disappeared from view, she heard a loud, gasping cry. She galloped to the top of the rise, reined in and stopped. Just over the rise, instead of the expected gentle slope, the ground dropped sharply away and became a steep hill. And a short way down, a low hedge unexpectedly cut the hill in half. Lucienne, her blood frozen in her veins and her heart arrested, could see nothing beyond the hedge—no sign of either horse or rider.

She guided her horse carefully down the slope to the hedge. Then she pulled him to a stop, slipped down and peered over the hedge. There, just below her, was Colin, sitting on the ground examining his left boot with a bemused expression. His riding hat and crop were on the ground beside him, his coat and breeches were smudged with grass stains and mud, his face was pale and his hair was disheveled. And his horse was nowhere to be seen.

She pushed through the hedge and knelt beside him. "Oh, Colin!" she said in a shaking voice. "You're *alive!*"

He lifted his head and said with an expression of utmost self-disgust, "Dash it all, Lucy, I've been *thrown.*"

"Yes, so I see," she said, patting his shoulder sympathetically.

"But how can it have happened? I've never been thrown in my life."

"That is hard to believe, considering the rash way you ride."

He lifted his head again. "Madam, it is a matter of pride with me. I tell you I've never been thrown."

"Well, you were this time. But don't be so downcast about it, Colin. You should be thankful you weren't killed."

"Good God, woman! You didn't think a little toss from a horse would finish me!" He hitched himself round to face her in an abrupt motion, but as soon as he did so, his face tensed with pain. *"Ouch!"* he cried out loudly. "My *foot!*"

"Colin, *please* don't move!" She reached out her arms to his shoulders to try to restrain him. "Something may be broken."

Wincing, he bent his left leg and stared at it. "I feel as if I'm bruised all over, but the real pain is in my ankle."

"Do you think it may be broken?" Lucy asked worriedly.

"I shouldn't wonder. Confound it, this is a devil of a fix! What are we to do now? I can barely move, much less get up and walk."

"My horse is just on the other side of the hedge. I can ride for help, I suppose, if you don't mind being left alone for a bit."

He nodded in dubious agreement. She stood up and went to push through the hedge to the horse, but she saw at once that their plan was doomed. "The blasted animal is gone!" she exclaimed.

"Dash it all, if that isn't the last straw," Colin muttered.

"Do you suppose he's gone back to the stables?" Lucienne wondered.

"That's more than I expect from *my* mount. *He* went tearing off into the woods down there. I hope he hasn't broken a leg on the underbrush."

"I may as well start to walk back, Colin. We can't have come more than a few miles, can we?"

"I don't know. But why don't you just sit here with me and wait? If your mount *did* go back to the stables, they're bound to send someone out to see what's become of us."

"That's true. I do hate to leave you sitting here alone with nothing to think of but your pain. If no one comes in half an hour or so, I can walk back then."

She took a seat on the grass beside him. The ground was cold and damp, but she made no complaint aloud. If he could bear his pain in silence, she could certainly keep her discomfort to herself. "Do you think we should take your boot off, Colin?" she asked. "It might ease the pain somewhat."

"No, I don't think the ankle could bear the jostling. But do you know what would be really soothing? If I could just lean back against you."

"Yes, of course." She edged closer, using one hand to brace herself and the other to help him ease himself against her shoulder.

Once in place, with his head nestled comfortably in the hollow of her neck, he sighed contentedly. "You, lovely Lucy, are a regular out-and-outer."

"Oh, pooh! Can you really say that when I pulled back at the edge of the rise and let you take the slope alone?"

"That only proves you have better sense than I." He looked up at her with a teasing smile. "Such a sensible wench. And so pretty, too. Do you know that, despite the hideous pain I'm in, I have an irresistible urge to reach up, pull your lovely head down to mine and kiss you?"

"If I were you, Colin Trevellick," she retorted, "I would use all my strength to resist that urge."

"No, you would not. I'm becoming more and more convinced that you're as wild and reckless as I am. In my place, you'd do just as I'm going to do."

"You're not going to do anything of the sort. Honestly, Colin, if I didn't know better, I'd think you'd arranged this accident just to get me in this awkward position."

"And so I might have done, if I were devious enough to think of it. But however I got you here, I shall certainly take advantage of the situation." And he reached up an arm and hooked it round her neck.

"See here, Colin," she objected, trying vainly to keep her head away from his, "if you don't let me go, I'll—"

But his lips were hard against hers, and, short of pushing him so brutally that the movement might cause him further injury, there was nothing she could do to stop him. For a moment she wondered if she might enjoy the sensation, for Colin had a great deal of charm and vibrancy. But the position of her head was uncomfortable, his moustache was scratchy against her upper lip, and his manner of taking advantage of her awkward situation was distasteful. In short, she did not enjoy the experience one bit, and she made up her mind that as soon as he released her, she intended to tell him so in no uncertain terms.

But when he did release her, a movement at the hedge drew her eye. A man was watching them from the other side, a man her heart recognized even before her eyes did, for she could feel it sink in her chest before his name came to her tongue. It was, of course, Lord Wittenden.

Oh, why, something cried inside her, *does he always come upon me at those times when I'm at my very worst? Blast the man, does he have an instinct for my moments of embarrassment?* It was not fair. She was not the reckless, impulsive, heedlessly passionate, headstrong person that she seemed to be whenever he was anywhere near. Why, dash it all, did he never come upon her when she was sitting quietly somewhere with a book of poetry on her lap?

Colin, feeling her stiffen, turned his head in the direction of her glance. "Ah, Wittenden! How did you find us so soon?"

"Too soon, I suspect," Perry said drily.

"Not too soon for me," Lucienne said, reddening. She helped Colin to sit upright and scrambled to her feet. "Did you discover my horse, my lord?"

"Yes. I was out riding with Miss Trevellick, and we saw a horse ambling his way back toward the stable. We didn't know who'd been riding him, but we assumed the rider had been thrown. Your sister, Trevellick, has gone back for help." He leaped over the hedge and came toward them. "From the look of your coat, I assume it was you who fell, but you don't seem to be much hurt."

"Only my ankle, but it pains like the devil. So much so that I can't seem to pull myself up."

"It seems a small price to pay to get oneself such delightful sympathy," Perry muttered, kneeling down and pressing his fingers against Colin's ankle to feel what he could through the boot.

"Oh, I quite agree," Colin said, grinning at Lucienne unashamedly.

Perry looked up at her. "If I thought I'd win an equal award, I'd break my ankle, too," he said quietly.

Her blush deepened. "That will be quite enough of that nonsense," she said sharply. "What we should be discussing is what to do next."

Perry stood up. "The ankle is already badly swollen, but whether or not it's broken I can't say. I think it would be best to wait until help comes. Then we can lift him up on a horse withut causing further damage."

In less than half an hour, help came. One of the Rutherford carriages, a light curricle drawn by two horses, came trundling down the hill, followed by Lord Rutherford riding a black mare. Two footmen carrying a litter emerged from the carriage. They loaded Colin on the litter, with many injunctions and words of caution from Colin as well as the onlookers, and they carried the injured rider back to the equipage, while Rutherford walked alongside cheerfully assuring Colin that there was a superior surgeon in the neighborhood who could be relied on to set any broken bones so that they'd knit "good as new." Leaving the black mare for Lucienne, Lord Rutherford climbed aboard the curricle, and the rescue party and the rescued drove off.

Lucienne and Perry found themselves alone. Perry, leading his horse with one hand, took the reins of the black mare and approached the still-embarrassed girl. "Come, my dear, there's no point standing about in the wind. You look almost frozen. Let me help you up so we may be off."

"No, thank you, my lord," she said, lifting her chin proudly. "I don't wish to go back just yet. I want to go down there to the woods to see what's happened to Colin's mount."

"What, *now?* I think it would be extremely foolish. For one thing, you're shivering. And for another, those dainty boots of yours, with their high heels, are completely unsuitable for tramping through underbrush."

"Thank you for your concern, my lord, but I am quite capable of deciding for myself whether I'm too cold or my boots too dainty. I intend to walk down there. I cannot bear to think that the horse may be lying somewhere among the trees with a broken leg or some such injury. But, my lord, please do not think it necessary to wait for me." She patted the horse's nose fondly. "I have this black beauty to carry me back."

"Then let her carry you back right now. If you won't be satisfied with my asking one of the grooms to look for Trevellick's horse, I'll do it myself."

"No, thank you. My mind is quite made up."

"Do you know, Lucy Gerard," he said in disgust, "that I think Applegarth was right? You *are* perverse."

"You may think what you wish," she said with her nose in the air. She grasped the reins of the black mare and proceeded to march down the hill.

He sighed in defeat and, leading his horse, followed her down. She turned and glared at him. "I said you needn't wait. And you certainly needn't accompany me."

"I know. But *my* mind is made up, too."

They edged down the steep incline in angry silence, tied their horses to a tree at the edge of the woods and stepped within. The dead leaves matting the forest floor were crisp with frost and crunched beneath their feet, and their breaths made thin white mists before their faces. Lucienne, still angry at having been discovered by Perry in that humiliating situation with Colin, tried to stride quickly ahead of him, but there were so many fallen branches and so much forest debris on the ground that walking was difficult. A limb caught the veil of her riding hat and ripped it badly. Another scratched the side of her face. She was shivering with the cold. And of course, the heels of her boots, inadequate as he'd said they'd be, caused her several times to twist her ankles. But she marched staunchly forward, the sound of his boots trudging behind her seeming to drive her remorselessly on.

At first the path the fleeing horse had taken was easily noticed, for the hoofprints on the ground and the breaks on the trees where he'd broken off the branches were fresh and clear. But these evidences of his route suddenly seemed to disappear, and Lucienne was not sure which way to turn. Too embarrassed to admit that she was floundering, she blundered on. But the woods were deeper here, the frost-rime on the ground untrammeled, and it was soon obvious that no animal the size of a horse could have come through. "I think, ma'am," Perry said quietly behind her, "that it's time to give up."

"I *won't* give up," she said stubbornly, trying to keep her teeth from chattering. She plunged on, and, not noticing a leaf-covered log in her path, stumbled and fell on her face.

He came up beside her and, placing his hands firmly under her arms, hauled her to her feet. "Hang it, Lucy," he said furiously, turning her round to face him and grasping her shoulders as if he were about to shake the life out of her, "is it your intention to go through life completely ignoring any suggestions but your own? Is your self-esteem so deucedly swollen that you can't believe you've ever made a mistake? Is it so impossible for the very superior Miss Gerard to behave stupidly, to make an error, to say she's sorry? If ever anyone needed to fall on her face, it's you! I'm *glad* you fell, do you hear me? I hope you're bruised from head to heel! If I were any kind of man, I'd leave you here to freeze to death! Or at the very least, I ought to wring your neck!"

She stared at him with mouth agape, for his diatribe had been as unexpected as her fall. Her breast heaved in her attempt to regain her breath, knocked out of her by her fall and then again by his cutting words. Her lips began to tremble, and, astonishing to him, two tears rolled down her cheeks. He'd never seen her so disarmingly pathetic, so vulnerable, as she was at this moment. Her ruined hat was askew, her face smudged, her riding habit covered with rotted leaves, and her tears had traced two streaks down her cheeks. Worse than anything, he noticed a tiny cut beneath the dirt under her right eye, from which a bit of blood had begun to leak. He winced, overwhelmed with shame at his unkind outburst. "Blast!" he muttered, trying to brush away the grime that covered the cut with one gentle finger. "I'm sorry, Lucy. I shouldn't have—"

Not quite knowing what he was doing, he cupped her face in his hands. The dark, tear-filled eyes had not moved from his face. They did not seem like the eyes of an arrogant, willful girl. They were frightened, confused and unutterably lovely. Whatever had possessed him to speak to her that way? "I'm sorry," he mumbled again, wishing only to unsay what he'd said, but before he realized it, he was kissing her. He did it without thought, with the same gentleness with which he'd brushed her cheek with his finger.

But once his lips touched hers, he couldn't tear them away. His hands slipped from her face, slid along her shoulders and down her back, drawing her closer and closer to him until he could feel her heart beating against his chest. In some part of his mind he knew he was crushing her mouth, crushing her ribs, holding her so tightly to him that nothing could wedge them apart, but he didn't care. He couldn't think, at this moment, of anything else but that this was what he'd wanted to do . . . to feel . . . since he'd first laid eyes on her. It was as if he'd known that, of all the girls he'd kissed before or would kiss again, only with her would he feel this mad rushing of the blood in his veins, this completely uncharacteristic explosion of passion.

But his characteristic restraint soon reasserted itself, and, slowly, reluctantly, he let her go. She backed away from him a step or two, her eyes never leaving his face. They spoke not a word but merely stared at each other while they both endeavored to catch their breaths. Then he said in his quiet way, "Lucy, I—"

"If you're going to say you're sorry, Perry Wittenden," she

interrupted in a choked voice, "don't b-bother."

"I was not going to say that at all."

"Then what *were* you going to say?"

"Only that, will-you, nill-you, I'm taking you back to the Grange." With purposeful determination, he pulled her to him, lifted her in his arms and, stumbling back along the path they'd trampled down earlier, carried her to the edge of the woods where their horses waited. He tossed her up on the mare, jumped on his horse and, without uttering another word, led her back home.

Chapter Seventeen

The curricle bearing the injured Colin arrived at the Grange just before luncheon was announced. Lord Rutherford informed his lady that the two missing guests would be following momentarily, and he suggested that luncheon be postponed for a quarter-hour to give him time to install Colin in a first-floor room and to send for the surgeon. By that time, he said, the other two would certainly be back.

But the delayed luncheon had passed and the surgeon had come and gone before Lucienne and Perry returned. The delay of their arrival had caused all sorts of speculation and consternation, and thus they were greeted at the door by a crowd of concerned and curious welcomers. Their explanation—that they'd gone looking for the missing horse—met with very mixed reactions. Chloe and her new friend Lily Dawes declared, with relief, that Lucy was the most heroic and courageous of females to have braved the cold and the unknown woods for a horse. Rutherford, on the other hand, said in disgust that the horse had turned up in the stables long before and that all they'd had to do was ask him about it when he'd come to pick up Colin, which, if only they'd done so, would have saved themselves all this trouble. Jenny Rutherford was concerned only that they might have contracted a chill, and she insisted that they be led into the sitting room and given seats close to the fire. Lady Trevellick, having learned from the surgeon that her son's injury was no more serious than a severe sprain, thanked both Lucienne and Wittenden for having assisted him, agreed with Jenny that they both looked "nigh froze," and went to make them a "hot Sampson" with her own hands. (The hot Sampson proved to be a mulled drink of brandy, cider and water, which they both drank with grateful appreciation.) Cora muttered under her breath that it was no surprise to *her* that a woman of Miss Gerard's wild reputation would disappear into the woods with a male acquaintance —and without a chaperone!—and not reappear for hours. Fortunately, no one but the Admiral and her sister overheard her. The Admiral merely looked amused, but Mabyn was undeniably chagrined.

The latecomers were cosseted and fussed over for the better part of an hour, until Chloe brought the scene to an end by declaring that she intended to put her niece to bed and to see to it that she stayed there for the rest of the afternoon. Lucienne readily acquiesced to this plan, for she'd been longing for a bit of privacy. It had been, for her, a very disturbing morning, and she wanted an opportunity to think about what had happened to her. But the most disturbing thing to happen to her that day occurred just as she was quitting the room. She glanced back over her shoulder and saw Wittenden and Mabyn Trevellick silhouetted in the sitting-room window, engaged in what seemed to be earnest and intimate argument. It was a sight that brought her spirits to their lowest ebb.

After her aunt had settled her on the bed and tucked the comforter around her, Lucienne closed her eyes and pretended to sleep, but it seemed ages before her aunt tiptoed from the room. When the girl was at last alone, she turned her head into her pillow and wept. She was not sure why. Her feelings were certainly in a turmoil, but until she could straighten them out, her emotions were a mystery to her.

She thought back to the morning. She'd started out the day cheerfully enough. Riding with Colin had been pleasant, and she'd been on the verge of deciding that a flirtation with him might be the very thing to make this sojourn in Suffolk entertaining. He was attractive, forthright, charming and even passably witty. But when he'd kissed her, she'd found him arrogant, and she hadn't responded to the kiss in the way she'd expected. She was, she knew, quite inexperienced in kissing, for the few men she'd known in Yorkshire had been too respectful of her to make the attempt; and, until today, the only man she'd kissed had been Owen. It had been very enjoyable to kiss Owen, she remembered, and she'd expected to feel the same about Colin's kiss. That, however, had been a disappointment. She'd suspected at the time that her judgment might be unfair—that the fellow's boldness, the unfriendly weather, their situation on the cold ground, and even the awkward position of their bodies put him at a disadvantage. But there had been many disadvantages an hour later in the woods, too, and *that* kiss—

But that kiss did not bear thinking of. The mere memory of it made her shudder. It had affected her like no other kiss she'd experienced. That moment with Perry Wittenden could not possibly be described as enjoyable, for the word had nothing to do with what she'd felt. *Shattering* might be more fitting. When Perry had taken her face in her hands, her knees had gone weak. And then, when he'd tightened his arms about her, the weakness had extended itself to her whole body. She'd felt suddenly overcome . . . spineless . . . as if her body were about to disintegrate into a million sparkling particles that would drift away, leaving only the warm, pulsing core of her in his arms. It was a feeling quite beyond pleasure, just as breathing after you've held your breath too long is beyond pleasure. Like that sort of hungry breath, the kiss had seemed, for a moment, to be something essential to her very being . . . so essential that, if stopped, she would die.

It was only a kiss, of course. She'd realized that as soon as he'd let her go. It had been nothing more than an impulsive act. She would be foolish to refine on it. And why should she? She didn't even *like* Perry Wittenden.

But then, why had his kiss affected her so profoundly? And why did her emotions churn up so fearfully every time he came near her? Was it possible that he meant more to her than she'd been willing to admit? Or, to phrase the question more honestly, was she in love with the fellow?

No, she told herself, it was not possible. One couldn't fall in love with someone one disliked. Could one?

She threw off the coverlet and sat up. *Let's be truly honest,* she commanded herself. *Do I really dislike him?* She suspected that a truly honest answer would be no. She didn't like what he'd written about her, but she didn't dislike the man himself. He was not a man one easily disliked. She'd called his good nature nauseating only because it seemed to be too good to be true. He was really quite lovable, when one thought about it. His face was so sweetly boyish, and the way his lips curved up on one side in that little smile was utterly adorable. He was a gentle, thoughtful, truly kind young man toward everyone in the world . . . everyone except her. The truth was that the only flaw she could find in him was his obvious dislike of *her*.

But if he disliked her, why had he kissed her like that?

Before she could find an answer, a knock sounded at the door, and Trudy poked her head in. "Miss Lucy, are ye ready to dress fer dinner?" she asked.

Lucienne blinked at her. More than two hours must have passed since she came upstairs! "I'll dress myself tonight, Trudy," she said, unwilling to surrender her privacy just yet.

Trudy nodded and withdrew, and Lucienne got up and began to pace around the room. It seemed to her that before the interruption she'd come to the real question at last: Did Perry care for her or did he not? There was certainly some evidence that he did. The poem Chloe had sent her, for one thing. Hadn't he said in solid black print, for all the world to see, that he couldn't forget a girl "with scornful eyes" who had argued with him and mocked him at every turn? Even Aunt Chloe had concluded that he'd been referring to her.

She flew to the night table, opened the drawer and withdrew a small clipping from its hiding place under her handkerchiefs. It was so worn that the paper was wearing thin at the folds. Her eyes searched the final stanza for proof. She tried to read it as if she'd never seen it before, so that she might bring to the words a fresh perspective, but she could not. How could she, when she knew the words by heart? She also knew that the girl he described there—the one whose name was so etched on his memory that "years of stormy waves" couldn't erase it—could have been anyone. She was certainly not the only girl he'd met who had scornful eyes and a playful smile. She could not use the poem as proof.

But there was other evidence. What about the look in his eyes when he came upon her unexpectedly at the Black Boar? If ever a man had gaped in admiration of a woman, it was he. But that evidence was not conclusive either. He might have goggled that way at *any* pretty girl who stood before him in such shameless half-nakedness.

And his behavior at the Black Boar the following morning was equally strong evidence that he *did* dislike her. He'd been as unkind and insulting to her that morning as he could possibly have been. Given his usual even temper, that morning's outburst surely had to be added to the list of points against her.

When all was said and done, who could blame him if he *did* dislike her? She'd behaved abominably toward him from the first. She'd been spoiled, headstrong, loud, abusive, stubborn and self-righteous. In the woods he'd said that her self-esteem was "swollen" and that she could never admit her errors. That certainly seemed to prove the extent of his dislike. Yet barely a moment later he'd kissed her. Was it any wonder she was confused?

She replaced her treasured poem in her night-table drawer and sat down on the edge of her bed, defeated. She could not guess what was in Perry's mind and heart. But at least she was clear about her own. She loved him; there was no longer a question about that.

It was too bad, really, she thought, dropping her head in her heads, that she'd realized the truth at just this time. This was not a propitious moment to discover that she was in love with him, for downstairs at this very moment, Mabyn Trevellick and he were showing signs of growing intimacy. It was strange how she'd sensed that the girl was a rival even before she'd understood her own feelings for Perry. It was not the girl's beauty, or sweetness, or even her talent for music that had made Lucy sick with jealousy—it was her immediate and instinctive awareness that Mabyn was a perfect match for Perry. Mabyn Trevellick was as sweet, as gentle, as good-natured, as generous and as talented as she, Lucienne Gerard, was short-tempered, reckless, spoiled, impulsive and foolish. The truth that she had to face was that Mabyn was as right for Perry as she herself was wrong for him.

With that discouraging conclusion, Lucienne rose to dress for dinner. The words *Mabyn Trevellick is right for him* echoed in her head as she plunged her face into the icy water of the lavabo and washed the dirt and tear stains away. They repeated themselves as she slipped a gold-colored jaquard over her head and buttoned the back. They reechoed in her ears as she put her feet into her black satin slippers. And they sounded loud and clear in her brain as she sat down at her dressing table to brush her hair. It was then that she noticed in the mirror the little cut under her right eye, the cut that Perry had touched so gently in the woods. She shut her eyes and felt again the sting of the wind through the trees and the pain of Perry's grip on her shoulder. She saw the look of fury in his eyes and their sudden, surprising change to a strange, almost unfathomable tenderness. And then his lips on hers, gentle at first, but soon changing to a furious, crushing, blood-tingling passion. Would he have kissed Mabyn in just that way? Impossible!

She opened her eyes and, breathing deeply, smiled at herself in the mirror. *He kissed me,* she whispered to her reflection. *She is perfect for him but he kissed me!* And with those words ringing in her ears, she went down to dinner.

At the table, Colin—already able to hobble about on a pair of crutches supplied by the surgeon—sat beside her and whispered flirtatious remarks into her ear that she took no notice of. Her eyes and her thoughts were fixed elsewhere, for on the other side of the table, diagonally opposite to her, sat Mabyn and Perry. They both seemed to be refraining from taking part in the general conversation, but Lucienne noticed that they whispered to each other from time to time, and more than once she caught the exchange of a smiling glance between them.

Perry never—not once during the entire meal!—looked in Lucienne's direction. He seemed not even to know that she was there.

Lucienne, sick at heart, could hardly eat. All the arguments she'd given herself as evidence that he might care for her were now proved false. Even if he *had* been thinking of her when he wrote that poem, for instance, it meant nothing now. Now it was Mabyn he was thinking of. Even the memory of the occurrence this morning in the woods was no longer a consolation. It seemed impossible to believe, but it was evidently true, that the kiss *she* would remember all her life *he* had already forgotten.

Chapter Eighteen

Nothing occurred in the next two days that Lucienne could find the least bit cheering. Even the weather was depressing. Trudy pulled the curtains back each morning to reveal a leaden sky, and Lucienne fell asleep each night to the sound of the wind whistling through the trees and rattling the shutters.

The hours in between she spent smiling at everyone and pretending to be enjoying herself. Depressed as she was, she remembered her pledge to herself to endure the fortnight with at least the *appearance* of high spirits, and she exerted herself to keep her word. Everyone else in the household seemed to be content. Little intimate groups were being formed within the larger one, and the daily routine was becoming comfortably habitual. The men went out on shooting parties each morning and returned each evening with braces of partridge, red noses and the most jovial of dispositions. The ladies, meanwhile, chattered over their embroidery frames, drank tea and played silver-loo to their hearts' content. Amidst all this revelry, Lucienne felt miserably alone. It was hard enough to be suffering unrequited love, but to be suffering it in a place where everyone else was exuding good cheer was the outside of enough.

Late in the afternoon of the fourth day, just after the men had trooped in from their shoot, the daily routine was interrupted by the arrival of Sir Owen Tatlow. He was welcomed warmly by almost everyone (for after four days of constant companionship, even the slightest rearrangement of groups necessitated by the addition of a new face was cause for rejoicing), less warmly by Chloe and Lucienne, and ecstatically by his bride-to-be. The whole party crowded about him until Lord Rutherford urged them all into the drawing room for refreshment.

Lucienne had anticipated with some trepidation the first time she and Owen would have to greet each other, fearing that the meeting would be fraught with awkwardness. It would be, she thought, particularly humiliating for him, for he was the jilted one, and he'd be uncomfortably aware that everyone watching them knew it. But the meeting turned out to be not at all as she expected. Owen came up to her with a positive swagger, his betrothed tucked under his arm like a trophy, and greeted her with all the arrogance of a man who has found himself a prize mate while the girl who'd spurned him was still unspoken-for. "Well, *Lucy!*" he crowed as if greeting an old friend. "Here you are at the Grange ahead of me, having all this time to get to know my little bride-to-be! What do you think of her, eh? A little Cornish charmer, isn't she?"

Lucienne stared at him for a moment, amazed that she'd ever found this insensitive clod attractive. "Yes, indeed," she murmured with as wide a smile as she could muster, adding under her breath after he turned away, "and much more charming than you deserve."

It was only after he was gone that she looked up and found Perry's eyes on her. She looked away at once but could not prevent a blush from spreading over her face. It was an irritating irony that the meeting with Owen turned out to be more humiliating for her than for him.

Snow began to fall that evening, but it was not much remarked upon by the guests at the Grange, for the evening ahead promised some new pleasures. In Owen's honor, Jenny Rutherford had arranged for three local musicians to play for them. "Tonight," she announced at dinner, "we are to have dancing!"

The men did not sit long over their brandies, and the assemblage happily gathered in the drawing room for the festivities. The center of the room had been cleared of furniture and the rugs rolled up and removed. It took no time at all for two sets to form on the dance floor: One was made up of the Admiral partnered with his hostess and Lord Rutherford with Chloe, while the other consisted of Owen with his beaming betrothed and Mabyn with Perry. Lucienne sat with the only other man in the room—poor, injured Colin—and had, for the first time in her life, to watch from the sidelines while other girls danced.

Colin, with his bandaged ankle propped up on a footstool, was perfectly content to sit out the dances with Lucienne at his side. And when her hand was sought for subsequent dances, first by Lord Rutherford and then by the Admiral, he was delighted that she refused. It was only when the country dances gave way to the waltz that Colin saw in her expression a look of yearning. "So you like the waltz, do you, Lucy?" he asked, feeling a twinge of guilt for keeping her from the floor.

"Oh, yes! Yes, indeed," she replied enthusiastically, turning her eyes away from where Perry and Mabyn were swinging in graceful circles round the center of the dance floor, in contrast to the stiff gyrations of the Admiral propelling his tall wife round the edge. "I love waltzing, don't you? I mean when you're able, of course."

"No, I don't much care for it," Colin admitted. "It's too energetic and leaves no opportunity for talking to one's partner. Besides, I was given to understand that the waltz is considered not quite the thing. Isn't it frowned on in polite circles?"

"As if you'd care if it were frowned on or not, black sheep that you are," Lucienne laughed. "I agree that it is somewhat frowned on in places like Almack's, or at large, formal balls, but it is perfectly acceptable at intimate gatherings like this. And it is beginning to come into vogue everywhere. Even at Almack's the hostesses permitted it once or twice last season. I waltzed there myself."

"And a lovely sight you must have made," Colin sighed, eyeing her with bold appreciation. A moment later, however, his attention was caught by something else. "Look there, Lucy. Tatlow seems to be heading this way. If he's approaching to ask you to waltz, please don't refuse him on my account. It would give these eyes of mine much pleasure to watch you twirling about. The only thing I'd enjoy more would be to twirl you about myself."

"I thought you just said you didn't much care for waltzing."

"I don't—with anyone but you," he retorted promptly.

Owen was now upon them, his purpose indeed being to solicit Lucy's hand for the next waltz. She refused, reminding him that his betrothed would no doubt wish to waltz with him herself. But Owen did not budge. "Cora doesn't waltz. She thinks it a shocking dance. I suggested that she watch us execute the steps. You and I were quite adept at it, if you recall. Perhaps, when she sees us perform, she will change her mind."

"Oh, go on, Lucy," Colin urged. "Show Cora what a prude she is."

Lucienne shrugged and permitted Owen to lead her to the floor. The Rutherfords were already standing there waiting for the music to begin, and they were soon joined by the Admiral with Chloe on his arm and by Perry and Mabyn. The musicians struck up a waltz with a stately rhythm, and Owen put his arm around her waist in his typical, authoritative manner and swung her into the dance.

Lucienne hoped that she might lose her self-consciousness in her delight in the intricate movements the waltz required, but the rhythm was too slow to make the dance challenging. She didn't have to concentrate on the steps at all but adjusted easily to Owen's familiar style. Thus she was aware of Chloe's smile as they danced past each other, of Colin beaming at her from the sidelines, of Perry's cheek resting on Mabyn's hair as they went gliding by. The dance seemed interminable, and Lucienne felt nothing but relief when it came to an end.

Owen, quite pleased with himself, led her to where Cora was sitting. "There, was that not a delightful exhibition?" he asked his betrothed.

"Oh, yes, quite," Cora replied in a tight, cold voice that would have revealed to anyone but the fatuous Owen the jealous irritation she felt inside. "I was wrong to say the waltz is improper. Perhaps Lucy can be persuaded to teach me the steps."

If Lucy could have boxed Owen's ears without causing a scene, she would have done it then and there. She would have liked to box Cora's ears, too. Why had the girl acted the prude in that way when her own sister was perfectly willing to waltz? But one couldn't box anyone's ears in polite society, worse luck. Therefore Lucy forced herself to smile at Cora and said with all the sincerity she could muster, "I'd be happy to show you the steps, Cora, at any time you'd care to try them. But your sister appears to be more adept at the dance than I, and she's undoubtedly a better teacher. Why don't you ask her? And now, if you'll both excuse me, I'll go back to Colin."

She walked swiftly away, leaving Cora to deal with her jealousy and her thick-headed bridegroom as best she might. She'd not taken a dozen steps, however, when Perry came up beside her. "They're going to play the last waltz," he said. "Will you dance it with me?"

"The last?" she echoed stupidly, her heart beginning to pound. "You want the last waltz with . . . me?"

"Yes, please. You haven't stood up with me once this evening. Isn't it time you did so?"

She shook her head, glancing guiltily toward Colin and then surveying the room hastily to see where Mabyn was hiding herself. "But I should be . . . And shouldn't you—?"

His little half-smile became wider as he cocked his head at her. "You seem so indecisive, ma'am" he remarked. "That's not like you. Will you dance with me or not?"

"Oh, dash it all, *yes*," she said abruptly, taking his arm.

They stepped on to the dance-floor and faced each other. Jenny and Spencer Rutherford were the only other couple on the floor. Lucienne was acutely aware that, being three or four inches taller than Mabyn, she was not as perfect a partner for Perry as the other girl was. But when the music started and he put his arm about her, she forgot all that. The rhythm of this waltz was much livelier than the last, and she found herself being spun over the floor before she was quite ready. Perry, however, was a better dancer than she'd expected, and he kept her feet moving in perfect rhythm. Soon she was whirling on his arm at a dizzying pace, her feet seeming not quite to touch the floor. Then something strange began to happen, something alarmingly like what she'd felt that morning in the woods— the feeling that her body was about to disintegrate into a million sparks. The music seemed to grow louder in her ears, colors swirled round her in unrecognizable streaks, and her body grew lighter and lighter. Only the strength of Perry's arm kept her from flying up and whirling away in the air. *Perry, hold me!* she wanted to cry. *Don't let me get away from you!* But she had no breath left with which to utter a word.

When the music stopped, the room around her continued to spin. She had to cling to him to keep from falling. *Oh, Good God!* she thought. *They've all seen everything!* She should never have agreed to dance with him. She should have known that the close proximity that the waltz requires of its dancers would be too much for her emotions. Now it would be clear to everyone how she felt about him! How could she lift her head and face them all? If only she could sink into the ground and disappear!

But as the room righted itself and the spinning stopped, she became aware that Perry was smiling at her and that everyone around her was applauding. She could see that the Rutherfords, who had obviously stepped aside and surrendered the floor to them, were clapping their hands enthusiastically, Aunt Chloe on the sidelines was beaming at her with pride, and Lily Dawes was shouting, "Bravo, well done!" Even Cora and Mabyn were applauding with apparently sincere enthusiasm. And Colin, whom she'd expected to be frowning in chagrin at discovering that she had strong feelings for another man, was grinning broadly and waving his arm at her in a gesture of triumph. She took a deep breath of relief as the startling revelation came to her that *what they'd seen had been nothing more than a nicely executed dance!*

"That, my dear, was waltzing indeed!" Perry exclaimed, bowing over her hand. "Thank you."

She gave him an answering curtsey. "You're quite welcome, my lord," she murmured in response. "I...er... enjoyed it."

Chapter Nineteen

The revelers in the drawing room, engrossed in the music and dancing, took little note of the snow falling heavily outside the windows. And they were even less aware of it as they slept. But when they awoke the following morning they could not avoid paying it some heed, for a blanket of it, two feet deep, covered everything in sight. And it was falling still.

There would be no shooting today, and no riding either. And an outing that Lady Rutherford had planned—to take the ladies to visit the ruined priory a few miles south of Mendlesham—was, of course, out of the question. In fact, if the snow continued to fall much longer, the accumulation might be so great that they would be kept indoors for days.

A mood of glumness seemed to fall over the party as the day advanced and the snow showed no signs of abating. All at once there seemed to be nothing amusing to do. The older members of the group managed to find ways of occupying their time—Lady Trevellick and Jenny Rutherford made themselves content by sitting near the fire in the drawing room and working at their embroidery frames, Chloe curled up on her bed with a book, Lily sat in the library quietly knitting while her husband dozed in a nearby chair, and Rutherford sequestered himself in his study to work on his long-neglected accounts—but the six younger guests wandered about the house in aimless dejection, gathering finally in the small sitting room to play a desultory game of piquet. It was not until Colin made a rather startling suggestion that their spirits began to lift.

What Colin suggested was a theatrical. He made the suggestion from his place at the card table, where only Owen and Cora still sat. Perry had gone to the fireplace to poke up the fire, and Mabyn and Lucienne were standing at the window staring out at the snow. "What we need to cheer us," he said in a loud, firm voice, leaning back in his chair and lifting his bandaged ankle up to rest on an unoccupied chair nearby, "is a large project that will engage our interest for a sustained period of time . . . like preparing a play."

Several pairs of eyes lit up at this suggestion, Owen's in particular. Mabyn and Lucy turned from the window and, curious to hear more, wandered back into the circle. Perry leaned on the mantel and studied Colin with interest. Only Cora's expression showed disapproval. She frowned at her brother, accusing him of being shockingly stage-struck. "I think he's always wanted to be an actor," she told the others.

"Yes, I have. I've always wanted to strut upon a stage, wearing a hat with a plume and dashing about brandishing a sword. It has always seemed to me to be the most enjoyable of occupations."

"But you cannot be dashing about a stage now, Colin," Perry reminded him. "Didn't the doctor order you to keep to those crutches for the rest of your stay here?"

"Yes, blast it," Colin said. "But perhaps we can find a part for me that I can perform on crutches. I can think of a few in which they would not be a hindrance, as, for example, Richard III."

"Good, God, you're not thinking of doing a Shakespearean tragedy, are you?" Owen asked, appalled. "I say it should be a comedy or nothing."

"But my love," Cora objected, "you are getting ahead of yourself, are you not? How can you speak of tragedies and comedies when we haven't even discussed the *appropriateness* of such a venture."

"What is there to discuss about appropriateness?" Colin demanded.

"You know, Colin," Mabyn pointed out, seating herself on the sofa near the fire, "not everyone believes that a private theatrical is proper at all."

"Why not?" Owen asked. "I, for one, think it is a fine idea."

"There's nothing sensible that can be said against it," Colin argued, "especially if it's a small private performance for our own entertainment."

Cora looked from her brother to her betrothed in some surprise. "Do you both forget yourselves? This is not our home. Lord and Lady Rutherford may not wish the Grange to be turned into a theater."

"Good God, Cora," her brother exclaimed, "do you think I'm proposing that we actually transform the house into a theater, complete with stage, pit, boxes and a gallery? That is not at all what I had in mind. One doesn't need elaborate trappings to enact a play. We need only to clear part of a room and hang a bit of cloth for a curtain."

"And perhaps a platform, if one of Rutherford's men can do some carpentry," mused Owen.

Lucienne burst into a trilling laugh, dropping down beside Mabyn on the sofa in her glee. "Oh, Owen, you sound exactly like a character in a novel by Miss Austen called *Mansfield Park*. Tom Bertram was his name, I believe, and he began by planning a modest little private theatrical with only a bit of green baize for a curtain. And before he'd finished, they'd built a stage complete with wings and a green room and had turned the whole house topsy-turvy."

"Yes, I read it, too," Mabyn said, turning toward Lucy and joining in her laughter. "And after all the fuss, and the squabbling over parts, and the rehearsals, and the sewing of costumes, and all the other preparation, Tom's father returned home and stopped the entire performance."

Lucy and Mabyn grinned at each other, their mutual recollection of the novel giving them a sudden feeling of warm friendliness. *If only Perry weren't somehow between us,* Lucy thought, *I might really like this girl.*

But Colin was glaring at them both. "What has that to do with the matter? Just because this Bertram fellow went too far doesn't mean that we have to?"

"But you were, don't you see?" Mabyn explained. "That's what Lucy was trying to tell you. Owen was already speaking of platforms and carpenters, wasn't he?"

"Well, I didn't mean . . ." Owen said, somewhat abashed. "I suppose we needn't go so far as to build a platform."

"I see no harm in a modest performance of a play," Perry said in a conciliatory way. "No one can think it anything but a wholesome way to pass the time. Why don't we ask the Rutherfords? Then, if they have no objection, we can go on to the next point of contention, whether or not we should do comedy or tragedy."

"Good!" Colin agreed. "Are the rest of you agreed?"

"I am," Owen said promptly. "I've never acted, of course, but I'm sure I could get the hang of it with no great difficulty. What do you say, my love? Other than the possible objection of the Rutherfords, you don't disapprove, do you?"

"No, I suppose I don't," Cora said, shrugging.

"As for me," Mabyn said, "I don't disapprove either. I would not care to act, of course, but I could help in other ways." She looked at Lucy and giggled. "I suppose, Lucy, that you'll think me too fastidious, like Fanny in the novel."

Lucy smiled back at her. "But Fanny was the heroine, so there's no fault to be found in her fastidiousness, or in yours either. While I, being quite *willing* to act, must be quite rakish and wicked, like the novel's villainness."

"Nonsense," Mabyn said seriously. "It was not her wish to act that made her villainous." She leaned toward the other girl and took her hand. "Please, Lucy, do not think I disapprove of acting in a private theatrical just because I'm too shy to wish to do it myself. You and Cora *must* do it, or there will be no play at all."

"Mabyn is right," Perry agreed. "If she's too shy to wish to perform, we must respect her wishes, but if *all* you young ladies feel uncomfortable about performing, then the whole venture is pointless."

"*I'm* quite willing," Cora admitted. "I don't want to spoil the fun, especially since Owen would enjoy it."

"And I've already said that I'm willing," Lucy added.

"Good. Then it's decided," Colin chuckled. "Well, then, shall I apply to the Rutherfords for permission?"

"Yes, of course," Owen said promptly.

"When do think would be the proper time to ask them?" Colin mused, half to himself.

"Why not right now?" Perry suggested.

Lucy looked at him archly. "Right now? You're very eager, are you not, my lord?"

"Eager, ma'am?" Perry smiled at her. "I suppose I am. Is there something wrong with that?"

"Perhaps there is," she said, suddenly struck with a desire to taunt him. "My instincts are warning me that you have an ulterior motive."

"I know I shall regret asking," Perry muttered, seating himself on the hearth and eyeing her suspiciously, "but what 'ulterior motive' do you suspect me of?"

"Of wishing to observe us, I suppose," Lucy said teasingly. "To give you grist for your mill."

"Grist for his mill? Whatever do you mean?" Colin asked irritably. He was both puzzled by her words and jealous of the little touch of flirtation he noticed in her manner. If Lucienne Gerard wanted to flirt, he asked himself, why wasn't she flirting with *him?*

"Yes, Lucy, what do you mean by that?" Cora demanded.

Lucy found herself vastly enjoying this unexpected opportunity to twit Perry. "Perhaps," she responded, "Lord Wittenden suspects that our efforts on this theatrical venture will bring out all our latent foibles and conceits. He wants to watch us all make fools of ourselves."

"But why?" Colin persisted. "Why would Perry—or anyone—want to watch us make fools of ourselves?"

"Surely you can guess," Perry said, shaking his head in mock despair. "She's hinting that I intend to lampoon you all later in the Whistledown Diary."

"Lucy!" Mabyn exclaimed in instant offense. "Perry would never be so unkind."

"No, I don't suppose Perry would," Lucy said, smiling at Mabyn in perfect agreement. "Perry Wittenden is the kindest of men. But when he picks up a pen, he becomes Peregrine Whistledown, and *he,* my dear . . ." Here she threw Perry a look of saucy challenge. " . . . *he* is a very different sort of fellow."

"Different in what way?" Mabyn demanded.

"Yes," Perry seconded, leaning forward interestedly, "in what way?"

Lucy's eyes sparkled gleefully. "You are all assuming that a man who behaves as a gentleman in your company behaves in the same way at all other times. You've all found Perry to be a perfect gentleman during this stay here, and you therefore assume that is his nature." She threw Perry another teasing glance before she went on. "But he is also a writer, you see. And as a writer his goals are very different, aren't they, my lord? I imagine that, for a writer, the temptation to describe the idiocies of the world around him must be very great, regardless of whom it may hurt. It is my guess that to be a good writer one *can't* be a gentleman. Isn't that so, my lord?"

"I don't think there's any *law* to that effect, ma'am," Perry retorted, smiling his quirky smile as he stretched out his legs before him in casual comfort, "though I admit that there were —and are—a good number of writers who were dreadful cads in print."

"But surely not *you!*" Mabyn declared firmly.

Lucy gurgled. "Well, my lord, answer the lady. Were you *never* a cad in print?"

"Really, Lucy," Owen cut in with avuncular superiority, "if you are referring to that verse he wrote about your accident, you cannot call that caddish. He didn't even know you then, remember, and never mentioned you by name."

"But even though he didn't name me, his description of me could not be called *gentlemanly,* could it?"

"Of course it could," Owen declared. "Writing in amusing terms about a nameless girl he didn't know is a very different thing from writing sarcastically about one's friends behind their backs. Even *you* must admit that Perry's too much of a gentleman to do that."

"Hear, hear!" Mabyn applauded.

Perry, eyes twinkling, rose and gave Owen a bow. "Thank you, Tatlow. That was as impassioned a defense as I've ever had."

"Yes, it was," Lucy agreed, throwing up her hands in surrender. "Perhaps, Owen, you should aspire to a career as a lawyer rather than an actor."

"Thank you, my dear," Owen said, preening, "but at the moment it is acting that interests me."

"And me," Colin agreed, eager to get on with the main

business—starting to work on a play. "Are all objections withdrawn, then? Is everything settled?"

Lucy made an airy gesture with her hands and rose from the sofa. "It's settled as far as I'm concerned. I only wanted you all to be aware that, if we proceed with this scheme, it is very possible that some day we might find ourselves described in all our vaingloriousness in public print."

Mabyn, all at once recognizing the teasing glints in Lucy's eyes as well as Perry's, realized that she'd been taking their little exchange too seriously. She rose from the sofa and went to the hearth beside Perry. "I think we may relay on Perry's gentlemanly qualities to override his urges to be a cad," she said, smiling up at him fondly.

Lucy, noting Mabyn's look and Perry's responsive grin, felt a chill in her chest. Her high spirits evaporated at once. She was suddenly beset with misgivings for having taunted Perry so persistently on the subject of his writing. She'd probably sounded like a sour old maid and appeared to everyone in the room in horrible contrast to Mabyn's sweetness. *Dash it all*, she said to herself, *I've behaved like an idiot again*. But there was nothing she could do about it now. She couldn't make an abrupt change in point of view or emulate Mabyn's tender loyalty. She could only finish the scene in the same way she started it.

She put up her chin. "By all means, Colin, go ahead and get permission from our hosts," she said, strolling in feigned casualness to the door, "but later, when we find ourselves the subject of a scathing satire, and we're all being laughed at in every drawing room in London, don't say you weren't warned."

Chapter Twenty

Colin soon followed Lucy out of the drawing room, explaining to those of the group who still remained that he intended to seek out their host at once. "If Lord Rutherford gives us his permission," he said excitedly as he hobbled from the room, "we may start on our theatrical venture this very day."

Perry did not long remain in the drawing room after Colin's departure. He found that his high spirits (which Colin's suggestion had engendered and which had been heightened by Lucy's teasing) had suddenly deserted him, and he wanted nothing more than to sulk in solitude. He excused himself with his usual calm politeness (pretending not to notice Mabyn's obvious disappointment) and made his way to his room. After shutting and locking the door behind him to insure against any chance intrusion, he took off his coat and, tossing it aside, threw himself upon his bed, crossed his booted ankles, linked his hands comfortably behind his head and stared up at the ceiling.

He knew quite well why he'd fallen into this ill humor. In fact, he could pinpoint the exact moment when his spirit had plummeted: when Lucy's playful tone had turned earnest, the moment before she'd swept out of the drawing room. She'd seemed at first to be indulging in a flirtatious badinage with him, which had sent his spirits right up into the clouds, but at the end her tone had seemed inexplicably vituperative, and he found himself falling back down to earth again.

What he did *not* know was why the stubborn, unforgiving chit could so easily affect his moods. He was a sad case, he admitted, to allow his emotions to be so mercilessly manipulated by a spoiled, self-centered, irrational female. How could he—a perfectly sensible, level-headed, logical fellow—find himself either dancing in alt or wallowing in despair in response to the whims of a creature like Lucy? Of course, he could make a guess at the answer. He loved her, he supposed. What else would explain this devilish turmoil?

He'd not been able to dispel the image of her face from his mind since the first day he'd laid eyes on her. He hadn't admitted to himself until today that what he felt for her was love, but he'd known that she churned up feelings in him quite unlike anything he'd ever felt before. He had to admit it now: He was in love with her. It was probably the biggest mistake of his life, but it was true. The problem was that she was the worst possible female for him to love. She was unpredictable, high-strung, short-tempered, stubborn, closed-minded, capricious and sharp-tongued. And she had no liking for him, either! She'd taken him in dislike from the first, when their carriages had collided, and it seemed that everything he'd said or done—or written!—since that day had only served to strengthen her first impression. It was quite hopeless for him to attempt to change that inflexible mind of hers. Besides, he didn't *want* to change her mind. She was not the sort of female who would make a proper wife for a calm, sensible man. Life with her would be much too chaotic. The whole situation was hopeless.

There was only one possible solution for this problem, he reasoned, and that was to get over this feeling for her. This ill-advised and hopeless sort of love was not unlike an illness, he told himself, and it was surely an illness that could be cured. He had only to reason the matter out with his usual common sense. If one was afflicted with, say, an inflammation of the lungs, one tried to rest, to avoid drafts, to keep oneself from becoming over-excited, to take appropriate medications and to give oneself sufficient time for the infection to pass out of the system. He could apply the same sort of curative devices to this emotional disturbance, couldn't he? He would remain calm, avoid emotional scenes involving her, "medicate" himself with whatever doses of other female companionship might be available, and wait for the "infection" to pass.

It was too bad that this infection seemed to make him immune to the charms of other females. Ever since he'd laid eyes on Lucy, no other female who'd crossed his path had made even the slightest mark on his consciousness. Even so charming and lovely a creature as Mabyn Trevellick seemed pale in comparison to Lucy, or at least it seemed so in the present phase of this disease. Well, he would give himself time. Wasn't it an unarguable truth that time heals all ills?

With that optimistic platitude, he felt his spirits rise, if not to elation, at least to normal contentment. Firmly pledging that he would not permit this love-disease to defeat him, he rose from the bed and made himself ready to rejoin the others.

Meanwhile, Colin had managed, without the slightest difficulty, to persuade the Rutherfords to approve his theatrical scheme. The Rutherfords not only approved with enthusiasm but offered to help. Lord Rutherford expressed a desire to take a part, and his lady undertook to sew up a curtain for them. By dinnertime, everyone at the table, utterly cheered by the prospect of new activity, was suggesting plays. Colin, still dreaming of playing hunch-backed King Richard with his crutches, argued long and hard for Shakespeare. Chloe suggested *The Conscious Lovers,* but Colin pointed out that there were too many roles in it for a small group. Owen continued to insist that only a comedy would be suitable, and after a great deal of pontificating on the subject, he won a majority to his point of view. Dozens of comedies were named and rejected, a few of them being fought for hammer and tongs. Lily Dawes was all for Sheridan's *Critic,* the Admiral for *Marriage a la Mode,* and Lady Trevellick for *The Country Wife.* In the end, however, Perry's suggestion that they do *She Stoops to Conquer* won the day. They could manage that play with seven or eight performers, if some of the servant roles were eliminated and some of the scenes revised. Once Perry was persuaded to undertake the revisions, everyone dropped their objections and eagerly agreed that the Goldsmith comedy was the one they'd wanted all along.

The rest of the evening was spent in discussing who among them was most suitable for each role. The entire group gathered round the long table in the library, passing a copy of the play from hand to hand. It was unanimously agreed that Colin, who'd suggested the idea in the first place and who was most vociferous in giving his opinion on every question, be made manager. Pleased, Colin took a seat at the head of the table to conduct the main business of the evening: casting.

Colin decided that the leading role—Marlow, the suitor who was bold with servant girls and bashful with ladies—should be the first role cast. Owen's name was immediately suggested, and, since there was no opposition, he was forthwith awarded the part. He accepted with a self-satisfied smile, feeling that, since he was obviously the handsomest of the men present, the leading role was no more than his due.

The next question to be decided, of course, was which of the lovely young girls present should play opposite him. Cora expected to be chosen without opposition, since, as his affianced bride, she would be a natural choice. But Colin insisted that only Lucienne could play the part. "Kate Hardcastle is the most difficult role in the play," he argued, ignoring his elder sister's obvious agitation. "She must swing easily from barmaid brazeness to ladylike decorum. Cora might do well enough with the ladylike part of it, but she's much too constrained to act sluttish."

Lucienne, not at all eager to have anything more to do with Owen than she absolutely had to, objected at once. "What makes you think that I would be more adept at playing the slut than your sister?" she demanded of Colin in offense.

"It's a question of temperament," Colin replied authoritatively. "The role of Kate Hardcastle requires a temperament more animated than Cora's. Take my word for it, my dear, you'll play the role to perfection."

"I think, Colin Trevellick, that if you consider Kate a slut, that remark is no compliment," Lucy snapped.

"Lucy, dearest! You can't believe that Colin meant to cast any aspersions on your character!" Mabyn said in her brother's defense.

"Besides, Lucy, in the play Kate is no slut," Perry put in in his mild way. "She's a lively girl who 'stoops to conquer' by masquerading as a barmaid. She is always essentially a lady. Colin was ill-advised to use that word."

"Nevertheless," Lucy insisted, "I prefer not to play her.

Cora has enough animation to play any role she wishes."

But Cora was unwilling to take even the slightest chance of being considered sluttish. "Now that I hear more about it," she murmured, backing down, "I'm not sure I *can* play the role."

"I would have chosen Cora for Miss Neville, from the first," Mabyn said. She looked at her sister with a smile. "Constance Neville's the girl who's trying to elope. It is a charming role."

"And really, Lucy," Chloe urged, "the role of Kate is *perfect* for you. Please don't let us down by refusing."

All the rest added their voices to Chloe's, and Lucienne had to surrender or be judged a spoilsport. She finally agreed, but the knowledge that she would have a play opposite that dead bore Owen Tatlow took away all her joy in the enterprise.

With the roles of Kate Hardcastle and Constance Neville cast, there were only a few parts left to be filled. Perry and Colin decided between them that the role of Tony, Kate's mischievous brother, could not be played on crutches, so that Perry would play that key role. Colin would therefore have to play the eloper, Hastings, but everyone assured him that the crutches would not spoil the effect if he played the part with enough bravado.

For the roles of the elder Mr. and Mrs. Hardcastle, Lord Rutherford and Lily Dawes were chosen. All the others in the group except the Admiral happily accepted backstage positions: curtain-puller (Chloe), costume-maker (Jenny Rutherford), property-keeper (Lady Trevellick), and prompter (Mabyn). As for the Admiral, he was given, much to his delight, all the roles that remained—the elder Marlow and all the servants. "Six roles!" he chortled happily to Lily as they all went off to bed. "Imagine that, my dear! Your husband is good enough for six!"

The work on the play began the next morning, happily distracting everyone from the action of the wind outside, which was piling the snow in huge drifts. While Perry sat at the library table revising scenes (with the Admiral bending over his shoulder begging him not eliminate this role or that word), Mabyn perched beside him and made copies in her fine hand. No sooner was a page copied than it was carried to the sitting room by one or the other of the waiting actors and immediately read aloud.

Lady Rutherford and Chloe, meanwhile, were rummaging through old trunks in the storeroom. Jenny had already compiled a scheme of the costumes and, list in hand, busily searched through the piles of old clothes for mob caps and wide skirts for the ladies and frilled shirts and cuffed-sleeved coats for the men. Lady Trevellick (who'd already bribed her abigail to compile a list of properties and gather them up for her) was the only member of the party who was doing as she'd done every day since her arrival—snoozing in her chair.

By evening, two full acts had been copied and read, and the performers were all busily memorizing their lines. Rehearsals began in earnest the next day. Colin organized a schedule requiring the actors to be present in the library (where half the room had been cleared and was designated as the stage) every afternoon from one-thirty to tea-time. At other times, however, one could hear ranting and declaiming from almost every room in the house, for each of the actors needed a secluded spot in which to practice his lines. But it was not satisfactory to practice alone. Each performer soon found that, when not rehearsing, a companion was needed to help with the memorizing, and before the day was out every actor had claimed a particular place in which to work and a particular partner to work with. Owen and Cora drilled each other in one corner of the sitting room, while the Admiral and Lily cued each other in another. Mabyn read lines with Perry in the morning room. Rutherford followed his busy wife round the house shouting his lines at her. And Colin and Lucienne invaded the dining room for their practice. The only sufferer in all this was poor Lady Trevellick, who could not find a quiet place in which to snooze.

Colin supervised the rehearsals with a firm hand, enjoying his newly acquired importance as manager as much as he enjoyed playing the eloping lover on the "stage." In truth, he enjoyed everything about this dramatic activity, not the least his hours with Lucy in their private rehearsals. There he not only played Marlow to her Kate, but she played Constance to his Hastings. Playing her lover in two guises began to effect him to such an extent that he convinced himself to play her lover in real life. "Marlow is an ass," he remarked to her after they'd done the lines of the humorous seduction scene in the third act. "He talks so much of his intentions to kiss the barmaid that he never gets to the business at all."

"Just as well he doesn't," Lucy muttered, her distaste of having to play the scene with Owen uppermost in her mind.

"If I were courting her," Colin went on, "I'd do things differently."

"Would you? How so?"

"I'd refrain from conversation and put my energies to purposeful action. I'd put my arm about the girl, like this, and pull her to me so quickly she'd have no breath to protest."

Lucy, pressed against his chest, was not at all breathless. *"Pray, Sir, keep your distance,"* she laughed, quoting the words of the play. "See? I've breath enough to stop you."

"But you can't stop me, my dear. I already have you where I want you. Struggle as you will, you won't be able to free yourself."

Lucy still did not believe that Colin was thinking of anything but the play. "Do you think such boldness would win Kate Hardcastle? I think she'd prefer a gentler suitor. As she herself says, *I want no such acquaintance, sirrah!"*

Colin pulled her closer. "Never mind what Kate would say. What would Lucy say?"

"Lucy would say the same." Realizing at last that the fellow was not acting a role but intending seriously to embrace her, she pushed at his chest to free herself.

"You're only saying that because I, like that idiot Marlow, have been talking too much. It's time for me to *act*." He tried to kiss her then and there, but she was struggling too hard to keep him from it. He needed the strength of both his arms to hold her and thus couldn't hold her head still.

She tried to reason with him. "Stop this, Colin! Please don't play the black sheep for me again."

"But you said that ladies *like* black sheep, he persisted, still unable to reach her lips.

"I said that *you thought* ladies like black sheep. If this is how black sheep behave, I, for one, don't like them a bi—"

But Colin, by the simple expedient of quick action (sliding one hand rapidly to her neck and holding her head steady), managed to place his lips on hers. Lucy wrenched herself free. "Dash it, Colin" she exploded, "if—!"

The door swung open. Perry, his eyes on a sheaf of papers in his hand, came into the room. "Colin, this scene in act five requires both a servant *and* the elder Marlow. Since the Admiral can't be in two places at once, I was wondering if we might—" He looked up and saw at once that something had passed between the pair. They were frozen in an attitude that gave clear evidence of an interrupted embrace. "Oh!" he exclaimed, backing off. "I'm sorry. . ."

"Not at all," Colin said with booming heartiness, infuriating Lucienne by throwing an arm about Perry's shoulder and giving him a wink of masculine triumph. "We were just . . . er . . . rehearsing."

Lucienne felt herself grow hot in embarrassment and rage. Why was this sort of thing always happening to her when Perry was near? Was it just bad luck or was there some weakness in her own character that created these situations?

Perry did not miss the blush that suffused her cheeks. He shrugged off Colin's arm, his eyes locked on Lucy's with an expression she couldn't read. "I do beg your pardon for not having knocked."

If she were not so furious, Lucy would have burst into tears. "There was no need to knock," she mumbled helplessly.

"Nevertheless, I need not keep you now. We can discuss this later." He strode quickly from the room, closing the door carefully behind him.

Lucy wheeled on Colin as soon as the door clicked shut. "How *dared* you wink at him that way!" she demanded, trembling with anger.

He looked at her in astonishment. "In *what* way?"

"As if . . . as if you were bragging of . . . of having successfully concluded a *seduction!*"

"I don't know what you're talking about," he said, the picture of innocence.

"Oh, yes, you *do!*" she stamped her foot impotently, wishing she could slap his face but convinced that someone else would come blundering in on them and be witness to yet *another* scene.

"You're not going to pretend that you're in a temper over a little kiss, are you?" Colin asked cavalierly.

"Pretend? *Pretend?*" She finished a fiery glare at him and then, realizing that he was too thick-headed to understand what he'd done, flounced to the door. "From now on, *Sirrah,* I will practice my lines by myself," she announced in a trembling voice. "And if you *ever* again attempt to take such liberties with me, Colin Trevellick, you can jolly well find another Kate for your blasted play!"

Chapter Twenty-One

Theatrical activities proceeded apace, all but Lucienne keeping themselves happy as grigs despite the news that the temperature had fallen, preventing the snow from melting and the roads to Mendlesham from becoming passable. The Grange Players' Theatrical Troupe, as Colin dubbed them, were too busy to care. The costumes were almost ready, the curtain was hung, the lines were being committed to memory, and the first three acts were already running smoothly. Thus it came as no surprise—although a great delight—when Colin announced at the dinner table that the performance would be held only three days hence.

Lucienne, having determined not to practice her lines with Colin any longer, sought Mabyn out to help her with her lines. Mabyn turned out to be an excellent coach, drilling Lucy in difficult scenes with gentle patience, and offering thoughtful, positive criticism whenever Lucy asked for it. The warmth between them, which had begun in their mutual admiration for Miss Jane Austen's novel, grew quickly into friendship. As long as Lucienne kept herself from remembering Mabyn's closeness to Perry Wittenden, she was able to express her admiration for the other girl's accomplishments and to enjoy her company. Mabyn, on her part, looked on Lucy with equal admiration. Lucy seemed to her to be a model of sophistication. Mabyn was convinced that she could learn much from the older girl's worldly charm.

It was only to be expected, therefore, that Mabyn would eventually be tempted to reveal to Lucy some of her private thoughts. "Do you not think that Perry is playing the part of

Tony most delightfully?" she asked Lucy shyly one morning as the two sat together on the window seat in the deserted library, having gone over Lucy's lines until they were sick of them. "For a gentleman with such innate reserve, he enacts the role of that brutish boy with amazing conviction, don't you agree?"

"Yes, he's the most convincing actor of us all, I think," Lucy said.

Mabyn smiled. "I didn't believe, at first, that he could ever make himself into a rudesby."

"Oh, I wouldn't go that far," Lucy said, smiling faintly at some very personal recollections. "I've seen him act the rudesby in real life, once or twice."

"Oh, no, Lucy, that can't be! I know you've taken him dislike for having written about you scornfully once, but you can't make me believe that he was ever *rude* to you."

"Not rude perhaps," Lucy equivocated, taken aback by Mabyn's impassioned defense, "but certainly short-tempered."

Mabyn shook her head, unconvinced. "It is hard to imagine him so. I suppose he is short with you because he knows you dislike him."

"But I don't dislike him. What makes you think I do?"

Mabyn shrugged. "Perry must have given me that impression."

"I'm very sorry that he thinks so. I must try to disabuse him of that idea."

"I wish you would. Then you would not *ever* find him short-tempered. He is never short-tempered with me," she said artlessly.

"Isn't he?"

Mabyn blushed. "He's never said a word to me that wasn't gentle and . . . and loving."

Lucy felt her heart clench. "Loving?"

"I should not have said so much," Mabyn murmured, dropping her eyes to the pages of manuscript in her lap. "But he is always on my mind. When something is on one's mind it invariably finds its way to one's tongue, I'm afraid."

"You didn't say anything out of the way, Mabyn," Lucy managed to say.

"Yes, I did. But perhaps you've already guessed my feelings. Cora says that the two of us have been smelling of April and May since the first day."

"The two of you? You and Perry, you mean?"

"Yes." Mabyn lifted her head and eyed Lucy curiously. "Didn't you guess?"

"Well, no. That is, I've seen you together, of course, but I didn't think . . ." She felt her fingers clench themselves into her palms. "You're not telling me that the two of you are . . . *b-betrothed?*"

"Oh, no! Perry has not yet made me an offer. But I . . . that is, *Cora* thinks that he is certain to come up to scratch by the time we leave the Grange. I think it unlikely, since we've known each other for so short a time. It is too much to expect an attachment of that sort to come to pass in less than a fortnight, don't you think so, Lucy?"

"I really don't know." Lucy's throat was so tight with pain that she spoke with difficulty. "I imagine that when two people are . . . truly suited, they can sometimes discover it quickly."

Mabyn beamed at her. "Oh, that is what I hope for! It would be lovely to have the matter all settled between us before I go back to Cornwall. Cornwall is such a dreadful distance from London, you know."

"Yes, it is," Lucy said absently, wondering how much longer she could bear to listen to Mabyn's effusions without bursting into tears.

Mabyn's expression suddenly changed. "You don't approve, I can feel it. What is it, Lucy? Do you think I'm being too hasty?"

"No, of course not," Lucy said with all the sincerity she could muster, willing herself to keep her emotions under control and her head clear. "What makes you think I disapprove?"

"Well, I know you dislike him—"

"But I've already told you that I don't dislike him at all. In fact, I . . . I admire him. I admire him enormously."

The glow returned to Mabyn's eyes. "Do you really? Then you don't think I'm being hasty?"

"As to that, Mabyn, you must be the judge. Only you can be sure of your feelings."

"Yes, you're right. But that is the very difficult part. How does one know how to interpret one's feelings?"

"Are you not sure of your feelings, Mabyn? Is that what troubles you?"

Mabyn nodded. "I *think* I love him, Lucy. But I've not loved anyone before. How can I be sure?"

But I'm sure, Lucy thought. *How is it that I'm so sure? Perhaps it's merely the pain of it that makes one sure. And Mabyn has not yet felt the pain.* "It is hard to be sure at first," she answered with great difficulty. "That is why it's often advisable to have a long courtship. But there is no *rule*, you know, and in your case . . ."

"Yes?" Mabyn urged. "In my case . . . ?"

Lucy couldn't go on until she'd taken a deep breath. "In your case . . . well, it has often seemed to me, Mabyn, when . . . when I've seen you together, that you and Perry have much in common."

Mabyn nodded. "Yes. Yes, we have. And that alone has made me sure of my feelings. But even when I'm sure," she went on thoughtfully, "how do I know that the feelings I feel at one moment will be the same the next? Why, you yourself changed your mind about Owen, didn't you? Yet you must have believed you loved him at first."

Lucy gazed at her, astounded. How could Mabyn possibly compare Perry with Owen? Owen, who was so greatly in love with himself, was not the sort who could inspire truly deep emotions in anyone else. Didn't Mabyn *see* that? Now that Lucy knew what the feeling of love really was, she knew that what she'd felt for Owen was mere fancy. A pleasant interlude. What she felt for Perry was something quite different. It was a feeling so deeply ingrained in her that she seemed to feel it in the marrow of her bones. And she knew that in ten years, or twenty—with Perry wed to another and completely gone from her life—she would still believe, even if she herself were married to a fine man and surrounded with his children, that Perry was the one real love of her life.

"You did love Owen at first, didn't you, Lucy?" Mabyn repeated, searching her face.

Lucy rose from the seat and sighed. She couldn't tell Mabyn what she'd really felt for Owen without disparaging her sister's choice. And she couldn't tell her what love was, either, without revealing too much of herself. She shrugged, helplessly, giving the younger girl a wan, weary smile. "I don't know how to answer you, Mabyn, except to say that Owen is not Perry." And with that enigmatic response, she quickly left the room, hoping that Mabyn would never be able to decipher what she'd really meant by it.

Chapter Twenty-Two

It was almost time for the official presentation of the play, but Colin was not pleased with the performances of either his leading man or his leading lady. Owen was so stiff in his acting that the character of the awkward Marlow became positively wooden. And Lucy played her scenes with him with so little warmth that no one would believe that Kate Hardcastle was at all taken with her sometimes-shy, sometimes-bold suitor. "Shut yourselves in the sitting room," Colin ordered them, "and try to put a little flirtatiousness in those lines. Dash it all, don't come out until some *sparks* fly between you!"

The pair dutifully closeted themselves in the sitting room and rehearsed their two key scenes together: the scene where Marlow flirts with the girl he takes to be a barmaid, and the scene in act five where he declares his love. Lucy, remembering Colin's remark that a good actor acts with his eyes, tried her best to look at Owen with flirtatious affection. After they played the scenes over several times, Lucy began to get the hang of it and was fluttering her lashes at him with what she hoped was convincing zest. Whether it was those fluttering lashes or something else that made him lose his head, she was never to learn, but all at once he threw his pages aside in a violent gesture and seized her in his arms. "Oh, Lucy," he murmured, trembling, "I *knew* you couldn't have forgotten what we felt for each other!"

"Owen, for heaven's *sake!"* she gasped in astonishment. "What are you *doing?"*

"It was bound to happen," he said, his lips on her hair. "I

knew that sooner or later you'd regret breaking off with me. Our love is not something we can easily ignore."

"Owen, let me go! You don't know what you're saying!"

"I know exactly what I'm saying. I can keep silent no longer."

"Owen, you don't mean it. You know you don't. Only stop and *think*. I *jilted* you, remember?"

"I can forgive you for that, my love. I know how head-strong you are. I've known from the first how you must regret it."

Lucy, struggling vainly in his grasp, tried desperately to think of a way to make him behave sensibly without causing an ugly scene and upsetting everything. "Please, Owen, listen to me," she urged as calmly as she could. "It's only the play, don't see you? You've let yourself become carried away by the *role*."

"The role? Don't be ridiculous. I don't care a fig about the role."

"Of course you do. You *must!* You're a *born* actor, you know. Everyone says so." By flattering him in that way, she hoped to turn his mind back to the play. "Actors of your talent always put so much of themselves into their roles. That's all this is. Really!"

But her words of praise only made her seem more desirable to him. "No, no," he insisted, crushing her to him, "it's more than that. There's much more than the play that binds us together. You feel it as much as I do, I know you do!"

"Owen!" she cried. *"No!"* But it was no use, for he was much larger, stronger and harder to control than Colin had been. Her cries were smothered by his violent kiss. She struggled with all her might to release herself from this strangle-hold, but it only made him more passionate. In the midst of the struggle, she heard the door open. *Oh, God,* she prayed in despair, *let it not be Perry again!*

It was not Perry this time, but Colin. He'd come in to see how their rehearsal was progressing. The sight that met his eyes touched off a towering rage in him, for not only was Owen molesting the girl he wanted for *himself,* the blasted muckworm was betraying his *sister!* *"Tatlow,* you damned *rotter!"* he shouted, swinging on his crutches into the room. "Let that girl *go!"*

Startled, Owen lifted his head, giving his prisoner the opportunity to squirm out of his hold. Owen tried to recapture her but only managed to tear the sleeve of her dress. "Damnation, Colin, mind your own affairs," he barked in chagrin. "Have the good taste to take yourself off. Can't you see that you're intruding?"

"Intruding?" Colin spat out. "I'll *show* you intruding!" Balancing himself on one crutch, he lifted the other and swung it in a wide arc toward Owen's shoulder.

Lucy caught it with both hands before it reached its mark. "Colin, *don't!"* she ordered breathlessly. "Don't make a scene! He didn't mean it. He was carried away by the play, that's all."

But Colin would not be placated. He wrenched the crutch from her hold and swung it again. "Play or no play, he had no right to mishandle you," he shouted as his crutch again missed its mark. "What on earth's the *matter* with you, you bounder?" he cried, swinging the crutch again. "Did you forget that you're betrothed to my *sister?"*

This time he managed to connect, giving Owen a smart blow on the arm. Owen, much larger than his assailant and not handicapped by an injury, easily pulled the crutch from Colin's grasp. "I told you, Colin Trevellick, to take yourself off," he thundered. "Do so at once, or I'll have to floor you."

"Floor me, will you?" the maddened Colin retorted, flinging himself upon Owen in complete disregard of his crippled condition. The impact caused Owen to lose his balance, and he toppled to the floor with Colin still upon him.

"Owen, *please!"* Lucy cried. "His *ankle!"*

But the two were beyond reason. They rolled about the floor, pummelling each other wildly. A chair that chanced to be in their way fell over, taking with it a sidetable that bore a large oriental vase. The crash of furniture and porcelain was hideous.

It didn't take Owen long to get the better of the smaller man. As soon as he was able to pin Colin's shoulders down with one arm, he made a fist of his free hand and raised it for the kill. "Owen, *no!"* Lucy shrieked in desperation.

Owen paid no heed. The blow was smashingly delivered to Colin's nose. But the noise had brought half the household to the door, and the Admiral and Perry ran in and hauled Owen to his feet before he could deliver another. Rutherford, with the assistance of a footman, then dragged Colin by the arms to the nearest upright chair and deposited him upon it. Noticing the blood seeping from Colin's battered nose, Lord Rutherford handed the fellow his handkerchief. "Are you all right?" he asked, not able to mask the disgust in his voice. "You haven't mauled your ankle, have you?"

"My ankle's all right, but I won't swear my nose isn't broken," Colin muttered in dejection, feeling his nose gingerly.

Everyone in the doorway, seeing Owen's hangdog look, Lucy's torn sleeve and Colin's battered appearance, was able to interpret the scene. Cora, white-faced and trembling, came into the room as if in a daze. She looked from one to the other of the principals in this unrehearsed drama and then gave a little cry in her throat. "Oh, Owen, how *could* you?" she whispered tragically.

"Please, Cora," Lucy said bravely, "it was a misunderstanding. It was the play, you see. It was only the play . . ."

Cora stared at her with unseeing eyes. Then, dropping her face in her hands, she ran from the room. Mabyn, who'd been watching from the doorway, turned and ran after her. Lucy watched them go with a feeling of utter helplessness. When she turned her back, she met Perry's eyes. There was nothing in them of warmth or sympathy. The look made her heart sink like a stone in her chest. The whole dreadful experience now smote her, and she began to shake. Chloe, who'd also been watching from the door, knew in her bones that Owen had caused this fiasco. She strode into the room, put a protective arm about her niece's shoulder and led her to the sofa. No one else moved.

Lord Rutherford, a frequent participant in the squabbles and fracases that occur on the floor of Parliament, was not easily overset by clashes of this sort. He knew from experience that these altercations required tact; he'd learned years ago that mishandling can frequently turn a minor mishap into a major calamity, while tact can deflate a major one. He cleared his throat. "I don't know what caused this dustup," he said with Parliamentarian authority, "and I don't want to know. I will merely state that there will be no more of it. We shall leave the two of you to settle your difficulty on your own. Neither of you is to leave this room until harmony has been reestablished. Come, everybody. Let's go and have our luncheon."

"With your permission, Lord Rutherford," Lucy said in a voice whose quaver she was making a noble attempt to control, "I shall remain with them. I think harmony will be more quickly regained if I am permitted to say a few words to these gentlemen."

Rutherford nodded. "As you wish, Lucy, as you wish." He herded the rest of the group out of the door. Chloe squeezed Lucy's hand encouragingly before she left, and Perry gave her a look as he passed her by, a look that might have been warmer than the earlier one . . . and then again might not have been.

As soon as the three of them found themselves alone, Owen opened his mouth to speak. But Lucienne raised her hand. "Don't you say a *single word!*" she ordered in a tone that brooked no argument. "You have said and done quite enough for one day." She got up from the sofa and faced him squarely. "You will now listen to me. And you will believe that what I say is the absolute truth, because I promise you that it is. I do not love you, Owen Tatlow, and what's more I never have. If you harbor any doubts on that score, it would be wise to rid yourself of the notion once and for all. You are betrothed to a fine young woman who evidently feels more for you than you deserve. If you have the sense you were born with, you'll go to her on your *knees* and convince her that what happened was a simple misunderstanding. You will explain that you were attempting to improve your performance in the play and *nothing more!* The fight occurred because Colin came in and misinterpreted what he saw. If she wants to be reconciled badly enough, she will believe you. Besides, Colin will be there to support what you say, isn't that right, Colin? I know you will, because you do not wish to be the cause of your sister's unhappiness, do you?"

"How can I be the cause?" Colin muttered sullenly, his

nose buried in Rutherford's handkerchief. "It wasn't I who was kissing you."

"You were the cause because you didn't trust me to handle my own affairs. I might have managed to bring Owen back to his senses without creating a dreadful scene, if only you hadn't come charging in like a maddened bull. And as for not kissing me, that is not true either. You yourself are guilty of the same crime as Owen. You assaulted me *twice* against my will, did you not?"

"Yes, but *I* am not betrothed to someone else."

"True, but you are not betrothed to me, either."

He lifted his head and eyed her warily. "You're not saying I never will be, are you?"

"Good God, Colin," she exclaimed in irritation, "does it need saying?"

"Yes, it needs saying. I was going to make you an offer after the play."

"Then it's just as well this happened, for you can be sure that I would not have accepted you. This has saved you the trouble of asking."

He lowered his head into the handkerchief again. "You're only saying that because you're irked with me. If I'd asked you properly, you might very well have said yes."

"*Why* will you two *dunderheads* never take me at my *word?*" she exclaimed in exasperation. "I would *not* have accepted an offer from you under any circumstances, Colin Trevellick. Whether I was irked with you or not. Nor will I ever in the future. I'm as sure of that as I'm sure of what I said to Owen. If you believed me sincere in what I said to him, you may believe I am just as sincere now. So let us have an end to all this."

Colin lay back in his chair with his legs sprawled out before him as if he'd ceased to care about anything. "Very well, I've done. You won't hear any more from me on that head."

"Good. Then go, both of you, and settle matters with Cora."

Colin looked up again with a glare. Then he pulled himself up from the chair like a rising phoenix. "Do you honestly expect me to speak up for this idiotic coxcomb after what he did to my nose?" he demanded, burying it in the handkerchief again.

"Yes, I do," she said flatly, picking up his crutches and handing them to him. "As Lord Rutherford said, it's the only chance we have to try to restore some sort of harmony to what's left of this fortnight."

"I don't much care if harmony's restored or not."

Lucy expelled a breath in disgust. "Do you care about the play, then?"

His head came up from the bloody handkerchief as he eyed her dubiously. "Of course I care about the play," he declared. "I've worked too hard on it not to care. But it's a dead issue now, isn't it?"

She shrugged. "If you and Owen can bring Cora round, I promise to do what I can to revive the deuced play," she bargained.

Colin nodded and, grasping Owen's arm, pulled him toward the door. But Owen hung back. "Lucy, I—"

"Don't say anything, Owen, please," Lucy cut in firmly. "Everything's been said. Just go and make amends to your bride."

When they'd gone, Lucy dropped on the sofa and lowered her head to its arm. She felt numb. What was wrong with her, she wondered, that she so often brought her life to the brink of chaos? She was not aware of having done anything to encourage Owen to maul her, except to try to act her part in the play. And it was Colin who'd encouraged her to do that. She couldn't be blamed for it, could she? But there was Colin, too. He'd evidently expected her to accept an offer from him. What had she done to make him believe such a ridiculous thing as that? She'd not felt—or shown—any affection for him, at least not that she was conscious of. It was a puzzle.

She heard the door open again, and she felt herself shudder. *What now?* she wondered. "Owen, enough!" she said without lifting her head. "Go away."

"It is not Owen. I've only come to bring you this to drink. It will make you feel better."

"Perry!" She sat up at once, her hands flying to her hair.

He sat down beside her. "Here. It's just some mulled wine. I thought you might need it."

"Thank you. That was kind." She glanced over at him nervously. "You are always kind."

He put the mug into her hands. "Not always, I'm afraid. You know that better than anyone."

Her hands were trembling so much she could hardly hold the mug. "I d-don't know what's the matter with me," she said uncomfortably. "I don't think I can hold it."

He took it from her and, putting an arm around her shoulders, held the mug to her lips. "There now. Drink it down."

She did as she was bid. The hot liquid burned her throat, but it warmed her insides with a pleasant glow. She shut her eyes, letting herself bask in the warmth of the wine and the equally warm protection of his arm. If only she had the courage, she thought, she'd turn her head into his shoulder and nuzzle his neck. Then he might put both his arms about her and console her with a kiss. The thought of it made her blush. *Haven't you had enough kisses for one day?* she asked herself severely.

She *didn't* have the courage. And after a moment he removed his arm. When she'd drained the mug, he got up and started away. Devastatingly disappointed that this one lovely moment of her day was being brought to an end, she put out her hand and caught his sleeve. "Perry?"

He turned. "Yes?"

"Do you think it was all my fault?"

He sat down again. "I don't know. Was it?"

She brushed back a lock of her hair in a hopeless gesture. "I didn't mean it to be. We were only rehearsing our scenes. Colin wanted us to 'spark', you see."

Perry's smile began to show itself. "And did you 'spark'?"

"I don't think so. It's hard to spark with Owen. I fluttered my lashes a great deal, but I don't think there was much more to my performance than that."

"But it was evidently enough for Owen to be carried away, eh?"

Her face clouded. "Then you're saying it *was* my fault."

"Damnation, Lucy, must you always be assigning blame? If you're not accusing *me* of being at fault, you're accusing yourself. There's not always someone to *blame* for the things that happen. They just happen."

"But they happen for a *reason*, don't they? You just said that Owen felt impelled to kiss me for a reason, didn't you?"

"The reason being the fluttering of your eyelashes, is that what you think I meant?"

"Yes. It sounds silly, I know, but if that is the reason, then I am at fault. The blame is mine."

"He didn't kiss you for that reason, you goose. He kissed you because . . . well, for the same reason that Colin kissed you the other day. And for the reason that I kissed you, too. You're not to blame if all the men you meet find you kissable."

She stared at him in astonishment. "Is *that* all it is? I'm *kissable?*"

"Yes. Very."

"Are you saying it isn't something I *do* but something I *am?*"

"I'm not sure, but for the purpose of this discussion—to prove the point that there's no blame attached to you—I'd say yes."

She thought about the matter for a moment. Then she turned back to him. "Do you mean that I shall have to expect this sort of thing to happen *again?*" she asked in horror.

He shook his head, biting his lip to keep himself from laughing. "There are techniques you can learn to control the problem," he said in feigned seriousness. "I once wrote a little essay on the techniques women used to rebuff over-aggressive gentlemen."

"Did you indeed? You must give me a copy," she said sardonically, throwing him a glinting look.

"I shall. It may help you to learn how to handle this little . . . er . . . problem of yours."

"I might have known you'd have written about it. Is there a subject you *haven't* written about, Lord Whistledown?"

"Several, but I intend to cover them *all* before I give up scribbling." He got up again. "Now that you've recovered your equilibrium enough to twit me about my writing, ma'am, it's plain you have no more need of me. So, if you'll excuse me—"

Her eyes fell to the hands clasped in her lap. "Yes, of course. Thank you for . . . for your kindness."

"If you're sure you don't find it nauseating, you're quite welcome." He nodded quickly and made for the door.

"When one thinks about it," she said, half to herself, "it's not really very complimentary to be called kissable."

He stopped and turned back again. "Isn't it? I'm sure there are many young ladies who would consider it so."

She looked up at him. "But it's not a truly commendable characteristic, is it? Not when compared to something fundamental, as, say, kindness . . ."

"No, I suppose not."

"Or modesty. . ."

"No . . ."

"Or gentleness . . ."

He stood poised at the door with his hand on the knob, regarding her with eyebrows quizzically raised. "No. I would say that it is not as truly commendable as gentleness."

"Or even talent . . ."

"Talent, ma'am?"

"Yes. As, for example, the ability to play the piano with true feeling."

"No, I suppose not even that."

She drew in a long breath. "Of course, if one had all those qualities and was kissable, too, that would be very delightful."

He looked at her curiously. "Yes, it would. Very delightful, indeed."

"Like Mabyn," she said quietly.

Now it was he who drew in a long breath. "Yes," he said, after a moment of profound silence. "Like Mabyn." And he walked out of the room and closed the door.

Chapter Twenty-Three

Owen bent his knee before Cora and, using the excuse that Lucy had suggested, pleaded for forgiveness. When his story was corroborated by her brother, Cora relented. As she told her mother later, it was a small mischance that somehow blew up to a large calamity, but now that Owen and Colin had explained it all, everything was forgiven and would soon be forgotten. If somewhere in her secret heart Cora felt a tiny pain that had not been there before, she did not acknowledge it even to herself. It was, perhaps, some wise and womanly instinct warning her that, if she was to live in any sort of serenity with the man she'd chosen, she would have to endure more of such pains, and that the best way to endure them was to ignore them.

By the time the party assembled for dinner, everyone knew that Owen and Cora were reconciled. There was in the air a feeling of enormous relief. The importance of the entire *contretemps* was reduced to the status of a minor to-do, everyone agreeing with Lady Trevellick that "noo we cin all be happy agin."

On Lucy's advice, Colin talked about the play as if nothing untoward had happened. Since his nose was swollen and discolored, his nonchalant attitude was not easy for the others to accept. No one wanted the performance of the play to be canceled, but no one expected that the rift between three of the principal players to be so easily smoothed over that a performance would be possible. Nevertheless, Colin insisted that the preparations go forward. The performance, he said, would go on the next evening as scheduled.

To everyone's amazement, the policy of not referring by word or deed to the disruptive occurrence seemed to work. Preparations proceeded at a frantic pace the next day. Finishing touches were made to the costumes, the properties were gathered together, a row of footlights was placed along the edge of the stage, seats for the invited servants and those few guests who were not actually performing were lined up, and scenes from the play that Colin thought still needed work were reviewed. Every hour the excitement grew. At dinner, everyone was almost too keyed up to eat.

And so the play went on. The first act was fraught with nervous tension, everyone watching with bated breath for the scene in which Kate and Marlow first meet. When they saw that Owen's performance was no stiffer than usual and Lucy no colder, they broke into spontaneous, relieved applause. The rest of the play was performed with admirable zest and, at the end, the dozen or so who made up the audience cheered with real enthusiasm.

Everyone agreed it was a triumph. If the growth of love between Kate Hardcastle and Mr. Marlow hadn't been particularly convincing, at least they hadn't come to blows. And the rest of the play had been charming. Cora and her brother had made a delightful pair as the two elopers; Rutherford and the Admiral, having shouted their lines at the top of their voices, convinced themselves and everyone else that their acting was superb; and, best of all, Perry and Lily had played the farcical roles of foolish mother and prankish son so well that they'd kept the audience—even those who knew the lines by heart—in stitches.

As a reward, Jenny Rutherford arranged for a celebratory supper to be served after the performance. They all repaired to the buffet that had been set up in the drawing room, the actors still in costume and still congratulating each other effusively. The room rang with laughter and good spirits, with hardly a remnant left of the dissension of the day before. Lucy, sitting on the window seat and watching the gaiety in front of her, could scarcely believe it. There was Colin in the center of the room, surrounded by admirers, proud as a peacock for his achievement in bringing the enterprise to so successful a conclusion and grinning broadly as he accepted encomiums from actors and audience alike. Lucy could see no sign at all in his demeanor of his being crushed by her refusal, only yesterday, of his offer of marriage. And there near the fireplace, leaning on the mantle and smoking his pipe with his usual *savoire-faire*, was Owen, accepting the compliments on his performance as if he believed every word of them. And standing right beside him, her hand in his, was Cora, blushing with joy at the realization that she'd earned more applause for her performance than the leading lady. Lucy looked round the room and shook her head. She couldn't believe how thoroughly all evidence of yesterday's ugly scene had disappeared. If it weren't for Colin's purple nose, she might have thought she'd *dreamed* it all.

"Not celebrating, ma'am?" Perry's voice at her ear made her jump. "I didn't mean to startle you, but the leading lady shouldn't be sitting all alone. I've brought you some champagne."

She looked up at him, feeling her spirits lift at the very sight of him. He was standing before her, looking utterly appealing in the breeches, full-sleeved shirt and leather jerkin that had been his costume, and he was carrying two glasses and an open bottle of champagne. Afraid that the gladness she felt would show in her eyes, she dropped them down at once. "Thank you, Perry," she said shyly, "but the leading lady does not feel much like celebrating. I know quite well how dreadfully I performed."

He sat down beside her and pressed a glass into her hand. "You'd have made a marvelous Kate in the right circumstances," he said, filling her glass.

"Would I? Properly sluttish, you mean?"

He laughed. "I think that word inhibited your performance as much as all the other inhibiting circumstances. It's too bad, really. I would have loved to see you let yourself go in the part. Your natural liveliness is just right for it."

"If you are trying to cheer me, Perry," she said, sipping her drink with what she hoped was convincing insouciance, "I assure you it isn't necessary. I'm not at all depressed about the play. There's no need for you to feel you have to be kind to me all the time."

"Was I being kind again?" he asked ruefully. "How nauseating!"

"And that's another thing. I wish you'd stop flinging that word back in my face." She brought her glass to her lips with a flourish, as if to underline her words, and downed the rest of her drink. "I never meant it, and I'm truly sorry I ever said it."

"Don't be sorry, my dear. I know you didn't mean it literally. And it turned out to be a really useful epithet for me. It taught me to see myself a little differently."

Her brow knit in confusion. "See yourself differently? I don't know what you mean."

"I hadn't realized before that certain qualities, regardless of their intrinsic worth, bring out different emotional reactions in different people," he explained, filling her glass again. "Let's take the quality of kindness, for example. Everyone would agree, I think, that kindness is, in itself, a quite admirable quality. But a kind man, to some females, is . . . well, if not nauseating, at least a bit of a bore. While to others he can seem attractive."

She stared at him, stiffening. "If you're saying, Perry Wittenden, in that prosy way of yours, that I think you a bore, you're fair and far off. I *never* meant—!"

"Of course you meant it. You said it just now. 'In that prosy way of yours,' isn't that what you said? What does *prosy* mean if not boring?"

"Oh, come now!" she said impatiently. "I was only teasing."

He sipped his wine, keeping his eyes on her over the wineglass. "In teasing, as in *vino, veritas.*"

"Nonsense!" she snapped, wondering how she could put things right between them. "There's not one word of truth in anything you've said."

"Then let's stop talking and drink our wine," he said, his voice as pleasantly calm as ever.

She took another swallow of the wine. "But I want you to *understand!*" she insisted. "Can't I *ever* make up for those awful things I once said to you?"

"What is there to make up for? I never took offense."

"Then perhaps you *should* have taken offense. We would

have had a battle royal and then made up, and all this . . . this misunderstanding would be over."

"But that's just it, you see. I don't *like* royal battles. I like things to be calm and quiet. I'm a very dull fellow at heart, I'm afraid."

She stared at him in utter frustration. What was the use of trying to tell him that she didn't find him dull if he didn't want to hear? she asked herself, holding out her glass for him to refill. Or was it *she* who couldn't hear? Perhaps he was trying to tell *her* something. *I don't like royal battles. I like things to be calm and quiet.* Was that his way of telling her that they just didn't suit?

Confused, hurt and angry, she drank the contents of her glass in one swallow. It made her head swim and loosened something angry in her. "Calm and quiet?" she echoed, turning on him abruptly. "You mean, of course, that *I* am anything but. I am turbulent and noisy, isn't that it? I drive my phaeton too recklessly, I get into embarrassing scrapes, I get myself kissed at all the wrong times and then I make scenes over it. In other words, I'm a shrew." She stood up and waved the empty glass in his face. "Lucienne Gerard, Whishle . . . I mean Whistledown's shrew! To you I'm always the shrew you saw the first time you laid eyes on me. I can never live it down, can I?"

"Do you know what I think, Lucy?" he asked, grinning up at her.

"Yes, I know what you think. You think I am too obsheshed . . . you think I am ob-sessed with the verses you wrote."

"I think, ma'am," he said, getting up and taking the glass from her hand, "that I have gotten you foxed."

She blinked at him in surprise. "Foxed? Do you mean *drunk?*"

"Yes, that's what I mean."

She pulled herself up proudly. "Don't be shilly. I've never been drunk."

"Then we won't call it drunk. We'll say you're tipsy. Or, if you prefer we can say tiddly, bewottled, wobbly, cupshotten, raddled, befuddled or shot."

She beamed at him admiringly. "You *are* a good writer! I've never heard such a lovely list."

"Thank you, ma'am, but I think we must get you upstairs to bed before you're noticed. We don't want you involved in yet another shocking scene."

"Oh, no, of course we don't," she said, her smile fading. "Not when Lord Wittenden's here. He likes things calm and quiet, he does. Can't bear to be embarrassed by a noisy shrew!"

He pulled her arm through his. "Now, listen to me, Lucy. We're going to walk directly across the room to the door. If you lean on my arm, you won't stumble. If we just look straight ahead, we may avoid having to exchange pleasantries with anyone. However, if anyone speaks to us, I'll reply. You say nothing. Do you understand me?"

"Of course I understand you. I'm not in the least befuddled, whatever you may think."

He propelled her as quickly as he could across the room. They were just about to make their exit when Colin came up to them. "I say, where are you two going in such a hurry? The celebrating's just begun."

"We're only going to the library to settle an argument about a line from Virgil," Perry said, keeping his tone casual but his stride unbroken. "We'll only be a moment."

Colin nodded and waved. In another moment, they were out of the room. As soon as they were out of the view of the celebrants, Perry put his arm about her waist and pulled her to the stairs. Even with that support, she stumbled several times. "Oh, dear," she giggled, "per'apsh I *am* a wee bit tiddly."

The footmen who were usually stationed at the bottom of the stairs were not present this evening, having been part of the audience and hence part of the celebration. Seeing that nobody was about, Perry scooped her up in his arms and carried her up the stairs. "Which is your room?" he asked.

"That way. Halfway down," she said, slipping her arms about his neck and nestling her head on his shoulder. "I mus' be foxed," she mused aloud. "Tha's how I found the courage. 'Pot valiant,' my father would shay."

"The courage for what?" he asked.

"Never mind. You can put me down now. That's m' room."

He set her on her feet, but she kept her arms wrapped round his neck. "Good night, Perry," she said, smiling at him whoozily. "Thank you for taking care of me. It wash very—"

"I know. Very kind." He reached up to remove her arms.

She resisted the attempt. "Don't you want to . . . kiss me?" she asked softly.

He wrenched her arms from his neck and held them down at her sides. "Good night, Lucy," he said firmly.

"Am I not kish . . . kissable anymore?"

He frowned at her. "You're always kissable. That doesn't mean I'm always going to kiss you."

"Now you're angry at me. I'm making another scene, I suppose."

"I'm not angry, Lucy. I just think you should go right in to bed. Is your abigail downstairs at the buffet? Trudy, isn't it? I'll send her up to you."

The polite detachment of his voice was like being doused with cold water. Her champagne-induced exhilaration died down at once, and she realized with a sickening feeling in her stomach that she'd behaved badly in his company again. "Thank you," she mumbled, turning away from him with a lowered head. "I won't say you've been kind, but I shall think it."

"You're welcome, my dear." He backed away a step or two but couldn't bring himself to leave her. "You needn't look so hang-dog, you know. It might happen to anyone who's not accustomed to drinking champagne."

"It wouldn't happen to Mabyn," she said in a small voice. "Mabyn would never get tiddly."

"No, I don't think she would."

She glanced over her shoulder at him. "Mabyn is calm and quiet, isn't she? Quite like you, in fact."

"Yes, I suppose she is."

"One could not imagine her behaving foolishly because of two glasses of champagne."

"See here, Lucy, why are you berating yourself like this? You didn't behave so very foolishly. And nobody saw you but me."

"That's right," she said, unable to keep her voice from cracking, "no one saw me b-but you."

"You'll feel a great deal better in the morning. Good night, my dear."

She watched him turn and walk off down the hall, but he'd gone no more than a dozen steps when she called his name.

"Yes?" he asked, turning.

"Perry," she mumbled timidly, "I know you wouldn't mention me by name, of course, but... you wouldn't ever... you wouldn't..."

"Wouldn't what?" he prompted, his brows furrowing angrily. He strode back to her and grasped her shoulders in a painful grip. "Wouldn't *what?*"

Her eyes fell from his face. "Never mind. I didn't really think..."

"Oh, yes, you did! You were going to ask if I'd write about my shrew again... about getting herself intoxicated, isn't that right?"

She made a little moan and lowered her head.

"Damn you, Lucy, what do you think I *am!* One moment I am kind to the point of dullness and the next I'm a slanderer of innocent young women! I ought to wring your *neck!* I swear to you, if you ever, *ever*, dare to ask me such a question again, I'll... I'll toss you out of the window into a snowbank and leave you there to *freeze!*"

He thrust her away from him in disgust, turned on his heel and strode away. She watched until he'd disappeared from sight and then ran into her room and threw herself upon her bed. She knew she ruined everything. If he'd ever had any feeling for her, she killed it tonight. He felt nothing for her now but disgust.

Her throat burned with unshed tears, but she felt too numb to cry. All she wanted now was to leave this place. There was only one place in the world where everything she did was approved and loved, and that was where she wanted to go. She wanted to go *home*.

Chapter Twenty-Four

The next morning the sun made its first appearance in five days, but when Trudy came in to her bedroom, Lucy didn't let her pull back the drapes. "Go away, Trudy," she mumbled from beneath her pillows. "Go away and let me die."

Her absence from the breakfast room was not remarked on, for several of the ladies were wont to keep to their beds in the morning, and she was therefore not particularly missed. But when there was no sign of her by eleven, Chloe came upstairs to see what was keeping her abed so late. She found the room still dark and Lucy completely buried in her bedclothes. "What is it, my love?" she cried in consternation. "Are you sick?"

"Unto death," her niece replied hoarsely.

Chloe bent over and felt her forehead. "You don't seem feverish. Shall I ask Jenny to send for a doctor?"

"No. Just let me die in peace." She rolled over and opened one eye. "You needn't be concerned, however. I understand that the affer-effects of drink are not really fatal."

"After-effects of *drink?* What are you babbling about?"

"Champagne. I drank too much of it last night."

Chloe sank down on the bed with a sigh of relief. "Oh, thank *God!* I thought you were seized with some dreadful affliction."

"It *is* a dreadful affliction. My head feels like a kettledrum that someone is incessantly banging, my eyes are burning, and my tongue is glued to the roof of my mouth."

Chloe smoothed back a tangled lock from her forehead with an affectionate hand. "Poor dear. How much champagne did you *drink,* you foolish child! I'll go down and have Cook fix a lemon tisane for you. It always has a soothing effect on my headaches."

"No, don't go," Lucy said, holding on to her hand. "There's something I must tell you."

"Yes, dear? What is it?"

Lucy pushed herself up and leaned back against the pillows. "I hope you won't be angry with me, dearest, but I've decided that as soon as the road is open, I want to go home."

"Really, my love? But why? We shall *all* be leaving in four more days."

"I know. But I don't think I can bear four more days."

Chloe's eyes opened in surprise. "Oh, my love, have you been as unhappy here as all that? I know that the business with Owen the other day was frightful, but I thought that you were quite content otherwise."

"No, I don't think I've had one minute of contentment. A few moments of ecstasy, perhaps, several hours of anxiety, and whole days of misery, but no contentment."

"Ecstasy? Anxiety? Misery? Good God, Lucy, that sounds like *love!*"

Lucy smiled wryly. "Does it really?"

Her aunt studied her face intently. "I know it can't be Owen. Don't tell me you've tumbled for Colin Trevellick! Is it Colin, my love?"

"Don't be foolish. Colin is a dunderhead."

"Then . . ." The bemused aunt suddenly gasped. "Oh, no! Not *Perry?* Not *now."*

Lucy cocked her head and gave her aunt a sidelong look. "Why not Perrry? Why not now?"

"Well, you see . . ." Chloe's voice faded, and her eyes fell. Then she lifted them up again and glared at her niece in irritation. "Dash it all, Lucy, if you were going to fix on Perry, why didn't you do it when I *wanted* you to . . . in London?"

"Love is not a play, Aunt Chloe. I don't think one can summon up the feeling on cue. Besides," she muttered as an afterthought, "no one showed me the manuscript."

"What do you mean by that, pray? I don't understand these cryptic asides."

"I mean, Aunt Chloe, that it is quite possible I *did* fix on

Perry in London. I just didn't recognize the symptoms."

"Oh, dear," her aunt muttered in wistful chagrin, "it's too bad you didn't."

"Because it's too late now, is that what you mean?"

Chloe nodded. "I'm afraid so."

"Why, Aunt Chloe? Have you heard something? Has Perry confided something to you?"

"No, he hasn't. But surely you've noticed . . . well, *everyone* has . . ."

"Noticed what, Aunt? You needn't be afraid to tell me. I'm quite prepared to face it. What has everyone noticed?"

"Perry and Mabyn. They've been almost inseparable." Her fingers nervously picked at the nap of the coverlet. "Lily and Jenny have both remarked on it to me. And yesterday . . ." She glanced up at her niece unhappily, unable to go on.

"Yesterday . . . ?" Lucy prodded.

Chloe sighed. "Yesterday, Lady Trevellick confided to Lily, who of course repeated it to me, that . . . that . . ."

"Yes?" Lucy braced herself for the worst. "Please go on."

" . . . that Mabyn is convinced he'll declare himself before the Trevellicks return to Cornwall." She'd spilled out the words in a rush of breath, and now she subsided into a glum silence.

Lucy stared out ahead of her with wide, unseeing eyes. "Yes, of course. I expected that."

"Did you?" her aunt asked, watching Lucy's face worriedly.

"They are very much alike, you know," Lucy said dully. "They are both so very good and kind . . ."

"Yes, they are, aren't they," Chloe agreed softly, biting her lip.

" . . . and calm and quiet . . ."

"Yes, my poor dear, I'm very much afraid they are." Chloe's throat burned with tears that she struggled to hold back.

" . . . and modest, too."

"Yes," Chloe whispered, wiping away a tear that insisted on making an appearance. "Very modest. B-both of them."

"He deserves a girl like Mabyn, Aunt Chloe. Besides being

wise and gentle and everything fine, she's also kissable, you know. He told me so."

"Did he?" For the first time, Chloe didn't like Perry very much. "That wasn't very kind of him," she muttered.

"Oh, but it was. After all, he did say I was kissable, too."

"He did? Good heavens, what sort of conversation were you two having?"

"It doesn't matter. We both understood that I wouldn't be right for him. You see, he doesn't like scenes and royal battles and . . . and shrews."

"Oh, *Lucy*," Chloe wailed, letting her tears burst forth, "I am so s-*sorry!*"

Lucy's eyes focused on her aunt's face. "Chloe, *dearest*, are you crying? Please don't. Please! You'll only make me cry, too, and we'll flood the bed! Besides, I'm quite reconciled. I want Perry to be happy, truly I do, and he'd never be happy with me. But you see, that's why I'd like to go home. I don't want to be here when they announce the betrothal."

Chloe reached out her arms. "Of course you don't," she murmured, taking her niece in a comforting embrace. "There, there, my love, cry if you wish. It won't hurt so much after a while, I promise it won't. And next season, when you come to me again, you'll take the town by storm, see if you don't!"

Lucy didn't permit their mutual weeping to go on for very long. By the time luncheon was served, they'd bathed their eyes, dressed their hair and were ready to face the world at large with their ordinary cheerfulness. But in the afternoon, when Lord Rutherford announced that the mail coach had made its way through from Mendelsham, Lucy took him aside and informed him that she intended to leave in the morning. "My father's health is delicate," she explained, "and I am uneasy about him when I've been away from home for long."

Rutherford patted her hand, said he completely understood, made admiring remarks about her filial feelings and promised to see to it that her carriage would be in readiness. And when she asked him to say nothing to the others until after she'd gone, explaining that she would not wish to put a damper on the party, he kissed her forehead and called her a jolly good sport.

Later that afternoon her trunks and boxes were brought to

her room, and she and Trudy commenced the packing. Trudy had at first been crushed at the thought of leaving, but when Lucy promised her that she could remain with her in Yorkshire until the spring, the girl cheered up. But to Lucy everything seemed depressing. There was even something depressing about seeing the luggage lying about all over the room. It seemed a tangible proof that a special part of her life was ending . . . that she was leaving something behind that would never come again, like youth itself. But she didn't dwell on such thoughts for long. She busied herself filling the trunks.

"Is this somethin' ye'll be wantin', Miss Lucy?" Trudy asked, holding out a folded bit of newsprint. "I found it 'ere under the 'andkerchiefs."

Lucy almost snatched it from her hand. "Yes, thank you," she said. "I'll pack it myself."

Seeing this remnant of Perry's writing in her hand was almost too much for her to bear. She dismissed Trudy, saying she'd had enough of packing for the time being, and sank wearily down on the bed. She unfolded the worn paper and let her eyes roam over the words. *A sweet and gentle girl I've now forgot*, he'd written. If his writing was to be believed, it was a scornful, mocking girl he'd wanted then, but of course *then* he'd not yet found Mabyn. If only Lucy had realized, then, what her feelings really were! But perhaps it was just as well that she did not, for she and Perry would have been no more right for each other six months ago than they were now.

A knock sounded at the door. "Lucy, are you there?" It was Mabyn's voice. "I must speak with you."

Lucy jumped up from the bed and glanced around the room hurriedly. Mabyn could not be permitted to come in, that was plain. Not with all the baggage strewn about. Lucy would just have to speak to her in the corridor. "Yes, I'm coming," she called. She went to the door, but when she reached for the knob she realized that she still had her precious clipping clutched in her hand. She folded it quickly and looked around for somewhere to hide it. There were dozens of places, of course, but she didn't want to forget where she put it or to have it carelessly discarded by one of the maids. She hesitated for a moment and then, still undecided, tucked it in the bosom of her gown. She could stow it away later, when she'd have more time.

She stepped out into the corridor, quickly closing the door behind her. "Yes, Mabyn?" she asked. "Is there something you want of me?"

"Something's happened, Lucy. Something I must tell you about. I must, or I shall burst. Can we go in to your room?"

"Well, I . . . you see, Trudy has been . . . er . . . going through my gowns and they are strewn all over the bed . . ."

"Then let's go to my room. It's only a few doors away." Maybn grasped her hand and pulled her down the hall. Before she could catch her breath, Lucy found herself ensconced on a chair before the fire in Mabyn's bedroom, with Mabyn perched before her on a footstool. "I hope you don't mind, Lucy," the girl was saying. "There's no one but you who would understand."

"I? But why, Mabyn? What is this about?"

"Do you remember the other day, when we talked about Perry?"

"Yes, of course I do. But, Mabyn, if this is about Perry, perhaps I am not the one you should speak to. There's your mother, you know. And Cora."

"No, I don't want to talk to Mama. She'd make too much of it. And as for Cora, she would spoil it all. Cora is so . . . so *practical*, you know. All she would want to know is if he'd actually offered, and that is not what I want to talk about."

"It isn't?" Lucy asked, bemused.

"No. Not really. Oh, Lucy, I must tell you," the girl said excitedly, looking up at Lucy with shining eyes. "I'm *sure* now. Absolutely sure."

"Are you, Mabyn?"

The girl nodded. "That's what I had to tell you. It is wonderful to be certain of one's feelings. Now, when he makes his offer, I shall not have a qualm in accepting him. Do you want to know how this all came about?"

Lucy felt herself grow taut as a violin string. "Isn't this subject a bit too intimate, Mabyn, for a relative stranger to—?"

"You are no stranger to me, Lucy. I *want* to tell you. It all came about so suddenly, you see, just this afternoon. We went walking in the snow, Perry and I. It was so lovely. The sun made everything dazzling, and the wind nipped at our cheeks, and we threw snow at each other and laughed and laughed. You know how it is . . ."

"Do I?" Lucy asked drily. "Please, Mabyn, I don't think you should—"

"Wait, I've only just started! As we walked along he took my hand and we began to talk more seriously, and he said that it was brought to his attention that he and I are considered to be alike in many ways."

"It was 'brought to his attention'?"

"Yes. I also thought the phrase was strange. In any case, he asked me if I thought it was true. So I asked him, what ways, and he said that we were both generous and good-natured and so on, and I said I supposed it was true, and then he asked if I thought he was *too* good-natured, boringly so, and of course I said he was being silly and that I never for one moment found him boring and *then* he said . . ." Here her lips curled up in a secret little smile, a rosy blush colored her cheeks and she looked down at the fingers curled in her lap. ". . . he said that it had also been brought to his attention that I was kissable." She peeped up at Lucy in girlish embarrassment. "Are you shocked at me, Lucy? Do you think I should have given him a set-down?"

Lucy did not find it easy to respond. "No, of course I'm not shocked," she said stiffly, "but I still feel that I'm not the one you should confide in this way."

"But you *are!* What you just said *proves* that you are. Mama would have been shocked. And Cora would have said that there'd be plenty of time for such talk after the betrothal. But Lucy, you may yet find me shocking, for there's more."

"Yes, I thought there might be," Lucy said tightly.

"Yes . . . well, where was I?"

"Where it had been brought to his attention that you were kissable."

"Oh, yes. I couldn't help laughing a little at that, you see, and I said that it was a strange thing to say and that I hoped he would have noticed it without it having to be pointed out to him. I thought that would make him laugh, you see, but he only looked at me with that smile of his—you've noticed, haven't you, how he seems to smile with one corner of his mouth?—and before I knew what he was about he ... he ...."

"He kissed you."

"Yes," she breathed. "It was ... lovely. I could taste the wind and snow on his lips, and my heart was pounding so hard I thought he'd hear it, and my head positively *swam!* It wasn't the first time I've ever been kissed, you know, Lucy, but it was the first time I'd ever felt quite like this. So, you see, that's why I'm sure!"

"Yes," Lucy said quietly, "I can see that."

The starry-eyed girl reached for Lucy's hands. "I knew you would. And you don't think I'm being goosish, do you? Foolishly precipitous? Overly romantic? Should I have pretended to be indignant and slapped him?"

"No, I don't think any of those things. I think ..."

"What, Lucy? What do you think?"

"I think, my dear, that you're a very lucky girl," she said, getting up slowly. "A very lucky girl. I ... envy you."

The younger girl jumped up from her seat and enveloped Lucy in an enthusiastic embrace. "Oh, thank you, Lucy, thank you! I *knew* you'd understand."

"And what's more," Lucy added as she stepped over the threshold, "I think Perry is very lucky, too."

She hurried down the corridor hoping to reach her room before her tears started to flow, but, strangely, when she'd closed her own door safely behind her, she found that she was not even close to tears. She was, in fact, *seething*. She was furious at Perry for having kissed the girl. It was a completely illogical feeling, she knew that. How could she expect him to refrain from kissing the girl he was going to wed? But logic had nothing to do with her feelings. It just felt so *unfair*. How could he have done it? Why had she permitted Mabyn to tell her about it? Mabyn had everything else, but Lucy had believed that the memory of the kiss he'd given her in the woods was her own. Now even that memory was degraded. He'd written in his blasted poem that he remembered only a scornful girl, but he'd taken sweet, gentle Mabyn out cavorting in the snow, and he'd kissed her! It made her *furious*. It was a senseless emotion, she knew, but she felt *betrayed*.

Well, everything was over now. She had nothing left to do

but put the traitor out of her mind. And the first step in that process was to take that poem, tear it in a thousand pieces and throw it in the fire. She reached into her gown for it but couldn't find it. She searched thoroughly. She even removed the gown and shook it out. But the little piece of paper was gone.

Chapter Twenty-Five

Perry did not sleep well that night. He'd tried all day to dismiss from his mind the memory of Lucy with her arms tight around him, nuzzling his neck in such a way that delicious little tremors had run down his spine, but nothing he'd done all the next day had succeeded in dissipating the spell she'd cast on him. And now that spell was interfering with his sleep.

For days now he'd tried everything he could think of to rid himself of his love-disease, but nothing had had a curative effect. He'd tried to feel revulsion toward her when he'd come upon her in the arms of Colin and then Owen, but he'd only felt a murderous jealousy. He'd tried to tell himself that she was a foolish, shallow, selfish creature, but every time he thought he'd convinced himself of that, she said or did something that he found charming, touching, honest or admirable. He'd even tried to make himself fall in love with Mabyn, going so far as to kiss her in the snow, but the kiss only reminded him of the feelings he'd experienced when he'd held Lucy in his arms, that day in the woods and that evening when they'd waltzed together; the overpowering recollection of those feelings made Mabyn's embrace seem something less than memorable. He loved Lucy, and there seemed to be nothing he could do to cure himself of it.

He still believed that they were completely unsuited, that she was too volatile for him and, should they ever make a match, that she would lead him a merry dance and give him a life full of chaos. But he didn't care anymore. He knew only that he wanted her and that his life would be forever barren and colorless without her. Should he admit all this to her?

Should he declare himself? This was the question that kept him tossing in his bed all through the night. He didn't know if he had the courage to face what would almost certainly be complete rejection. After all, he was the fellow she'd called nauseatingly good-natured. Though she'd denied it of late, she surely found him a very dull fellow. As Wittenden, he was a bore, and as Whistledown, he was a cad.

But when he'd carried her to her room yesterday, she'd clung to his neck with undeniable, if inebriated, passion. And there had been many other little signs that she might have some feeling for him hidden away inside her. He had to learn the truth; there was no hope for him at all without it. If she refused him, he might finally be able to make a real attempt to banish her from his mind; and if she accepted . . . well, then he would at last find himself a completely happy man.

He would ask her tomorrow. He could not bear another day of this hideous indefiniteness. Whatever it cost him, whatever courage was necessary, whatever pain or joy was in store for him, tomorrow his future would be decided.

But by the next morning Lucy was gone. Her carriage had left the Grange just before dawn. Only the Rutherfords and Chloe had known she was leaving, and they were the only ones who'd waved her off. By breakfast time, however, the news had been heard by everyone. Lily and the Admiral were sorry, for Chloe's sake, that Lucy was gone; Lady Trevellick said she regretted that she'd not had time to teach the girl the "auld tongue"; Colin sulked; Owen seemed indifferent; Cora was relieved; and Mabyn was crushed. "Why did she not say good-bye to me?" she asked Chloe at breakfast. "I thought we'd become the best of friends."

"She didn't wish to cause a stir or put a damper on the party," Chloe apologized for her. "I'm sure she'll write to you about it herself."

"Yes, but then it will be too late for. . ." Mabyn stopped herself and compressed her lips.

"Too late for what, my dear? Is it something I can help you with in Lucy's place?"

But the girl only shook her head. "No, thank you, Lady Chloe," she murmured. "It wasn't anything important." And she wandered off looking to Chloe's eyes just a bit forlorn.

Perry, who'd gone for a solitary stroll that morning and had missed breakfast, heard about Lucy's departure from Mabyn a little later. Excusing himself from her company as soon as he could politely do so, he went seeking Chloe. He found her in the sitting room, staring out of the window gloomily. "Was there any particular reason for Lucy to leave so precipitously, Lady Gerard?" he asked without preamble.

Chloe turned round and frowned at him. "No, no particular reason. Why do you ask?"

He ran his fingers through his tousled hair. "I ask because I hadn't expected . . . that is, we left so many matters . . . unresolved."

"Oh?" Chloe peered at him curiously. "What matters were those?"

He shrugged and took an impatient turn about the room. "They were not matters of any special import, I suppose. I just would have wished . . ."

"Wished what?"

There was no answer. Chloe watched the young man pace about for a moment. "Come, Perry, sit down here beside me. It's been some time since you and I have had a chance to talk."

"Yes, I know," Perry said abstractedly, taking a seat beside her on the sofa. "The play kept us all so busy."

"Well, there is no play now. So tell me, my boy, what you meant a moment ago when you said you would have wished to conclude some business with my niece."

"Did I say that? No, there was no particular business. I would have liked, however, to have had the opportunity to say good-bye. The last time we spoke, you see, we'd had a bit of a quarrel."

"Oh? A quarrel? Nothing very bitter, I hope, Perry."

"Bitter enough," Perry admitted, frowning down at his booted left foot as if he didn't know whose it was.

"Oh dear! That *is* too bad," Chloe murmured.

"You needn't make too much of it, ma'am," he said drily. "Your niece and I always indulged in bitter quarrels. It was the essence of our relationship from the first."

"I'm sorry to hear that, Perry. I'd always hoped that the two of you would be friends."

"Did you?" He looked over at her with a rueful smile. "Even after you learned that I'd turned her into Whistledown's shrew?"

"Heavens, my boy, I never took those verses at all seriously. I wouldn't have given them a second thought if Tatlow hadn't bruited it about all over town who your shrew was."

Perry sighed. "It's kind of you to say that, Lady Chloe. I only wish your niece were so forgiving."

"She *is* forgiving. She wasn't bothered by those verses any more than I was, once she realized that the gossip it created was a mere tempest in a teapot."

"Wasn't *bothered?*" Perry gave a bitter snort. "Are we speaking of the same Miss Lucienne Gerard? I don't like to contradict you, my dear, but I don't think you know your niece as well as you think you do."

"What are you saying, Perry?" she asked, turning to him with a startled look. "Are you telling me that *that's* what you've been quarreling about?"

"We've been quarreling about everything, but my writing always seems to be at the bottom of it."

Chloe shook her head. "You must be misunderstanding her, Perry. Perhaps you're overly sensitive about your writing. I think she's only been twitting you on that head."

"*Twitting* me? Oh, no, ma'am, don't deceive yourself. She's so angered by those blasted verses that it's made her dislike everything about me."

"Now I *know* you've misunderstood her," Chloe insisted. "As a matter of fact, she told me herself how much she . . . admires you."

Perry gave her an arrested look. "Admires me?"

"Yes, Very much, I think."

"That's strange. Mabyn said the very same thing to me the other day. In fact, she used the very same word. 'Lucy admires you enormously,' she said."

"Well, then, you see? I'm right."

Perry shook his head. "If you are, then I can only surmise that your niece is capable of the prodigious feat of both disliking and admiring someone at the same time."

"I cannot believe you're right about that, but there's no use in my persisting in this disagreement," Chloe said, fearful of pushing this interesting conversation too far. But she could not give the subject up entirely. It was too good an opportunity to probe Perry's feelings. "Speaking of Mabyn, dear boy, am I being precipitous in offering you my sincere felicitations?"

"What?" Shaking himself from the grip of a thought that had been occupying him for the past few seconds, he turned to her with an expression of complete bewilderment. "Felicitations, Lady Chloe? For what?"

"Surely you can guess what I'm alluding to. We have all been expecting an announcement."

"Announcement? I don't understand."

"About you and Mabyn. Oh, dear! It seems I *have* been precipitous. Forgive me, Perry dear. It is only my fondness for you that makes me so eager to bestow my good wishes on you. I know you will tell us all when the time is right."

His eyes widened as the import of her chatter dawned on him. "Good God! You are not under the impression that Mabyn and I . . . ! What could have given you such an idea?"

His unequivocal and sincere bewilderment came as a shock to Chloe. Although in her heart she *hoped* he had no intention of offering for Mabyn, she had been quite sure her hopes would be dashed. But here he was, looking at her as though the idea of asking for Mabyn's hand had not until this moment crossed his mind! "But . . . *Perry,*" she stammered, *"everybody* at the Grange has that idea."

"Everybody? How can that be? I never . . . ! Mabyn and I haven't even *thought* of such a possibility."

Chloe regarded him pityingly. "Are you certain, Perry, that *Mabyn* didn't think of it?"

"Of course I am! That is . . . I never gave her any cause . . . at least, not consciously." He got up and began to pace around the room again. "We have been close, I suppose. We both have an interest in poetry, you see, and she was always so eager to . . . but I never thought . . . Good God, Lady Chloe, are you suggesting that she believes me to be *courting* her?"

"We *all* believed it, my boy."

He stopped in his tracks, stared at her and made a gesture of despair. "But *why* did you believe it? We *all* were thrown together as house-guests, were we not? We intermingled at meals, in the evenings, at breakfast, at all sorts of games and activities. I did not single her out for special attention, any more than I singled out Colin or Cora or . . . or *Lucy,* for that matter."

"That is not how it seemed to the rest of us, my dear," Chloe said gently. "You and Mabyn were very often with your heads together."

He gave her a stricken look. "Were we? I didn't realize . . . She would bring a poem to my attention, and we'd take a walk and discuss it. Or we'd go over my lines in the play. Her company was always pleasant. I suppose I didn't notice how it might appear to others. I never *courted* her, Lady Chloe. There was never any flirtatiousness between us . . ." At that moment he remembered something and winced. "Except perhaps . . . yesterday . . ."

"Are you saying, my boy, that you don't love Mabyn?"

"*Love* her? How can I love her, when I'm . . . ?" He ran his fingers through his hair again, utterly distraught. "God, I've made a mull of it! What am I to *do?*"

"I think, Perry," Chloe said, rising and putting a motherly hand on his arm, "that you should speak to the girl. But if, wittingly or unwittingly, you've raised her expectations, you must make good on them. I would be very sorry—much more sorry than you know—to see you wed to someone who hasn't captured your heart, but Mabyn doesn't deserve to have her hopes so cruelly dashed if indeed you raised them."

He nodded his head slowly. "Yes, you're quite right. Thank you, Lady Chloe, for being so forthright with me. It seems I've been in need of a mother's advice. I'm glad you were here to give it to me." He gave her one of his little half-smiles. "Now that I think of it, I realize that ever since I was a boy, what little I knew of mothering I learned from you." He lifted her hand to his lips and then strode from the room.

Lady Chloe is right, of course, he told himself as he betook himself down the hallway in search of the girl. If he'd truly raised Mabyn's expectations, he was honor-bound to offer for her. It didn't matter that he'd never had the slightest intention of courting her. What mattered was that he'd misled her, and in so doing he'd obligated himself. In his turmoil over Lucy, he'd attended his conversations with Mabyn with only half a mind. It was quite possible he'd said things that the girl could have misinterpreted. He tried to recall what he might have said during those exchanges, but he could remember them in only the vaguest way. There was nothing vague, however, about the fact that he'd kissed Mabyn yesterday. How foolish his behavior had been, to be sure!

His footsteps slowed as the full realization of where he was heading burst upon him. At the end of this corridor was . . . marriage! To *Mabyn! Good God*, a voice within him cried, *my whole life is about to take a turn I neither expected nor desired! How could I have permitted myself to come to this pass?* He had a sudden urge to run for the nearest doorway, make straightway for the stables, saddle a horse and ride for town, leaving the entrapments of Rutherford Grange behind him. But he mastered the urge at once. He was raised a man of honor, and a man of honor he would remain, whatever it cost him.

He found Mabyn at the piano in the music room, playing Bach with intense concentration. He waited in the doorway, not wishing to disturb her. He could not help but admire the strength and sensitivity of her playing. Lucy was right about her; Mabyn's musical talent was quite beyond the ordinary. In truth, the girl was beyond the ordinary in many ways. Any man might consider himself most fortunate to win the affection of such a young lady . . . any man whose heart was not otherwise entangled. But *his* heart had become entangled months ago, and he knew that even so extraordinary a creature as Mabyn could not pry it loose.

As if she sensed him there, Mabyn looked up from the keyboard. "Perry!" The cry was eager, but as soon as it had left her throat, she blushed. "How long have you been standing there?" she asked shyly.

"Only a moment. Please go on playing, Mabyn. I was enjoying just standing here listening to you. We can talk later."

"Did you wish to speak to me?" She jumped up from the piano bench and came toward him. "I'd much rather talk to you than practice," she said, taking his arm. "Come and sit beside me on the window-seat. It will be so cozy, with the sun shining in that way."

They sat down together, and Mabyn looked up at him. The look was both expectant and uneasy. Perry was as uneasy as she. He couldn't bring himself to speak for a moment, but he took one of her hands in his and stared down at it. "Mabyn, I—" he began at last.

"My, how serious you look! Am I about to be scolded for something?"

"No, of course not. You could never do anything that would require a scold." Then, as if he'd heard his own words for the first time, he gaped in surprise. "Good God," he muttered, half to himself, "I suppose that sort of remark could be construed as courting, couldn't it?"

"Courting?" She gave a little, nervous giggle. "Very *mild* courting, if you ask me. *Are* you courting me, Perry?"

"That's what I wished to ask you. Has it seemed to you that I've been courting you these past days?"

"That's a strange question. What makes you ask?"

"Well, you see, it's been brought to my attention—"

"Goodness, not again!" she cut in. "You said that yesterday, remember?"

"Did I?"

"Yes. You said that it was 'brought to your attention' that I was kissable. I was quite offended at that, you know."

He sighed. "I can't say I blame you."

"Well, you needn't look so downhearted, sir. I forgive you. Now, what has been brought to your attention today?"

"It seems that it's been generally assumed that I've been courting you. Under the circumstances, therefore, I thought we ought to discuss the matter. If you, too, have been under that impression, Mabyn, I want you to know that I'm quite ready to go to Cornwall and ask your father for permission to marry you as soon as you say you'll have me."

Her hand trembled slightly in his grasp. "And if I have *not* been under that impression?"

"What?" he asked, bemused.

"You said you're ready to speak to my father *if* I had the impression you were courting me. Does that mean that if I *hadn't* that impression, you're *not* ready to speak to him?"

He winced. "Dash it all, Mabyn, I'm a clod. I know I'm doing this very badly. Please forget everything I just said, will you? Let's start again. Mabyn Trevellick, in the simplest, clearest English possible, will you marry me?"

She withdrew her hand, very slowly, from his grasp. "Are you asking me because it was brought to your attention that I *expected* it, Perry?" she asked, lowering her head.

He felt as if his stomach had been tied in knots. He stared at her bent head, hating himself, this houseparty, and the fates that had brought him to this pass. He didn't want to marry her, but she looked so young and vulnerable, sitting there with the sun lighting her burnished hair, that he couldn't bear to hurt her. "I'm asking you, you goose," he said with what he hoped was hearty enthusiasm, "because you're so kissable, of course."

She glanced up at him for a fleeting moment and then turned her head away again. "But you don't love me, do you?" she murmured.

He grasped her shoulders and made her face him. "Mabyn, why do you ask that? You are everything that's lovable, don't you know that? I've never known a girl as sweet, as gentle, as—"

"As sweet and gentle as the girl whose name you wrote upon the sand?" she asked, her voice choked.

"What?" His hands dropped from her shoulders. He could feel something within him clenching, but he didn't know why.

"You don't remember? 'From sand and memory she's washed away.'"

He recognized those words as his own, but somehow they weren't making sense. "Where did you hear *that?*" he asked. "It's only a foolish verse, you know. I wrote it as an exercise. The villanelle is a real challenge to a versifier. How did you happen to come across it?"

She put a hand into the décolletage of her gown and took out a folded piece of paper. "I found this yesterday," she said, handing it to him. "On the floor of my room."

He unfolded it and peered at it, completely baffled. "My *villanelle?* On the floor of your *room?*"

"Lucy was there with me yesterday. She must have dropped it. I was going to ask her about it today, but she'd gone." Her voice began to tremble. "I read it very carefully, Perry. Several times. Even those words scribbled alongside the last stanza. Can you read what they say? 'I think he means you.'"

Perry felt his pulse begin to pound in his ears. "Are you telling me this is *Lucy's?*" he asked, peering in disbelief at the shabby paper with its yellowed edges and worn folds. "That she kept it all this time?"

"So it seems," Mabyn said, her voice so low he could hardly hear her. "I knew when I'd read it that she loved you. But I didn't realize until this moment how much you still love her."

"No," he said hoarsely. "No!" He put a hand to his forehead and tried to think. Was it possible that what Mabyn was saying was true? Had Lucy recognized herself in the poem, and had she carried it with her all this time, looking at it over and over until the folds were worn through? But he couldn't think about that now. There was Mabyn, looking at him with brimming eyes. He had to be fair to her. He forced himself to concentrate on her rather than on the tantalizing significance of the piece of paper in his hand. "You are jumping to conclusions, my dear," he said firmly. "Lucy and I don't even like each other."

"That, my dear Perry, is not my concern," Mabyn said, getting to her feet and walking proudly across the room, "but I don't think you really believe that."

He followed her and grasped her arm. "Mabyn, don't refuse me for so foolish a reason as a discarded bit of verse. Lucy and I could never suit, but you and I are as well matched as any couple I know."

"Perhaps there's some truth in that," she said, removing her arm from his grasp and going to the door, "but I think I'd prefer to wait until I find someone who wants to write poems about *me*."

Chapter Twenty-Six

Lucienne was home. She was back where she belonged, in the familiar and safe surroundings of her youth. But the charm of her pretty blue bedroom, the glad welcome of her neighbors and friends, and even the warmth of her father's unyielding affection seemed not enough to gladden her deeply depressed spirits. And, to make matters worse, she had only to lift her eyes to see outside her window the icy grey landscape of the Yorkshire winter.

She had hoped that her return home would restore her previous state of mind, but the contentment of her youthful days seemed now to be gone forever. None of the old, familiar sights seemed quite so delightful as they once did, especially when she realized that she would be spending the rest of her life among them, an old maid doing, seeing and saying the same things year after year. For she'd made up her mind (although she'd not yet informed her aunt) that she was not going back to London in the spring. One season in society had been quite enough; she was not going to endure another. She'd had her fill of men, matchmaking and love.

She'd always thought that by the time she'd reached this advanced age, she'd be married to a proper gentleman and be living the life of a society matron, but evidently that was not to be. Perhaps it was just as well. She'd always lived in a style that was not particularly admirable; her life had been, she'd begun to realize, a self-indulgent, wasteful and useless one. Now that she'd had her fill of girlish pleasures, she determined to live the rest of her life usefully, and as a woman of good character. She pinned her hair back neatly in a bun, put aside her Paris gowns and took to wearing plain muslin dresses with neat tuckers at the neck and workmanlike aprons tied round her waist. She took a sudden interest in supervising the housekeeping, visiting the sick and reading books of high seriousness. Her father, watching her in astonishment, wondered if she were afflicted with some mysterious illness.

One day, a little more than a week after her return, Trudy came into the upstairs sitting room where Lucienne sat sewing shirts that she was preparing as gifts for the servants on Boxing Day. "Parcel fer ye, Miss Lucy," she said, holding out a large, flat, squarish envelope. Lucy took it with some surprise, for she was not in expectation of any mail. Besides, it was too large to be a letter. She looked at the envelope curiously. Her name was scrawled on the outside, but there was nothing more to identify it. "How did you come by this, Trudy? There's no frank or postage mark on it." But Trudy had already gone.

Lucy picked up her scissors and slit the envelope's flap. Inside was a magazine, and she knew even before she pulled it out what it was: the *West-Ender,* of course. Her heart began to thump alarmingly as she opened it at once to page three, where the Whistledown Diary always appeared. It was there, just as it was every month. She barely glanced at the heading, for the first two words of the poem leaped out at her: *My shrew...*

That BOUNDER! something inside her cried out in fury. *He said he wouldn't write about me! He PROMISED!*

Her hands shook as her eyes flew over the words:

> My shrew has eyes of flashing fire,
> It takes not much to rouse her ire—
>   A brat, she!
> She pouts like any spoiled child,
> Her temper's something like a wild
>   Apache.
>
> No kind words ever pass her lips,
> I've seen her soused on just two sips
>   Of wine;
> With accusations she'll assault

Whoever's near, but soon the fault
                              Is mine.

Her moods they change like late fall's breeze,
She won't admit her slips when she's
                              Mistaken;
I never know when she deceives,
Her wit is sharp and always leaves
                              Me shaken.

Her voice is proud, her manner grand:
Whenever she's put out her hand
                              I've kissed it;
She is, in short, a stinging bee!
I'd wed her in a trice, if she
                              Insisted.

Lucy reacted to each and every line with an apalled *Oh, no!*, each one louder and more distraught than the last. By the time she'd read the verses through, she'd jumped to her feet, scattering spools of thread and pins heedlessly on the floor, and was striding like an enraged tigress about the room. "How *could* he do this to me again?" she cried out to the empty room. "How *could* he?"

With the magazine clutched in her hand, she ran to the door. "Trudy! *Trudy,* where are you?" she shouted. "Why in blazes are you always in hiding when I need you? Get our cloaks, do you hear me? And pack us a small portmanteau. And tell Samuels I want a coach with two pair. *Two* pair, mind! Dash it all, where *is* that blasted girl?"

She ran down the stairs, colliding with the hurrying Trudy just as she was about to take the first turning. "Oh, *there* you are! Did you hear what I said?"

"Yes, Miss Lucy, I 'eared ye," the abigail said, looking strangely uneasy. "But I don' unnerstand. Are we goin' some-wheres?"

"Yes, we are. To London. Right now!"

"Right *now,* Miss?" Her look of uneasiness increased, and she began to make strange pointing motions in the direction of the bottom of the stairs. "But ye cain't go right now, Miss," she said, whispering agitatedly. "I think ye ought t' go up an' take off yer apron."

"What on earth is the matter with you, Trudy? Why are you whispering? And what's my apron to do with anything? I said we are *going*. So bestir yourself, my girl! Now!"

"But, ma'am," Trudy croaked, still hoarsely whispering and still pointing urgently toward the turning of the staircase, "I don' see why ye—"

"Why? *Why?*" Lucy snapped, striding past her and rounding the turn. "Because I'm going to *murder* someone, that's why!"

As soon as she made the turn, she understood why Trudy had been gesticulating so urgently. A man in a greatcoat, with a shock of unruly red hair on his head and a pair of incongruous spectacles perched on his nose, was standing at the bottom of the stairs. "I'm the one you're going to murder, I suppose," he said, flashing his boyish half-smile up at her.

"Perry!" she gasped, freezing in her tracks.

"In the flesh, ma'am. I knew you'd come seeking me out with murder in your soul, so I came up to Yorkshire to save you the trouble."

She gaped at him for a moment until the shock of seeing him subsided and the rage at what he'd written stirred up in her again. "I *do* have murder in my soul," she said, stomping down the remaining steps. "How could you have done this appalling thing!" She waved the magazine under his nose threateningly. "It's . . . it's . . . *slander!*"

"Yes, I know," he agreed mildly, grasping her wrist and forcing the offending hand out of his face. Then, without the slightest change of expression, and without any apparent effort, he slipped an arm about her waist, pulled her to him and kissed her. She beat at his back and shoulders furiously, but the more she struggled, the closer he pressed her to him. After a moment, and much to her chagrin, she found her rage subsiding and that wonderful feeling of being about to disintegrate in his arms creeping over her. She let herself surrender to the feeling for a little while and then, with an enormous effort of will, wrenched herself away. "Perry! Have you gone *mad?*" she asked breathlessly. "What do you *mean* by this insane behavior?"

"I'd be happy to explain," he said, "but I fear we're not alone."

She looked round, startled. Her father was standing in the library doorway observing the scene with amused fascination, Trudy was looking down from the stair-landing open-mouthed, and several of the servants were peeping out from behind doorways and corners. Lucy blushed to the roots of her hair. "Papa," she said with becoming bravado, "this is Lord Wittenden. You may remember that I spoke to you of him. He's the gentleman who slandered me."

"Is he indeed?" her father chortled, snapping his fingers at the servants, who all disappeared at once. "I must say you've given him an interesting reward for his efforts."

Her blush deepened. "Yes, well . . . I'll explain it all to you later, Papa," she said, taking Perry by the arm and pulling him toward the door of the small sitting room at their right, *"after* I've discovered the explanation myself." With that, she pushed Perry over the threshold of the sitting room, gave her father a wave, scooted quickly inside and shut the door. "Now," she said, leaning her back against the door and taking a deep breath, "you may tell me what this is all about."

"Yes, of course," he said, pulling off his greatcoat and tossing it over a chair, "but first I must kiss you once more."

Before she could object she was again summarily and thoroughly embraced. "Do you know, my love," he murmured with his lips against her hair, "that even with your hair in a knot and a misshapen apron tied round your waist, you're absolutely lovely?"

She found it quite impossible to remain angry at him while he held her in his arms, so it was many minutes before she was able to resume her scold. Finally, however, some recollection of her previous indignation returned to her. "Go and stand over there, Perry! Yes, there, across the room where you can't . . . distract me." Obediently, he backed away. She took the opportunity to remove her apron and drop it behind a chair. With chests full of beautiful clothes, she thought ruefully, she had to pick *this day* to don a veritable housemaid's gown!

With Perry safely across the room near the fire (where he made himself comfortable leaning on the mantel), Lucy was able to get down to business. "Now, will you please explain yourself, you gudgeon? You have me completely confused."

"I don't see what's so confusing. You read my verses, didn't you? Didn't they make it clear? I want you to marry me."

"Is *that* what those verses said?" she asked sardonically. "It seemed to me they said that I was not only a shrew but a spoiled child, a wild Indian, a souse and a stinging bee."

"Yes, they said that, too."

"Just the sort of creature *any* sane man would wish to marry," she muttered bitterly.

"I suppose, then, that I'm not quite sane." Ignoring her stricture that he remain on the opposite side of the room, he crossed the distance between then, took her hand and drew her down beside him on the sofa. "You see, Lucy, what the verses don't say is that I love you. Quite to the point of insanity."

Lucy couldn't trust her ears. "That's not *possible,*" she gasped. "You love Mabyn, don't you? You *must* love her. She is everything fine and lovely . . . and so *perfect* for you."

"Yes, I know. But ridiculous as it is," he said softly, lifting her fingers to his lips, "it is you I love."

"Oh, Perry!" She closed her eyes and let the beautiful words sink in. But after a moment they flew open again. "But Mabyn said you . . . you *kissed* her. In the snow. And that it was *dizzying.*"

"Not for me," he said softly, gathering her into his arms. "Every second I held her I kept remembering those moments in the woods when I held you. Those moments were, to me, much more than dizzying."

"To me, too," she whispered, lifting his hand to her face and rubbing her cheek against it. "But, Perry, Mabyn was expecting you to offer for her, was she not?"

"Yes," Perry admitted, trying to answer her question but finding himself woefully distracted by the delicious smell of her hair. "I don't know what I did to raise those expectations, but I did. Your aunt Chloe pointed out to me that I was therefore obligated. I offered for her the very day you left. She refused me."

She lifted her head abruptly. "She *refused?* I don't believe it! She told me herself of her deep feelings for you. They couldn't have changed in a day!"

"But she *did* refuse me," he said, firmly replacing her head on his shoulder. "She said she didn't wish to wed a man who wrote poems for someone else."

The word *poem* caused a cloud to cross Lucy's face. "I shall refuse you, too, you know," she said, suddenly glum.

"Will you?" he murmured abstractedly, removing two hairpins from the knot in her hair and watching with delight as the loose waves uncurled upon his chest. "Why, my love? Are you going to pretend that you don't love me? I shan't believe it, you know. I have the proof." Moving one arm very slightly, he withdrew from his pocket the folded clipping that Mabyn had given him. "Any female who'd carry these silly verses on her person for months has to be besotted," he said, obviously pleased with himself.

"I am besotted," she admitted, pulling the clipping from his fingers in embarrassment and hastily tucking it into the bosom of her gown. "But not so besotted," she added dolefully as she lowered her head and began to twist a button on his coat, "that I'd wed you and thus admit to every gossip in London that I'm the revolting creature in your most recent opus." She lifted her eyes to his face in utter bewilderment. "How *could* you have published such an unkind portrait of the girl you claim to love?"

"But my love," he responded with a grin, "I *didn't* publish it."

"What?" She pushed herself away from him, blinking at him in bafflement.

"I didn't publish it."

"What do you mean? It's right here in the magazine!"

"Yes, I know. But no one else will ever see that magazine."

She shook her head in confusion. "How can that be? Half of London reads the *West-Ender*."

"Yes, but not this copy. This is a special edition." His grin widened in mischievous amusement. "It's the only copy in existence containing that poem. You see, I had it specially printed."

She continued to stare at him for a moment. Then her eyes dropped down to the magazine that began to tremble in her hand. "Specially p-printed?"

"Yes. Just for you."

Her eyes flew to his face, reflecting both the relief and the anger that were warring in her breast. "You . . . you *dastard!*" she exclaimed, rising to her feet and throwing the magazine at him.

"Dastard?" He looked up at her in surprise. "Just because I had the poem specially printed?"

"No! Because you did it just to *infuriate* me!"

"No, ma'am," he declared, pulling her down beside him again and forcibly restraining her from moving, "that was not the reason. I did it to teach you a lesson. I knew, when you read it, you would think the worst of me—that I had maligned you again."

A wave of mortification washed over her. "And I *did* think the worst, didn't I?" she murmured, her throat tightening.

"Yes, you certainly did. You were ready to murder me."

"I . . . I'm sorry," she mumbled, abashed.

He lifted her chin and forced her to meet his eyes. "How many times must I tell you, my love, that I'm not that sort of rotter? I am as nauseatingly good-natured a writer as I am a man."

"Oh, Perry," she sighed, sinking against him in shame, "forgive me. I should have known. I won't doubt you again." Throwing her arms about his neck, she added fervently, "And I *love* your nauseatingly good nature!"

"Do you? I'm very glad to hear it," he said, contentedly permitting her to snuggle into his embrace. "If that matter is finally settled," he added, pulling out the magazine that had somehow lodged itself between them, "we can rid ourselves of this slanderous nonsense forever." And he tossed the magazine into the fire.

"No!" she cried, leaping to her feet. She ran to the fire and gingerly lifted the already burning magazine from the coals. Dropping it on the carpet, she quickly stamped out the flames with her foot. Then she rifled through the black-edged pages, found page three and carefully tore it out.

"Good God, Lucy," Perry exclaimed, "what on earth did you do that for?"

"I couldn't let you burn the only copy," she said, smiling at him fondly as she folded the page and tucked it in her bosom with her other treasure. "A girl doesn't get a love poem like this every day."